M000204822

Angel Beneath My Wheels

K. S. Moore

FIREFLY

ANGEL BENEATH MY WHEELS BY K.S. MOORE
Published by Firefly Southern Fiction
An Imprint of Lighthouse Publishing of the Carolinas
2333 Barton Oaks Dr., Raleigh, NC 27614

ISBN: 978-1-938499-67-8

Copyright © 2016 by K.S. Moore
Cover design by Elaina Lee, www.forthemusedesign.com
Interior design by AtriTex, www.atritex.com

Available in print from your local bookstore, online, or from the publisher at:
www.lighthousepublishingofthecarolinas.com

For more information on this book and the author visit: KathrynSueMoore.com

All rights reserved. Non-commercial interests may reproduce portions of this book without the express written permission of Lighthouse Publishing of the Carolinas, provided the text does not exceed 500 words. When reproducing text from this book, include the following credit line: "*Angel Beneath My Wheels* by K.S. Moore published by Lighthouse Publishing of the Carolinas. Used by permission."

Commercial interests: No part of this publication may be reproduced in any form, stored in a retrieval system, or transmitted in any form by any means—electronic, photocopy, recording, or otherwise—without prior written permission of the publisher, except as provided by the United States of America copyright law.

This is a work of fiction. Names, characters, and incidents are all products of the author's imagination or are used for fictional purposes. Any mentioned brand names, places, and trade marks remain the property of their respective owners, bear no association with the author or the publisher, and are used for fictional purposes only.

Scripture quotations are taken from the HOLY BIBLE NEW INTERNATIONAL VERSION r. NIVr Copyright c 1973, 1978, 1984 by International Bible Society. Used by permission of Zondervan Publishing House. All rights reserved.

Brought to you by the creative team at Lighthouse Publishing of the Carolinas:
Eva Marie Everson, Jessica Everson, Jan Powell, Jennifer Leo, Shonda Savage, and Eddie Jones

Library of Congress Cataloging-in-Publication Data
Moore, K.S.
Angel Beneath My Wheels/K.S. Moore 1st ed.

Printed in the United States of America

PRAISE FOR ANGEL BENEATH MY WHEELS

Creating stories has always been a powerful tool to communicate truths that need to be heard in a relevant way. *Angel Beneath My Wheels* captivates you and takes you on an ages old journey of the potential to discover trust lost. Often hidden beneath the surface of our personas we create resides, in many of us, a need to trust once again, and in the process receive healing. Kathryn has written a wonderful and creative novel that will take you beyond fiction to fact…that trust is healing, and when built upon a foundation of faith in Christ, saving, and conquering.

> Billy E. Mauldin Jr., President and CEO, Motor Racing Outreach,
> co-author of *The Race: Living Life on Track*, and spiritual adviser
> to **Season 13 American Idol** contestants

Having been married for more than 40 years, and having ministered to late-stage cancer patients for more than 10 years, I had thought that perhaps my heart might have lost its ability to be moved and made emotionally vulnerable. *Angel Beneath My Wheels* reminded me of the sweetness and innocence of "first love," the complexities of life and the importance of forgiveness to move forward unhindered by regret. My heart was touched by this story and I believe yours will be too.

> Rev. Dr. Michael Barry, author of *A Reason for Hope, A Season for Hope,*
> *The Art of Caregiving* and *The Forgiveness Project*

Kathryn Sue Moore's inspiring debut, *Angel Beneath My Wheels*, is brimming with romance, passion, and heart. With a spunky protagonist who can turn heads and change carburetors—how cool is that?!—Christian romance readers and NASCAR fans will flock to this charming, uplifting novel.

> Lori Nelson Spielman,
> Best-selling author of *The Life List* (Random House) and
> *Sweet Forgiveness* (Penguin)

ACKNOWLEDGEMENTS

Some very special people have helped me get this story to print and I would like to thank them for all they have done.

To my loving husband, Alan – we got lucky and met – and to my amazing children, the most wonderful blessings on God's earth and the inspiration for my writing.

To my agent, Les Stobbe, whose online article about crossover fiction caught my eye. Thank you for taking a chance on me. Your vast experience and profound insight have been invaluable.

To my editors, Jessica and Eva Everson, whose patience, I'm sure, was sorely tested as we worked through some of the tough spots. I am forever grateful for your wisdom, guidance and kindness. You are extremely gifted.

To my talented critique partner, David Stricklen, and my beta readers, Myra Moore, Nancy Mosier, Heidi Phillips, Nellie DeVries and Cathy Boynton. Thank you for your honest feedback and unending encouragement.

I am truly blessed to have worked with each of you.

DEDICATION

This book is dedicated with love to Rachel, my daughter and
the angel beneath *my* wheels.

Prologue

SPRING 2012

Is it possible for me to imagine the person I want to be, and make myself over to be that man? Or am I forever bound by experience and upbringing?

It's well before dawn as I park my pickup at the clearing and turn off the engine. My stomach growls, and I can't remember the last time I've eaten. With nothing but a heart full of hope, I set off on foot across the meadow beneath a moonless sky, then enter the pitch-black woods beyond. I can't see squat, but I know the way like a duck knows south.

I make it to my spot, lean against a tree, and stare toward the willow twenty-some yards away. The silent night is broken only by the resonant chirp of crickets and the occasional deep-throated croak of a bullfrog near the creek.

Will she ever return here? A voice within whispers. *She will.* The possibility keeps drawing me back.

Like every story, ours has a beginning and, for me, it started right here where I first saw her, curled up asleep on the soft grass beneath the willow, her hands palm to palm beneath her cheek as if in prayer. At the time, I thought she'd been sent from heaven above.

I still do.

I'm hopeful we're still in the early part of our story, somewhere nearer to boy-meets-girl than happily-ever-after—or, worse, the tragic end. I can't bear the thought our story could be over. For me, it's just begun.

I knew when I stole that first kiss I wasn't simply going to fall in love with her; I would love her forever. And if she ever comes back I'll tell her. I should have told her right then. Fact is, there are a lot of things I should have told her. I reckon if I had, she'd know how much I love her, she'd know she can trust me, and she wouldn't be running from me.

1

The woods are cool and moist with the pungent, earthy aroma of an early Tennessee spring. I stand alone in the darkness, my existence monotone, the color of my life washed away like chalk art in the rain. My only warmth comes from memories of her. The honey-sweet voice whispered to me in those precious few private moments we shared. The subtle fresh scent of her as I held her in my arms. The delicate feel of her hand in mine as we hiked these woods not so long ago, on a beautiful Sunday afternoon, bright with the sun and the promise of newfound love. I close my eyes, let my head fall back against the tree, and I see her; the way we were and could have been surround me.

My father was fond of telling me, "Luke, love is the one thing—the only thing—that makes life worth living, and once you've tasted it, you'll never savor anything more. It'll turn your whole world upside down, redefine the man you are, and you'll never once regret it."

Now I know what he was talking about. The intoxicating flavor of her lingers, and I find my heart starved for her, yearning with every ounce of my being to have her back in my life. And I'm a different man than I was when we first met. Of that much I'm sure.

But can I be the man she deserves? Can I love her and live to make her happy?

I've always held a man's destiny is made with his own two hands. Don't just dream of the life you want to live; go out and live the life you dream of. I could make it happen with her. We could have a happy ending, a life as pure and promising as the ring she wears. Haven't I succeeded at about everything I ever set my mind to? And I know the type of hero she's looking for. I know I can be that man.

But she's gone.

And though it churns my innards to think it, the thought is there all the same: she may never come back.

I can't breathe. The knot of fear in my stomach twists violently as I think about all the dangerous people out there looking for her. I fall to my knees because there's no place left to fall, and I can barely make out shapes in the darkness through the hot tears stinging my eyes.

Desperate to ease my helplessness, I bow my head and pray for the one hope that dominates my life—to find her there, asleep beneath the willow. And when I wake her she'll nestle into the safety of my arms, never to be parted again.

I hear the birds now, the night songs fading to a dull hum. As light begins to peek over the eastern tree line, bathing the willow in the first faint blush of daybreak, my heart lifts.

Maybe, just maybe, she'll be there.

Sleeping Angel

Fall 2010

Wait for it. Wait for it.

Luke sat silent and still in the early morning light, his patience sorely tested as he watched the beautiful whitetail buck hesitate, then continue to amble into the clearing. His rifle was raised, safety off, aimed, ready to fire.

The buck sported a huge rack, at least a ten-point, maybe more. Head held erect, nostrils flared, the magnificent creature proceeded with caution, striving with every ounce of its raw animal instinct to sense the danger in the air. In seconds it would be in the open. Luke waited, his heart hammering inside his chest, pulse pounding in his ears, his whole body taut with anticipation—like always right before the shot. The buck took another step, paused, sniffed, another step, paused, then one more. Luke squeezed the trigger. The gun roared and the buck bolted.

Luke exhaled, and a wide smile lit up his face. He'd gotten a good shot on it. Breathless, he leaned back against the tree and stretched his neck and shoulders inside his camouflage hunting jacket, inhaling deeply the crisp morning air. Allowing the animal time to collapse and die, he waited another twenty minutes, then climbed down from his tree stand to track it.

Luke loved the early mornings, often waking well before daylight to head to the woods to hunt or watch the sun rise. His favorite time was the hour near dawn when he was sure to see more wildlife, hear more earthly sounds, and feel closer to nature than in the whole other twenty-three hours of the day combined. He especially enjoyed watching the smaller creatures emerge from their night places to begin their daily dance to the subtle music of the waking earth, scurrying about to the soft refrain of a mild breeze whistling through the trees. The crickets and bullfrogs bleating out a steady rhythm. The high delicate notes of the songbirds flitting about, adding their own unique beauty to the multilayered melody.

It was an incredible thing to experience, and Luke relished the ability to enjoy it whenever he was home. In all of his travels across the country, he'd never come across a more glorious sunrise than the one over his own property in the hills and hollers of north-central Tennessee.

Luke walked to the spot in the clearing where the buck had stood, a satisfied smile curving his lips at the telltale signs of his accuracy: splashes of blood, still shiny wet and bright red on the tall blades of grass and mottled leaves on the ground. He walked in the direction the buck had run, tracking it as far as the creek. It hadn't crossed, but instead had run along the edge. Luke followed the fresh tracks in the mud for several hundred yards, searching among the thickets for the wounded animal. When he glanced up, a far-off spot of bright pink on the opposite bank caught his attention.

Luke raised his gun, double-checking the safety was on, and peered through the high-power scope. His jaw dropped. He hurried down the creek to a place he could cross, then crept up the other side to where he'd seen the spot of bright color. He inched closer, ducking beneath the long branches of the giant willow tree, and spotted a young woman lying on the ground, her head partially covered by the hood of a bright-pink sweatshirt. He watched the steady rise and fall of her rib cage in relief.

He bent closer. Now why would a pretty little thing like her fall asleep in the woods on such a cold night? His head tilted as he studied her face. She didn't look injured but ... were those tear stains on her cheek? Maybe she's lost. He considered waking her and rubbed his stubbled chin, contemplating. He'd more'n likely scare her half to death dressed the way he was, out in the middle of nowhere and carrying a rifle.

Curled on her side, her legs pulled beneath the hem of her dress, she looked tiny. Long hair escaped the edges of the hood, light brown and flowing in loose delicate curls. Her lush coal-black lashes contrasted with her fair skin. Her hands were together, palm-to-palm, her head resting upon them, as if she were praying. Like an angel. A slow smile spread across his face.

Luke longed to see the color of her eyes, watch her smile, hear her voice. Maybe she lived with the old farmer who tended the corn down yonder. He thought again of waking her, but he remembered his appearance and resigned himself to simply walk away.

He took a step backward and paused. But then he might never see her again.

He could have a sit and wait for her to wake, to make sure she was all right, knew how to get home. But he didn't have time. He had to find that buck and get on down the road. His daddy was expecting him for breakfast and then he had to head to work.

He turned to go and she shivered. Easing his gun to the ground, he removed his coat and draped it over her. It was his favorite hunting jacket. Had been with him for years. Once while pheasant hunting a buddy shot a hole clean through the sleeve. Afterward, they'd both laughed until they cried about the near miss. He hadn't hunted with Dirk Jansen since.

As silently as he'd come, he retreated, looking back once more to commit the scene to memory: the sleeping angel, covered by his worn coat, lying peacefully beneath the ancient willow in the soft morning light. It was a beautiful sight.

Auto Auction

FALL 2011

"Up next, ladies and gentlemen, auto auction item number one-ninety-four," the booming staccato voice of the auctioneer rambled off. "A nineteen-sixty-six Ford Galaxie, five hundred XL. High-powered four-twenty-seven FE race engine. Rated at over four-hundred horsepower. Who wants to start the bidding? Do I hear five thousand? Five thousand, five thousand, do I hear five thousand?"

Rachel Tate waited in the hot, dusty parking lot, not wanting to be the first to bid. She took a deep breath and let it out slowly. This was the one she'd come for, the one she'd been waiting for, the one she'd driven three hours and stood waiting two more to bid on.

"Do I hear four thousand? Come on, folks, she's not much to look at, but she's got it under the hood where it counts," the bawdy auctioneer prattled on. "Four thousand. Do I hear four thousand? Four thousand?" He acknowledged a raised hand in the crowd, "Four thousand! Do I hear forty-five hundred? Forty-five hundred, forty-five, forty-five, anyone, come along, come along now, forty-five, forty-five, forty-five hundred."

Rachel raised her hand, dropping it as soon as the auctioneer nodded in acknowledgement.

"Forty-five hundred! Do I hear five? Five thousand, five, five, five, five, five thousand."

After twenty minutes the bidding came down to her and one other person. Rachel made eye contact with her competitor when he spun around right after she outbid him once, but he'd gotten it in the end. She'd had to let it go at a little over nine thousand. She wanted the engine in that piece of junk, but she didn't have enough cash. "Waste of time," she mumbled, slapping her ball cap against her thigh. It was the only 427 here today. And she'd driven all this way, for what? For nothing. She shoved her hat back on her head, and turned to leave.

"Ladies and gentlemen, can I have your attention, please? We have a late entry—another classic muscle car. A raucous nineteen sixty-four Ford Fairlane Thunderbolt, stock four-twenty-seven FE under the hood. According to Ford, all you need for racing is the ignition key. This is auto auction item number two-fourteen. Do I hear a starting bid of three thousand dollars? Three thousand, three, three, three thousand …"

Rachel perked up. Did he say Thunderbolt? With an original 427? She turned around.

There was a lengthy pause as the auctioneer leaned his ear to an associate. "Two thousand dollars! Do I hear two thousand, two thousand …?"

Two thousand was a low opening bid. It must be in pretty bad shape. She hurried to the front to check it out as the bidding started to pick up. It looked bad but not much worse than the Galaxie. She raised her hand at $3,500 and proceeded to bid, finally stopping at a little over $7,000. It wasn't worth that much. She glanced behind her to see who was bidding against her—the same guy who had gotten the other 427. What in tarnation did he need with two of them?

She stomped away, furious she'd come up empty-handed. Now she'd have to wait at least another two months and hope there would be another at the next auction, or figure out a way to retrofit her design into a smaller engine. The 427 would have been perfect.

"Hey, beautiful. Hold up," an intensely male voice called after her.

She turned to find the man who'd outbid her running to catch up. She stopped and watched him approach, eyes narrowed, lips tight. She'd lost out not once, but twice, to this jerk.

He was tall, six-foot-three or six-four, lean, and well-muscled. His black tee shirt fit snugly across his chest and around his biceps. She guessed him to be close to her age, maybe a couple of years older, with dark-brown hair and sun-bronzed skin. He had an unshaved, strong, square jaw which gave him a rough bad-boy look—attractive in a rugged, down-to-earth way.

He stopped and flashed a bright, even smile. "So, you're into old muscle cars?" He took off his sunglasses and pushed up the bill of his "Team Brandt" ball cap, no doubt for a better look at her.

She shook her head. "I wanted it for the engine." She noticed he had a dimple on one cheek and the most amazing soft-blue eyes. She had to look away to keep from staring.

"Yeah? Why?"

"None of your business." She turned to walk the last few steps to her car.

"Sor-ry." He hurried to keep pace with her. "I'm Luke Brandt, by the way."

When she stopped and turned back to him, he held out his hand and gave her a well-practiced smile. *As if that's supposed to impress me.* "I know who you are." She ignored his hand. She didn't care that he was a well-known race car driver, but had never realized how gorgeous he was up close, which was probably the reason he had the reputation he did—fast cars, fast women. She opened her car door and slipped in. Looks aside, the last thing she needed or wanted was a guy like him.

"Nice car." He disregarded her lack of civility. "Did you do the restoration yourself?"

She scowled. "Why'd you do that?"

"Do what? Outbid you? I need the engines for my race car." He flashed his gorgeous smile.

"Both of them?" She couldn't believe it and her angry glare let him know exactly how she felt.

"You never know what you're getting. Especially when the car's not running when you buy it. It could be totally blown and you wouldn't know it until you start it up and see the oil run right out the bottom. But then, you'd know that if you knew anything about old engines."

"I do know. I also know you don't even run Fords." She started her car, pulled the door closed, and, in one fluid motion, shifted into first gear, popped the clutch, and gave the car enough gas to leave him standing in an angry spray of gravel and dust.

"Jerk." She laughed at the cloud of dirt forming in her rearview mirror.

Luke ducked to avoid the worst of it, but when the dust settled, he couldn't help but grin ear-to-ear. She was fantastic. More sparks and fire than the Fourth of July.

He laughed out loud and smacked his hand on his thigh. She not only knew who he was, she knew what kind of engine he ran.

He liked girls who liked cars; not many did. They'd tell him they did, but when it came down to it, they knew absolutely nothing and had no appreciation for the beauty of a nicely restored classic or the sheer power of a well-tuned engine. But she did; her Nassau-blue, sixty-six, soft-top Corvette was one sweet set of wheels.

And she was smokin' hot. He'd thought she was a real looker when he first glimpsed her during the bidding, but up close she was even prettier. She was a petite little thing who wore a ball cap atop her long, light-brown ponytail that fell in front of one shoulder. Her sun-kissed skin was flawless and lent her a natural beauty that shined from the inside out. And those gorgeous green eyes—deep and dark, like the dense woods he loved, although her glare of unmistakable distaste wasn't nearly as inviting. No doubt, she was mighty angry. This was a woman who might keep his attention for more than a night or two.

She turned onto the highway, leaving another spray of dust and gravel in her wake. He laughed again. Yup, she was surely something. "Mmm, mmm, mmm," he muttered, shaking his head as the little blue car disappeared down the road.

Sparks

B ack home, Rachel pulled into the driveway and parked in her usual spot at the front of the huge red pole barn. She turned off the engine and sat for several minutes, looking straight ahead, unwilling to accept she'd wasted her entire Saturday at the auction to come home empty-handed.

Her father's John Deere stood at the far end of the driveway, facing one of the two sliding barn doors that opened to the fields on the long side of the rectangular space. Beyond the tractor lay an assortment of well-used farm implements. The empty concrete floor between the farm equipment and the hood of her Vette taunted her.

Her project beckoned from the workbench that ran along the wall opposite the sliding doors where it sat amidst the tools, rags, and parts she'd used to put it together. She got out of the car, walked to the small, front-entry door, flicked on the lights, and pressed the button to close the overhead door.

She glanced at the time on her phone. She was supposed to meet her friends in town in an hour and she still had to get ready. Lateness was one of her pet peeves. She'd vowed long ago never to be one of those people. Still, she figured she had ten minutes to tinker and think of a backup plan.

The air in the closed-up space felt heavy with the familiar smells of oil, stale exhaust, compost, and earth as she picked up the carburetor and turned it over in her hands, unconcerned about the grease that smeared her skin. She'd so wanted the 427 to test out her redesigned carburetor. It was a big enough engine to pull the horsepower she was after, and the cars it came in had plenty of room in the engine compartment for the additional cooling unit. She contemplated again how she could make it work in her Corvette.

She and her father had spent a good deal of time over the past several months trying to figure it out, but nothing had worked. The Vette simply didn't have enough room under the hood. Defeated, she set the unit on the workbench, turned off the lights, and shut the door behind her.

At eight o'clock on the dot, Rachel walked into The Old Hickory Inn, a trendy country music joint near the campus of Tennessee State University and one of her and her friends' favorite downtown Nashville hangouts. She spotted them at their usual table and said hello to Gil the bartender on the way to join them.

She sandwiched herself between her girlfriends, Allie and Becca, as Jackson slid a fresh beer her way from across the table and let her know she had some catching up to do. Along with her other friends, Cole and Reese, they'd all gone to the homecoming game at TSU. While football wasn't Rachel's favorite pastime, she loved going to the college games and tailgating. She looked forward to homecoming, when the alumni returned. It was always fun to run into old friends she hadn't seen in a while.

Rachel was disappointed to have missed the game, especially for such a fruitless expedition to the auto auction.

Luke spotted the little blue Corvette sitting at the curb in front of The Old Hickory Inn as he passed by in his pickup, pulling the Galaxie behind him on a flatbed trailer. He slammed on the brakes, almost causing the car behind him to crash into his trailer. The car honked several times but Luke didn't move. He stared across the street at the pretty little Vette, not believing his good fortune.

It was her car. There was no way there could be another one like it within two hundred miles. He drove around the block and contemplated what to do with his trailer.

The inn was twenty-five minutes from home, but he wanted to clean up before he saw her again. 'Course, if he went home it would be an hour or more before he got back into town, and she might be gone. As he rounded the block a second time, he stopped in the road and jumped out of his truck, which provoked more honks from annoyed drivers as he ran across the busy four-lane street.

He felt the hood of her car; still warm. He decided to take his chances. If she was gone when he got back, well, at least he'd know where he might find her again. Her car would make her easy to find, even in a city the size of Nashville.

He raced home, unhooked the trailer, showered, shaved, and changed into clean jeans and his favorite shirt—a blue pinstripe his mother once told him matched his eyes. In no time flat, he jumped in his truck and raced down his winding driveway.

Luke checked the clock on the dash and laughed, realizing how fast his pit stop had been, then laughed again as he placed his cowboy hat on his head and glanced at himself in the mirror. Why was he even doing this? Was she that special?

His thoughts drifted back to the parking lot at the auto auction and his lips curved into a smile. Yup, she was something special, all right. She was into cars. He imagined how a girl like her might be dressed for a night on the town. She couldn't possibly have gotten any prettier, but maybe with her hair down and a beer or two in her, she'd be a little friendlier.

He walked into The Old Hickory and caught sight of her with a large group at a table in front of a low stage. He beamed. She wore a TSU sweatshirt like most of her friends, but with a skirt and cowboy boots, she looked totally feminine. Her long hair shone and her green eyes sparkled when she laughed.

He settled onto a stool at the bar and glanced back as she and a guy made their way to the small stage. She had beautiful legs, although her skirt was a tad on the long side for his taste. With legs like that she should wear short skirts—*real* short.

There were microphones and a few instruments set up on the small stage. Luke ordered a beer and leaned against the bar to watch.

It was a slow country song, romantic, and they both knew it well … maybe too well. He frowned. It unsettled him, watching her sing a song like that with someone else. His eyes narrowed as he took the measure of the man playing the guitar and singing with her. He was tall and built like a football player, but he looked pretty rough, with a mottled complexion, thin blond hair, and watery blue eyes. He couldn't imagine her going out with a guy like that. She could do better.

He watched and listened, surprised by her lovely voice—sweet and smooth like fresh country honey—and awed by the raw beauty of the music they made together. She didn't sing directly to the guy, but she did look his way every so often to grace him with a nice smile.

When the song ended she took an exaggerated bow, and as she straightened, the guy leaned over to kiss her on the cheek. They both laughed, he took her hand and led her off the stage as their friends led the crowd in a raucous applause.

Luke turned to the bartender. "She come in here often?"

"Rachel?" The bartender looked her way, his eyes following her back to the table. "Fair amount," he said in a pure southern Tennessee drawl.

"Is she dating him?"

"Naw, pretty sure he's only a friend. *Her* man's gonna come drivin' up in a white Charger," the bartender offered up with a laugh.

Luke's brows shot up, "How's that?"

"A joke," the bartender said with a chuckle. "Rumor is, she's waiting for her dream guy to pull up in a white Dodge Charger. You know, her knight in shinin' armor?" He laughed again.

"Is that right?" Luke laughed with him. A white Charger. Chargers were nice; the older ones had plenty of power, and he liked the looks of the newer version reintroduced a few years back.

Several minutes later another guy wearing jeans and a sport coat approached the table and got Rachel's attention. Her eyes narrowed and her lips stretched thin as she looked up at him. She shook her head, said something, then turned back to her friends. When he put his hand on her shoulder, her singing friend jumped to his feet, his chair crashing to the floor behind him. He exchanged a few words with Sport Coat Guy.

Luke wondered if a fight was about to break out. Rachel said something to both of them and Singing Guy picked up his chair and eased back into it.

Sport Coat Guy stood at the corner of the table for several more minutes. His back was to the bar so Luke couldn't tell what was being said, but it looked like he was being ignored. After several minutes, Sport Coat Guy knelt down beside Rachel and whispered something in her ear.

When she gave him a look of utter disgust and bounded to her feet, he stood with her. She pushed at his chest, then turned to walk away. But when he grabbed her arm, she pounced like a roped wildcat, wrenched her arm free, whirled around, and slammed his nose with the heel of her palm. He stumbled backward, grabbing his nose. Without hesitation, she kicked him in the chest with her boot, sending him reeling back toward the bar.

Luke jumped up as Sport Coat Guy headed his way. He caught him under the arms, preventing him from crashing into the barstools, and turned him toward the door and helped him out the rest of the way.

"This isn't over, Rachel," Sport Coat Guy shouted, his hand still holding his bloody nose while he tried to shake off Luke's hold.

"Go on now," Luke said, giving him a final shove out the door. Satisfied the guy would stay gone, he walked back to where she stood. "Rachel, is it? You all right?" he asked, tipping his hat back.

"You," she said, obviously surprised to see him. Her eyes narrowed in an angry glare. "I'm fine," she said through clenched teeth. She winced as she shook the hand she'd used to smash the guy's nose.

"Hey, I'm sorry. I was only trying to help." He felt an overwhelming urge to pull her into his arms, to hold her. She looked hurt and afraid. "Let me see that," he said, reaching for her hand.

She yanked it away. "Does it look like I need a cowboy hero?"

"I—"

"Well, I don't. Just so you know." She anxiously looked toward the door, as though expecting Sport Coat Guy to storm back through.

Luke raised his hands in mock surrender. "Okay, calm down there, sweet thing."

Her eyes blazed back at him for several long moments, wide, disbelieving, as though he'd insulted her. And then she turned and walked away.

What had he done wrong? He took a step toward her. "Hey, wait. I ... I actually saw your car out front and hoped you'd be here. I want to apologize for this afternoon."

She spun around. "For what?"

"For making you angry."

"That's it?" she said, brows raised. "Not for being selfish and inconsiderate, but for making me angry?"

"Well, yeah, for all of that." Man, she was tough.

She shook her head, dismissing him. "I'm going back to my friends now."

"I was hoping maybe we could hang out." He hesitated. "I don't know anyone here tonight."

"I'm not surprised. You have to be a friend to have a friend."

"Aw, come on now. That's a little harsh, don't you think? Look, I'm sorry. I was selfish and inconsiderate today." He hoped it was enough of an apology to suit her.

She stared at him long and hard, the beginnings of a smile curving her full lips. And then, with a sigh, she looked away.

"I would like it if *we* could be friends."

She looked back at him as though considering.

"Come on."

A hint of regret flitted across her face, followed by an angry frown. "I don't need a cowboy like you for a friend." She walked away and rejoined her friends.

Luke shook his head. She was one angry little girl. He returned to his seat at the bar, keeping an eye on her, wondering how to get on her good side. Or if she even had a good side where men were concerned.

"She's not usually so rowdy," the bartender said. "In fact, mostly she's a real sweet girl. But I reckon she can take of herself." He slapped his palm on the bar with a hearty laugh. "Now ain't that the truth?"

"You got that right," Luke agreed, shaking his head in disappointment.

He looked her way every now and again. A half hour later, she and her girlfriends got up and sang another country song, and they laughed in the middle of it, messed up quite a few of the lyrics, but everyone clapped anyway. He had to admit, it was fun to watch. They were cute, and she had a nice voice, a great laugh. Her sexy innocence totally drew him in. What he wouldn't do to get her to laugh with *him*.

"What do you suppose a fella's gotta do to turn her head?" he asked the bartender.

"Hard tellin' with her. I don't see her with other guys, aside from her friends. She sure seems to like the music though. Maybe if you sing her a song."

Luke laughed. "Yeah, right."

"Aw, come on now, I could play the guitar for you," the bartender offered. "Tonight's open mic night. Anyone can get up there. And the crowd's not that picky. In fact, I've a notion to do a song myself so's more folks will get up on their own. You think on it a bit." He checked with his other customers at the bar, got a couple of them another round, then grabbed his guitar and headed to the stage.

The bartender was pretty good and the generous applause confirmed it. As he made his way back to the bar, Luke reconsidered. He'd never even been up on a stage before, let alone sung for a room full of strangers—and for a woman? Maybe for this one he oughta give it a try.

He shook his head. He couldn't do it. He glanced back over his shoulder at Rachel again. She was so pretty, so full of fire. She was still holding her sore hand, massaging the heel of it under the table with the thumb of her other one.

He stared down at his beer. He could do it. He got up in front of crowds all the time at the track. Women were always telling him he had a great voice. There were a lot of country songs for a guy with a deep voice. "A shot of whiskey, please," he called to the bartender. "You reckon I can get a small bag of ice too?"

Luke tossed back the shot and slid the glass back. "What song are we going to do?"

The bartender thought for a minute. "How about 'Cowboys and Angels'? Do you know it?"

Luke searched his memory. "Not well, but … sure. Perfect." She'd called him a cowboy earlier. That was the ideal song for him to sing to her. "Got a pen and some paper?" He brought up the lyrics on his smart phone, chuckling when he saw his good friend listed as the songwriter. He scribbled down the words, then watched the video a couple of times. He looked at the bartender, adjusted his hat, rubbed his chin, and finished off his beer.

"Ready?" the bartender asked.

Luke's insides felt as if he'd swallowed a hornet's nest. "Ready as I'll ever be."

"Let's do it then." The bartender picked up his guitar.

"I'm Luke Brandt." Luke extended his hand as the bartender rounded the bar. "Gil Mason." They shook.

Luke went to Rachel's table and handed her the bag of ice. "This'll help your hand." Then he followed his new friend up onto the stage.

Luke raised the microphone. "Ladies and gentlemen," he said, "I'd like to dedicate this song to the angel out there who called me a 'cowboy hero' earlier." He let his gaze span the room. "As if that's a bad thing." When he chuckled, several in the audience laughed with him. "This is my first time up on stage so …" He glanced back to Gil, who strummed a few chords, then back to the crowd and Rachel. "Please be kind."

He looked her way and almost missed his cue. But when his voice filled the room, her eyes softened and he relaxed. She knew the song was for her. As the music ended, the place erupted in thundering applause. Luke grinned, pleased and surprised. "Thank you." He shook Gil's hand, then waved to the audience. As he glanced down at her table, he caught her stare and flashed a smile. Then, with a subtle wink, he turned and made his way back to the bar.

Luke thanked Gil again as the bartender put his guitar behind the bar.

"My pleasure, man. Hey, I think she liked it," he said with a tilt of his head in Rachel's direction. He set a fresh beer in front of Luke.

Luke raised the glass to Gil with a wide grin. "I reckon she did."

He turned and leaned against the bar, watching her. He planned to talk to her again and hoped she'd be nicer. He'd apologized profusely, even sung her a song. She couldn't still be mad, could she? He thought about what he would say.

Borrowing a chair from a nearby table, he sat down at the end next to her. "Howdy."

She gave him a shy smile, her gaze darting to the stage then back to him. "That was real nice."

What a smile. That was worth it right there. "I'm glad you liked it. How's the hand?" He leaned over to look under the table. She was still holding the ice against it.

"Better. Thank you for the ice."

He nodded. "Good." He wanted to know why she'd decked the guy, but didn't want to spoil their positive momentum. He wanted to keep her smile in place. "You know, I am a pretty nice guy." He leaned close so only she could hear, inhaling her subtle sweet scent like ripe peaches over homemade ice cream.

"Yeah?" She pulled back to look at him.

"Yeah. I feel bad about this afternoon. I'd like to make it up to you, if you'd let me." Asking her out to dinner seemed lame. He needed something better, something impressive, sincere.

Rachel looked down. "It's not necessary."

"Do you like NASCAR?"

"Sure. Who doesn't around here?"

Ah, there was that beautiful smile again. "Come watch me race. I'll get you tickets."

"You don't have to."

"I want to. I have to confess, it's a bit selfish. You know me, selfish, right?" He laughed at himself. "If I know there's someone special there rooting for me, I run a whole lot faster—even win sometimes." He gave her a mischievous grin. "You'd come if I got you tickets, wouldn't you?"

She stared. "Probably."

"Done deal then. I'll send you tickets." He brought up a blank contact screen on his phone and handed it to her. "So, Talladega or Charlotte?"

She held the phone as though debating whether she should give him her information. "Talladega is closer, but either would be fine." She entered her name and address and handed it back.

He looked at her. "Aw, come on now. Your address, but not your phone number?"

She looked sideways at him, bit her lip, then grinned and took the phone back. She entered her number and gave him the phone.

Satisfied, he dropped it back into his pocket as he stood. "Thanks. So, I'll see you at Talladega then." He tipped his hat.

Rachel nodded. "Talladega."

Happy as a pig in acorns, he made his way back to the bar. He had her phone number and she was coming to watch him race. He settled his tab, gave Gil a firm handshake, and thanked him again for doing the song.

Rachel's gaze followed Luke as he made his way back to the bar. Did he really call her *sweet thing*? Another man had called her that once. Austin. She should've pressed charges against him, sent him to jail. She hadn't felt safe since the incident on his birthday almost a year ago. She was sick and tired of him showing up everywhere.

And now Luke Brandt had her phone number. Luke Brandt, of all people, even after the way she'd treated him. She cringed, remembering her harsh, cruel words. *"I don't need a cowboy like you for a friend."* What a mean thing to say. He didn't even know her. Why should he care that she'd wanted one of those cars?

He *was* good looking—intoxicating baby-blue eyes, perfect boyish grin, and his deep voice, strong, yet gentle. And he'd sung for her. The corner of her lips turned up into a wide grin. Relax. He's sending race tickets. No big deal.

Her excitement faded as she watched him walk out. She twisted the ring on her finger, her heart racing. No, he was definitely not the type of guy she needed in her life.

Once outside, Luke looked around. Good, no Sport Coat Guy.

His gaze landed on the Vette at the curb. He looked it over as he circled it. What a beauty—an amazing restoration. Every fender and line flawless, as if right from the factory molds. He peeked through the window. The interior was clean too. The white leather seats looked brand-new and the chrome shifter was polished and shiny. Even the carpeting was immaculate. He straightened and eyed the hood, wondering if she was as meticulous about the motor. He could pop the hood and have a look-see. He glanced at the bar's door and back to the car. Nah, better not. He sure didn't want to get back on her bad side. He could wait. Maybe she'd show it to him one day.

With a grin he turned toward his truck. He couldn't remember ever being so excited about a woman's phone number. Satisfied, maybe, but never excited. His heartbeat quickened as he thought about seeing her again. He'd have to wait for Talladega. She'd been hesitant to give him her number; probably would have turned him down outright if he'd asked for a date. He'd best wait.

Maybe he'd get those muscle cars running and give her one. Hopefully, they were both viable. It might take a few weeks, but he'd run the Galaxie down to the shop tomorrow and start the guys working on it first thing Monday.

He pulled his phone out, slid behind the wheel of his truck, and closed the door. He brought up her contact information—Rachel Tate. What's your story, little girl? Why in the world would a pretty little thing like you spend a whole Saturday afternoon alone at an auto auction? And why only Fords? Why not another Corvette? She'd been mad as a drenched cat about being outbid on those muscle cars. Was it the 427 engine she was after? What was so all-fired special about that particular motor?

He pictured her singing in her skirt and boots, laughing and having a great time. And her beautiful smile when he'd finally gone over and sat beside her. He still couldn't believe he'd gotten on stage and sung for her. He glanced at her name and number. It had been worth it, though.

He looked into his rearview mirror and laughed at himself. What he wouldn't do for her. He'd figure a way to wrangle a real date with her soon, and find out her story, including why she wanted those cars.

Breakthrough

"Want to join me for the race later?" William Tate asked his daughter as they pulled into the drive.

Rachel grinned. Her daddy loved his Sunday afternoon NASCAR racing. "No, thanks. I'm going to work in the barn today. I'm getting real close on my new carburetor. *Real* close."

He put the truck in park, shut off the engine, and looked at her sideways. "Well, I reckon I may have to come take a peek in a bit."

She pushed the truck door closed behind her and joined him on the sidewalk. "I'll let you know when." She patted him on the shoulder.

After a quick change from church clothes to coveralls, Rachel entered the barn, flipped on the lights, and went to the workbench. She contemplated the huge empty space in the middle where her new Galaxie or Thunderbolt should have been. It had taken forever to save the cash. She hoped it wouldn't take as long to find the right car. The next auction wasn't for two months, and would there be another 427?

If only she could get her reengineered carburetor to work in her Vette. She surveyed the barn, her gaze landing on her daddy's old John Deere at the far end. They'd worked on the old green tractor for as long as she could remember, and it still ran great. The simple old farm machine had been her toy box when she was cutting her teeth on engines. She'd replaced every belt and serviceable part on it at least once. Daddy was a good teacher.

She was nine when she'd had to leave the farm to go live in town with her mama after their divorce. From then on she spent every weekend at the farm with her daddy. He'd pick her up after school on Friday for the weekend. He taught her about raising corn and beans, took her for long walks to find wild strawberries along the railroad tracks, to pick fruit from the orchard in late summer, or fishing down at the creek. But what she loved most was working on the tractor with him.

While they worked side by side, she told him about her week at school, her friends, dance class, tennis lessons, all that was going on in her life. He told her stories, shared his insights, and talked freely of God's plan and the beauty of life, love, and nature.

She thought about fourth grade when she'd gotten caught passing a note in class intended for a boy. Bodie Breeden. She needed to ask him straight out if he liked her or not. She thought her friends were silly with their he-said/she-said drivel. She wanted to know.

Bodie, embarrassed by her note passing, had simply yelled "No," in front of everyone. She'd been steaming mad, but once home, she'd cried her eyes out.

"Sweet pea, it's hard to imagine right now, but one day a handsome young man is going to come along and sweep you off your feet, and you'll *know* he's the right one. You won't need to ask." Her father handed over a washer and a nut, then followed with a wrench. "These go next."

She held the tractor belt in place with one hand while she put on the washer and nut with the other, using the wrench to tighten them down. "Yeah? What kind of car is he going to drive?" For Rachel, a person's car told her everything she needed to know. If their car was well taken care of, it meant they cared about things, people too. Was it fast? A performance vehicle? That meant they enjoyed life, lived on the edge. Was it extra big? They were timid, afraid of getting hurt. Was it small, economical? They cared more about saving money than enjoying life to the fullest.

"He'll drive a classic Corvette," her father suggested, knowing his little girl loved the old Corvettes.

"No. That's my car. He can't drive the same car as me."

"A brand-spanking-new Corvette then."

She pondered the idea. "Nah, don't you think that's a bit … showy? People who drive brand-new expensive sports cars are trying to say, 'Hey, look at me. Look at how successful I am.' I don't want a show-off." She thought her father should know her better.

"Okay, let's see." He paused. "How about a Charger?"

Rachel chewed that one over, picturing the car. Yeah, a Dodge Charger—powerful, fast, fun, and style, but not so much that it was boastful. And plenty of horsepower, at least in the bigger engine. If the guy was smart, he'd drive the V8.

"Good, Daddy. Like in *The Dukes of Hazzard.* A fast one … white." The good guy always rode a white horse.

"A white Charger then," her father agreed.

Rachel loved that memory. Her daddy always knew what to say to make her feel better. And she knew he loved her the way she was. He encouraged her in everything she wanted to do; never tried to make her fit into what he thought her life should be.

Like her mama did.

Rachel didn't want to think about her mother. She popped the hood of her Corvette and stared at the engine for a long while, focusing on the small space around the carburetor. She looked at the old green tractor, then at her carburetor on the workbench. There had to be a way. It was going to work; she was certain of it. All she needed was a real test in an actual engine.

She opened the two sliding barn doors, then fetched her laptop from the house, setting it on the counter and pulling up a stool.

Hours later she was smothering flames on her arm and picking herself up off the floor after her project blew up in her face. Her father came running from the house as she knocked out the last of the flames on the workbench. He grabbed the fire extinguisher from the wall and sprayed the burning pieces scattered across the barn floor.

"What in tarnation are you doing?" Setting aside the extinguisher, he checked her over, touching her face, her hair, and the burnt sleeve of her coveralls.

She tore off her goggles and jumped up and down. "It worked!"

"Yeah, I can see that," he said as he looked down at the charred remains of her project.

"No, the explosion was because the temperature got too hot. But now I know exactly what the too-hot point is."

"You couldn't have found that online?"

"I used what it said … kept it below, but it still blew up," she explained. "It wasn't right. But now I know *exactly*. And it worked, Daddy. You should have seen it. It ran for over three minutes, perfectly, on the gaseous fuel. It was amazing, like I knew it would be." Her excitement was so intense she could hardly stand still. She started to give her father a hug, but at the sight of the soot and grease on her arms, she withdrew and simply grinned at him.

Her father took her hand and inspected her forearm beneath the burnt fabric of her sleeve. "Are you all right?"

"I'm fine. It's just a little burn."

"Sweet pea, this is not a *little* burn." He pulled back the edges of the fabric to reveal a large patch of bright red-and-black flesh. He glanced at her face and she grimaced. "We're going to the hospital, young lady." He kicked at burnt remains on the floor, making sure nothing would reignite. "Come on."

They took his old pickup to the hospital. He insisted she call her mother on the way to let her know what happened. When she rushed into the emergency room, she took one look at the grease, soot, and ash, and was close to hysterical. She scolded Rachel up one side and down the other for not taking better care of herself. For spending way too much time in that "dirty workshop" of hers. Rachel finally had had enough.

"Mama, please. I'm fine. This is what I love to do. Truly." She gave her mother a hopeful stare, wishing she could make her understand. She wasn't like other girls who were content to dress up and be pretty all the time. She wanted to do something important. She loved to figure things out, make things work, dirty her hands. Sometimes she envied gorgeous, self-indulgent women and the attention they garnered from men. But she knew it wasn't in her blood. For all the years she'd tried to be the proper young lady her mother wanted, she'd been miserable.

She had started college as an art major—her mother's idea. She was creative, but her guidance counselor pointed out she also had a remarkable aptitude for math, logic, and mechanics. After several changes of her major, often against her mother's wishes, she graduated with a double major in mechanical engineering and computer science with a minor in chemistry. She hadn't found a job as an engineer, so she'd taken a position as a computer programmer at an engineering firm. She disliked the work because it was too easy, but she was good at it and it paid well.

"What about the hospital benefit gala?" her mother asked in a panic, reaching out to pick at a strand of Rachel's scorched hair.

Right. The fundraiser for the new trauma center at the hospital was only a few weeks away, and Rachel had promised her mother she would go. They'd even gone shopping together for a new gown. "I guess I'll have a bandage on my arm. Maybe I could wear a jacket."

Her mother's eyes held disappointment. With a sad tilt of her head, she glared at her daughter with scornful pity. Rachel's shoulders sagged. She frowned like a dejected child and stared down at her grimy hands fidgeting in her lap, her earlier excitement a distant memory. "I could not go?" she offered, not bothering to look at her mother, knowing full well there was no way she was going to let her miss one of Nashville's major social events.

Her mother patted her shoulder, "We'll figure out something, sweetheart."

Several hours later, Rachel was back in her shop, cleaning up the mess. She looked at what was left of her project and couldn't help but giggle. It was completely destroyed, but she'd made a huge discovery. She had a lot of work to do to build another one, but she was confident the next prototype would work. She backed out the Corvette so she could sweep beneath it. Out in the drive, she checked it over carefully, thankful the explosion hadn't done any damage. She grinned as she remembered finding it.

She was in a junkyard looking for an alternator for the pickup when she saw the glimmer of Nassau-blue paint in the distance. She'd circled the Vette, assessing its condition. It was in terrible shape. It had no top and had been sitting in the elements for who knew how long. The body wasn't too bad. It was missing one of the quarter panels, but, when she popped the hood, the engine seemed to be intact.

She'd negotiated with the owner of the yard, landed a fair price, and promised to pick it up within twenty-four hours. Then she'd gone home and talked her daddy into lending her the money. "Just until I can sell the Mercedes. Please, Daddy?"

"Rachel, your mother will have your hide if you sell her graduation present to buy an old junker."

The new Mercedes sport coupe was her mother's idea of what a proper young Nashville debutante should drive. Rachel stood her ground. "But it's my *dream* car. And I can do the restoration myself, with your help, of course." She hoped the idea of a new project would entice him. "And with the sale of the Mercedes, I'll have enough money left over for the parts I'll need."

He relented, and they'd bought it. A few days later she sold the Mercedes. Then she asked her mama to brunch at the country club, thinking that would be a good place to tell her. A woman like Emily Rose Tate wasn't likely to go ballistic in public. But when Rachel shared the news, her mother grew eerily quiet. After several minutes of unsettling silence, her eyes filled with tears. She patted them away with her napkin.

"You really love that old car?" her mama asked.

"I do, Mama. Please don't be sad. It's what I always wanted." How could she make her mother understand how much it meant to her? "Please try to understand."

"Well," her mama forced a weak smile, "I'm sure it will be beautiful when you're done with it."

It was about as close to an encouraging word as Rachel could ever remember coming from her mother. And it was beautiful.

Rachel caressed the steering wheel affectionately. Looking up, she caught a glimpse of herself in the rearview mirror. Startled by the black-streaked face that stared back at her, she studied her image for several minutes. No wonder her mother was distressed when she'd caught sight of her in the hospital. She looked like three-day road kill. What man would be attracted to that?

Rachel felt a huge weight on her heart. Why was she always such a huge disappointment in her mother's eyes? She loved her mama, she truly did. But why couldn't she accept Rachel the way she was? She wanted different things out of life. Couldn't she at least try to understand that? There was more to living than making yourself pretty, more to hope for than getting married and having babies.

Wasn't there?

If she were at least dating someone, Mama might ease up. But she hadn't had a date in almost a year. Not since the incident with Austin.

Rachel hadn't told anyone about that night. When she'd gone back to Holly's the next morning, she had planned to tell her. But when she arrived, she found Austin there. He'd spent the night with Holly. Her boyfriend had turned to her best friend, and she had given him everything. *Everything.*

Rachel was beyond stunned that her best friend would do that to her, but what shattered her more was that Holly had broken their pact. In fact, she'd broken it several years before, but chose that morning to let Rachel know.

Rachel twisted the purity ring on her finger as she fought back the tears the memory evoked. She had cried more over what Holly had lost than what had almost happened between her and Austin. She thought about all the times she and Holly had talked about sex and encouraged one another to wait. About all the times they'd lifted each other up, reciting Ecclesiastes 4:12 together: "Though one may be overpowered, two can defend themselves. A cord of three strands is not quickly broken."

For weeks afterward, Rachel felt diminished, like she was a single strand, afraid she wouldn't be able to withstand temptation the next time. Maybe that's why she hadn't had a date in almost a year. It wasn't that she hadn't been asked. She always said no.

Rachel ran her fingers through what was left of her hair and grimaced as more burnt strands fell into her lap. She jumped out of the car and shook her head, running her hands through her hair to shake out the broken pieces. She slammed the car door and returned to the shop to finish cleaning up, trying to push away the self-disgust as she questioned whether she was following the path God intended for her.

Or was it the path *she* wanted to follow?

Fundraiser

R achel stared at her reflection in the mirror of the dressing table that had graced her bedroom at her mother's house since she was nine. The young woman who stared back at her could pass for pretty, but was so small—"petite" her mother would affectionately say. She searched for her shoes. Finding them peeking out from underneath the bedskirt, she slipped them on. There, that was a little better. At five-foot-two she was always the shortest one in her group of friends. Squaring her shoulders, she pushed the thought away. God made her this way and there wasn't anything she could do about it. She focused instead on her face and smiled, pleased. She'd gone with her mother that afternoon to have their hair and makeup done. She'd even had her nails done, despite the fact that she'd be wearing gloves. She actually felt pretty.

She looked at her right arm and the new bright-pink flesh from her wrist to her elbow. The still-healing burn that covered most of it looked much worse than it was. She slipped on the long cream-colored gloves her mother had bought for her, satisfied with her image in the mirror. There. All covered up.

The gloves were an elegant touch. They matched the color of the gown perfectly, and even though they didn't go with the delicate beading or the overall design of the dress, they did the job. Oh well, they would have to do.

"Cole is here," her mother called from the bottom of the stairs.

Rachel took one last look in the mirror and steeled herself for the evening. She loathed these charity events her mother insisted she attend. She always felt like a piece of meat being paraded among the wealthy young lions who were the sons of her mother's generation. Her mother would bring well-to-do young men to meet her throughout the night in hopes that one of them would sweep her off her feet. In the past, it was always more than a little awkward for her date, and she was often embarrassed enough for both of them. When she showed up alone at the last event, her mother had been furious, calling it "unseemly," but Rachel had had a good time. She spent most of the evening talking about racing and football with a bunch of old men who were perfect gentlemen and appreciated her attention as well as her mind.

Determined to make the best of the unavoidable obligation, Rachel descended the steps to meet her date. Cole was a good friend—her only friend that actually owned a tux—and he'd happily volunteered to be her escort. And he knew exactly what it was going to be like for her.

Since meeting in a freshman engineering class, he'd heard enough about these parties to understand how she felt. It would be nice having him at her side tonight. He'd probably even get her to laugh about it. He was a good friend, and she was lucky to have him.

As Rachel and Cole approached the wide stone steps of the Tulip Grove Mansion, Cole deftly switched sides with her and offered his arm. She slipped her arm in his and they gracefully entered the expansive front hall of the historic home. Tulip Grove Mansion was a lovely antebellum house built in 1836, which sat across the road from the Hermitage, President Andrew Jackson's home. The president had built it for his nephew, Andrew Jackson Donelson. Now it was a local favorite for large, elegant weddings and lavish parties like the hospital fundraiser.

"You know Andrew Jackson's wife's name was Rachel, right?" Cole asked.

"I do. In fact, if you asked my mother she'd let you know I was named for her. It's sad though, if you know her story."

Cole looked her way, waiting for her to continue. Had he not heard it before?

"She had a very unhappy first marriage, then married Jackson before she was even divorced. During the election campaign, her virtue was questioned and she was degraded to the point where the stress and resulting depression affected her health. She died before her husband moved into the White House."

"Wow, sorry I brought it up."

"Don't be. I actually like my name. And I'm not going to be anything like her. I am strong," she said, with exaggerated confidence, "and I am *going* to have fun tonight, despite my mother."

"Okay, let's have some fun then, already. How about something to drink?"

"Sure." They both glanced around the various doorways that opened onto the front hall. "I think it might be this way." She pointed toward the ballroom through the wide double doors on the left.

While Cole made his way to the bar, Rachel stood back and surveyed the room. It was a perfect place to hold a fundraising event and she had to give her mother credit for planning it. She excelled at these types of occasions and always seemed to have everything under control. You would never know, talking with her at the party, that she was the lead organizer. It was her special gift, and she took great pride in the amount of money they raised. That was always the final measure of her success. It wasn't how many people showed up or how much fun was had by all. It was always, "Did they meet their fundraising goal for the evening?" And the answer was usually a resounding *yes*, and then some.

"Rachel Tate?" She heard a sweet, feminine voice call from behind her.

Rachel spun around to see her high school friend Cassie Walsh approaching with—of all people—Luke Brandt on her arm. Rachel's eyes momentarily fixed on him. Her stomach twisted. She forced her gaze back to Cassie as she settled a calm, controlled expression on her face. "Cassie. Oh, my land. It's so good to see you." She held out her arms.

Cassie's arms went around her. "It's Cassandra now," she whispered, as she hugged Rachel back. "How are you?" she asked, her voice bubbling with excitement as she pulled back to give her friend the once-over.

"Great. I'm doing great," Rachel said. "And you?" Cassie was a stunning, tall blonde, flawlessly feminine in a way Rachel had always envied. From the tips of her perfectly manicured nails to her beautiful up-do, she was everything Rachel thought she never wanted to be. Suddenly self-conscious, Rachel wrapped her arms around her middle.

"Amazing. Life is good." Cassandra turned to her date. "I'd like to introduce my boyfriend, Luke Brandt. Luke, this is a dear friend of mine from high school, Rachel Tate."

Boyfriend? He sure hadn't acted like he had a girlfriend the last few times they'd met. What a player. "Mr. Brandt," Rachel said, holding out her hand, her polite smile firmly in place.

"Please call me Luke," he said as he gently squeezed her hand and flashed his gorgeous grin.

"You do seem to keep showing up all over the place," Rachel said.

"Oh. You two have met before?" Cassandra asked.

"A couple of times," Luke answered, not taking his eyes off Rachel.

As Luke continued to stare, a flash of discomfort darkened Cassandra's brow, but was quickly replaced by her picture-perfect happy face. "Did you know he's a race car driver? Oh, silly me, of course you would." Cassandra had been addressing Rachel but then turned to Luke. "Rachel loves cars. And everything about them—driving, racing, you name it. Why, she even likes fixin' 'em up. Can you imagine?"

Luke's brows shot up as he looked at Rachel, "Is that right?"

"I'll bet you still watch all the NASCAR races on television with your daddy, Rachie, now don't you?" Cassandra nudged Rachel's shoulder.

Cole was suddenly at Rachel's side, extending a glass of red wine to her and smiling at the others.

"Thank you." Rachel took the offered glass. "Cole, this is a good friend of mine from high school, Cassie—uh—Cassandra Walsh, and her friend Luke Brandt. Cole Ritter."

As Cole shook their hands, Cassandra smiled sweetly, but her eyes betrayed her as she looked him over with a disapproving stare.

"Luke Brandt, as in the NASCAR driver?" Cole asked, ignoring Cassandra's none-too-subtle perusal.

"One and the same," Luke said.

"I hear you may be switching over next season to start running a Ford?" Rachel asked, as if she had an inside scoop on the matter.

"I may," Luke said, his knowing gaze confirming for Rachel he hadn't forgotten the auction.

"Yeah, ain't it so excitin'?" Cassandra exclaimed. "Luke invited me to come watch him race at Charlotte. Says he always runs a whole lot faster when he knows there's someone special up there rootin' for him. Now, won't that be so thrillin'?"

"Oh my." Rachel mimicked Cassandra's exaggerated enthusiasm. "Indeed. Why, with you up there in the stands cheering him on, I'm sure as sugar he'll run faster than ever—maybe even win. Now wouldn't that be somethin'? Luke Brandt wins Charlotte." Rachel looked at Luke, disappointed he'd used that same line on her friend.

Luke's pleasant demeanor vanished and he narrowed his eyes at Rachel.

Cassandra noticed Luke's reaction, but her smile never faltered. "Rachel, we'll have to catch up some more later, you hear?"

Rachel wanted to gag at the pretense. "Why, of course." She smiled sweetly.

"Good to meet you," Luke said to Cole. "Rachel," he nodded to her as Cassandra led him away.

Rachel turned to Cole, rolled her eyes, and laughed, "Shoot me now. I should not have done that."

"Done what? You were fine." Cole looked confused.

"Oh, nothing," Rachel watched Cassandra and Luke make their way through the room. She should have known he'd be dating someone like Cassandra Walsh. Just as well, too. All the more reason for Rachel to forget about him.

Rachel's mother arrived and within minutes was introducing several young men and their families to her and Cole. Cole was the perfect gentleman, greeting each one with impeccable manners and a genuine home-bred Southern charm. As Rachel watched him interact with them, she felt a sudden sense of longing. Why couldn't he be the one for her? He was a good friend and a real gentleman. He came from a good family, was extremely intelligent, a project manager for an aeronautics company, and they enjoyed each other's company. Why couldn't she feel anything for him? She admired the confident way he put everyone at ease, including her mother. But she wasn't attracted to him, plain and simple. Rachel tipped her head and studied him. Nope, not at all.

She searched the room for Luke and Cassandra. They made a beautiful couple. He was striking in his tux, tall and lean, his gleaming smile shining like the white of his dress shirt. She looked from Luke to Cole and back again. Luke caught her stare and smiled at her. She instantly focused her attention on the people in front of her.

When they finally had a break, Cole asked her to dance.

"Are we having fun yet?" he asked, as he swept her onto the dance floor.

"Oh, yeah. A real blast." Rachel's words dripped sarcasm.

"Hey now. Some of those guys aren't half bad."

"Which ones?"

"Well, take that Bryson fella. He seemed like a real smart guy. And the senator's son too."

"Ugh. He's almost as short as me and nearly as wide as I am tall." She laughed.

Cole laughed with her and spun her around.

Luke was suddenly behind Cole, tapping him on the shoulder. Cole glanced back.

"May I?" Luke asked.

Cole looked at Rachel with a questioning glance. Her laughter disappeared. She was trapped. She forced a smile and nodded. Cole politely stepped aside, allowing Luke to take over the dance. Rachel took Luke's hand. He placed his other hand at the small of her back, and they moved with the music.

His warm touch on her bare skin sent an unexpected shiver up her spine. She looked around the room, wishing she were anywhere but there. "What makes you think I want to dance with you?"

"Don't matter. I want to dance with you and a gentleman can cut in anytime he's a mind to."

"Is that so?" She hated certain one-sided society rules. They made a woman put up with intolerable nonsense, like dancing with a guy she'd have never said yes to, even if he'd had the gumption to ask outright.

Luke scowled. "Why do you keep doing that?"

"Doing what?" she snapped.

"Making me feel like a total jerk."

She looked away then back up at him, tilting her head. "Walks like a duck, talks like a duck …"

He stopped dancing and let go of her, backing away with his hands raised.

She painted on her best debutante façade, did a slight curtsey, and turned to walk away.

He reached out and grabbed her by the arm, turning her to face him. "Oh, no you don't, little girl. You're not walking away like that."

"Ow!" She cringed when his hand clamped over her still-healing burn. He let go and she pulled her arm in to her side and held it with her other hand as she glared back at him. *Little girl?*

"I'm sorry. I didn't mean to hurt you," he said, glancing at her gloved arm. "Can we start over, please?" He held out his hand to her. "Rachel, may I please have this dance?"

His soft-blue eyes bored into hers, pleading, the depth of his voice breaking through her defenses. After a moment's hesitation, she held out her hand and they resumed the dance.

"What's wrong with your arm? I didn't hurt you, did I?"

"No, well, yes, actually, you did. I, um … I burned it cooking." It was misleading, but she didn't need to tell him that she'd been cooking gasoline, trying to heat it to its boiling point.

"Oh, I'm sorry. Do you like to cook?"

"No. In fact I'm a terrible cook … obviously." She laughed at herself. Golly, he was a big man. Tall and hard but with a gentle grace that defied his size. She could make out the subtle scent of his aftershave or cologne. It was nice, masculine, and Rachel breathed deeply, enjoying it. Then she realized with a start the effect he was having on her. "Isn't your girlfriend going to get jealous?"

"She went to powder her nose. She'll be gone at least a half hour. And she's not my girlfriend. We're just dating."

Tempted to ask how many women he was "just dating" and whether Cassie realized she was one of the many, Rachel decided to let it go. It was none of her business and besides, she could not care less. She wasn't going to be one of them. "A half hour?" Rachel laughed out loud.

"No lying. Time her; you'll see for yourself." Luke looked down at her, and they enjoyed the laugh until he pulled his gaze away. After several moments he glanced back to her and let his eyes roam down the length of her, finally returning to gaze into her eyes. "You look beautiful tonight." His deep, warm voice made her insides shiver. "Like an angel," he added.

"Thank you," she replied, suddenly shy, getting lost in the depths of his eyes.

"So what do you do, Rachel Tate?"

"I'm a computer systems analyst for an engineering company."

His brows shot up. "Really?"

"I have an engineering degree, which is what I'd rather be doing, but I haven't been able to find a job as an engineer yet. Companies don't hire women for those jobs. Not in the South, anyway. At least not often."

"What kind of engineering degree?"

"Mechanical."

"You don't say. Well, I'd hire you in a heartbeat. You should come work with me."

She laughed and looked up at him to see if he was serious. "Doing what?"

"Working on my race team, building cars, helping me win. It's a lot of fun and we do win every now and then." He gave her an encouraging nod. "You know, the other day I read an article about how women were a huge asset for a race team. They're so much better than their male counterparts at keeping their cool in the pits when problems or emergencies come up. But they're hard to find, since not many women have the interest or the necessary skills. But you do. You love everything about cars, *including* working on them. Or 'fixin' 'em up' as Cassandra put it, right?"

The music ended and the band announced they were taking a break. "Thank you for the dance," Rachel said, eager to leave.

"You didn't answer me."

"About what?"

"About coming to work with me."

"Right. I'll think on that." She started to turn away. Cole walked toward them, and she watched Luke's eyes as he, too, saw Cole approaching.

"Don't you want to talk about it some more ... like pay and hours? Don't you want to know some details?"

"I'll think about it, okay?"

"Thank you for the dance. Cole." He acknowledged her friend as he came to stand beside her.

"Luke," Cole said.

Luke reached into the pocket of his coat and pulled out a card. "Hey, if you change your mind." He handed Rachel his card.

She took it. "Thanks." She turned away, and Cole placed her arm in his.

"What was that all about? He gave you his card?"

"He wants me to come and work for him ... be part of his race team."

"Wow. That'd be fun, wouldn't it?"

"I suppose."

"But you're not even considering it. Why?"

Rachel was amazed at how well her friend read her. "I told him I'd think about it."

Cole looked at her sideways. "But you've already decided, haven't you?"

"Yeah, pretty much. I … I don't like him, Cole. I don't trust him." He was too good-looking, too smooth, too … *everything.* He was trouble, and her instincts told her to steer clear.

Luke stood near the French doors that opened onto the gardens and leaned his shoulder against the door frame. It was a lovely evening, cool but not too cold, with a harvest moon shining brilliant white against the black Tennessee sky.

He closed his eyes and relived the dance, remembering how good she felt in his arms. She had a tiny waist and seemed to float right along with him, effortlessly following his lead. Her long beaded gown had ribbon-like straps that crossed in the back and molded to the gentle curves of her lithe frame. It was the ideal color for her—creamy white, like the wings of an angel. With her matching gloves that went up past her elbows, she was the picture of pure innocence and elegance, as full of grace and goodness as a Sunday morning.

He imagined leading her on his arm down the stone path out into the gardens to a quiet place where he could kiss her in the soft moonlight, wrap her in his arms, and whisper sweet things in her ear, telling her exactly how he felt about her. What *would* he tell her if he got the chance? That she'd set his world on fire?

Luke shook his head. If she worked for him, he couldn't have those kinds of thoughts. As he mulled that over, he decided he didn't want her to work for him after all. He wanted her, period. And he was going to get her … somehow.

He'd have to do some figuring.

Talladega

On race morning, Luke made his way to the front of the pit area and looked across to the stands that were starting to fill. Overpowering smells of rubber, fuel, and exhaust hung in the air, stirring his senses. His pulse raced with anticipation as his stomach floated up into his throat. He swallowed hard, forcing it back down.

Luke lived for weekends spent at the track. Racing was part of his blood: the roar of the finely tuned engines, the sheer exhilaration of speed and danger, the near-deafening cheers from the fans. He never felt more alive than right before a race and couldn't wait to share it with Rachel.

He practically danced where he stood, alternating his weight from one leg to the other. He wondered how many races she made it to and how much of a fan she was. She'd known who he was and even what kind of engine he ran, so she had to follow the sport to some degree. He was excited to see her. Wouldn't it be great if he took a first place finish with her watching?

He was due. He'd had a great season so far—finished every race, more than half in the top ten and two wins. He wasn't quite in the running for total points, but it was the best season he'd ever had and there were only five more races left in the year.

Nashville to Talladega was a little less than a four-hour drive. Maybe she and her friends drove down the night before or maybe they got up early. He'd sent her six tickets, enough for all of the friends she was with the night at The Hickory. He stood behind the cement half-wall of the pit area and scanned the crowd, letting his gaze systematically traverse each row of the lower section of stands directly across from the pit area where he knew her tickets were. Nope— not there. Not yet.

Finally, a large group walked down the steps toward the lower section, and he was certain it was them. Great. She was early. He knew she would be.

Luke headed toward them, using the tunnel that crossed under the track to the stands.

Rachel stood to meet him in the aisle.

When he noticed her watching him make his way up the steps, he waved and began taking them two at a time. He was already wearing his race suit and he looked amazing. Tall, athletic, excited. Rachel had to remind herself he was bad news. This was her week. Next week, it would be Cassie. Who knew after that?

"Hey there, beautiful," he called. "You made it."

Rachel's friends joined her in the aisle, and Luke and Cole shook hands. Rachel introduced the others—Allie, Becca, Jackson, and Reese. He shook their hands as well, welcoming each of them. "I'm so glad y'all are here today."

"Can I get your autograph?" Allie asked.

Rachel laughed at her friend's boldness. Allie was never shy.

"You bet." As Allie reached into her bag for a pen, Luke asked them, "You got a particular car you're all rootin' for today?"

"Yours, of course," Allie said, without hesitation, handing him her pen and race program.

"That's good—just checking." Luke grinned mischievously. He signed her program and handed it back. "Hey, if y'all can stick around after the race I'd love to buy you a beer."

"Thanks, but we have to head back," Rachel said.

"No, we don't," Allie countered.

"Actually, we do, Allie. I have to work tomorrow. Several of us do," Rachel reminded her.

"It's okay. Another time maybe. If you change your mind, we'll be up the road a piece at the Rogue River Sports Bar."

"Thanks," Rachel said.

Luke looked at her, his gaze lingering a bit too long. "I'm glad you're here."

Rachel forced a smile, as if she were holding a screaming child. "Thanks for the tickets. You running one of those four-twenty-sevens today?"

"No, those are test engines."

She knew there was no way that big block engine would fit into his race car, even if his crew had been able to rebuild and calibrate it for the race. "Good luck today," she said, anxious to wrap up the conversation.

"Yeah, good luck," her friends echoed.

"And thanks for the race tickets," Reese added. "These are great seats."

"You're welcome anytime. It's always good to know I've got a few folks in my corner." Luke turned to Rachel and captured her gaze. "Enjoy the race."

"Thanks. Good luck today." When he continued to stare, she looked away, more than a little uncomfortable.

Luke shook his head, turned and jogged down the steps, stopping to look back and wave before he disappeared into the tunnel.

Rachel turned to find Allie in her face. "Rachel, he is so *hot*. What is your problem?"

Rachel rolled her eyes.

"I can't believe you, Rach. A real live NASCAR driver actually came up to talk to you and you blew him off."

"He's a guy, Allie. Okay? He's good-looking and drives a race car. So what? He's bad news. Trust me." Just because he gave her free tickets didn't mean she had to drool over him, like Cassie and apparently every other woman he met.

"You're crazy," Allie shot back, falling into her seat.

"Maybe." Rachel sat beside her. "But I'm going to trust my gut on this one."

Luke made his way back to the pit area. What was her problem? Did she not like him?

He recalled the way she'd stared at him when he sang for her. And the way her sweet words afterward had touched his heart. No, she liked him fine. He'd seen it in her eyes.

She couldn't possibly still be mad about the auto auction, could she? He mulled it over in his head and realized that every time he'd seen her, she'd mentioned the engines, not the cars, only the engines. It must have been far more important to her than he'd realized. Why'd she even want a car like that anyway? She'd done an excellent job restoring the Corvette she drove, and a well-restored Vette was worth three or four times what a Galaxie or Thunderbolt would pull in. Why not another Corvette?

Maybe it *was* the 427 engine she wanted. That was the only thing those two cars had in common; that, and they were both Fords. He knew why *he* wanted the 427, but why would she want one? She was an engineer. Was it possible she wanted it for the same reason he did?

He'd have to push his guys to finish up on the Galaxie, make sure it was viable, so he could give her the other one. Maybe then she'd soften up toward him. He gazed across the track to where she and her friends were all seated. Was she worth the trouble? Luke pictured her in his arms and as he'd danced with her at the fundraiser. He closed his eyes and imagined the subtle sweet scent of her, the feel of her warm, smooth skin as his hand rested on her lower back.

His heart skipped a beat. His eyes flew open. She affected him something fierce. He found her again in the crowd across the track and grinned. Yeah, she was worth the trouble, all right. Whatever he had to do, he was going to get her to warm up.

Luke ran a good race that afternoon. His crew came through when he'd gotten bumped midway through, spun out in the middle of the track, and narrowly missed being smashed by another car. He'd had to head to the pits for major body repair, but the alignment was unaffected, and he'd captured third place position with only ten laps remaining.

Luke pushed it, but had a hard time slipping in under the leaders, so he held tight to the third place spot. With only two laps to go Jimmy Johnson, the leader, ran out of gas. Dale Jr., then running a close second, got stuck behind him, and, like a gift from above, Luke was able to pass them both wide on the last lap to win.

Afterward, despite the all-out celebration with his crew, he couldn't stop thinking about Rachel watching it unfold. Was she scared for him when he'd spun out and almost gotten creamed? Did she cheer like crazy as he'd fought his way back up to third place? Was she happy for him when he won? He sure would have enjoyed celebrating with her. He was going to have to invite her again soon. Maybe she was his good luck charm. An angel beneath his wheels.

Luke laughed. Cowboys and angels ... yeah. He liked that.

Charlotte

Race mornings were usually quiet at the track. Everyone was finished unloading and setting up, having done most if not all of it the day before. Interviews, autograph sessions, and qualifications were behind them. The starting lineup was set, and any last-minute adjustments to the cars had already been made. It was simply a time to relax and wait for the stands to fill, the anthem to be sung, and the green flag to drop.

As Luke sat in a lawn chair outside his motor home, enjoying his morning coffee, he watched a family playing in the grass beyond the parking area. If only he could have a family like that one day.

A little boy—maybe seven or eight years old—and his mom and dad were kicking a soccer ball around, playing keep-away. They laughed, having a great time. After a while the winded parents sat on the grass to take a break. The husband put his arm around his wife, and she looked up at him and gave him a kiss while the little boy continued to run around kicking his ball. What would it have been like to be that little boy, with both parents playing with him, watching over him, loving him?

An image flashed in Luke's mind of himself as a little boy, left alone, standing on an expanse of grass, dark clouds moving in overhead. No one around, no one to play with. He had waited, afraid, hoping, then fell to his knees, praying for them to come back.

Luke shook himself out of it, ran his hand through his hair, and looked back to the parents. The wife relaxed in her husband's arms, while the man watched his son with a loving gaze, his pride shining forth as his son basked unaware in the love and warmth of his family.

How could his father have walked out on something like that? What kind of man leaves his wife and son and never comes back? Luke couldn't fathom an excuse to explain it. Even if the woman wasn't all the man hoped for, how does a man abandon his child forever?

How could his father not be the least bit curious about what happened to him? Did he even know that the wife he'd abandoned had died, leaving their son in a children's home?

He wondered if he looked like his father. If he got his deep voice from him. He could remember playing catch with a man once in a garage on a faded beige rug. He was tall with dark hair. If the man was his father, it was his only memory of him. It would explain his height and his dark-brown hair. He wondered what other traits he'd inherited, but most of all, why his father hadn't loved him enough to stick around.

As self-pity and despair rose, he thought about his adopted parents. They'd loved him—or at least they'd tried their best. He was seven by the time they adopted him and, in his young mind, way beyond needing hugs and kisses from a stand-in mother. Deep down he had craved the affection, but was too afraid to accept it. There were still times when he felt his adopted mom wanted to hug him, but he'd always held back, maintained a safe distance. He didn't know why. Trust? If you let someone love you, they could hurt you.

Maybe that's why he'd never fallen in love. At twenty-six, he'd never been in love. He'd had plenty of girlfriends who came and went, but he never let anyone get close enough to hurt him. Was he destined to be a lonely bachelor? Was he capable of loving someone? Letting someone in? Trusting a woman with his heart … trusting that she wouldn't leave him?

He thought about Rachel Tate and a wide grin brightened his face. What a little firecracker she was, and pretty as a bug too. Could he make her fall in love with him? If only he could be her knight in the white Charger, sweep her off her feet, be everything she dreamed of, they could have one of those happy-ever-after endings. But would he be able to love her back, to give her what she needed?

He watched as the family made their way back to the motor coach area, the husband and wife walking arm-in-arm, the little boy holding his mother's hand. He wanted that more than anything else in the world. Longed for it with every fiber of his well-intentioned heart. He wanted a family like the one he never had.

He wanted to believe he could be a great husband and father. If there was anything in this life worth living for, it was that—to love and be loved, fully, faithfully, forever.

Was Rachel the one? He smiled as he recalled her fire and passion at the auction, the way her green eyes had watched him while he sang at The Hickory, and how she'd touched his heart with her kind words afterward. A soothing warmth settled over him as the memory of her honey-sweet voice lingered. If she wasn't the one, she was the closest he'd ever come.

Luke's cell phone rang and he jumped up to grab it from the motor home. "Yeah?"

It was Jimmy Ray, his crew chief. "Where are you, man? We have ten minutes to roll time. You gonna race today or what?"

Luke checked his phone. Where had the time gone? And where was Cassandra? She should have arrived over an hour ago. "I'm on my way."

He grabbed a bottle of water from the fridge, rushed down the bus steps, locked the door behind him, and turned to see Cassandra strolling his way.

"Hey there, sugar," she called.

Luke stopped. "Hey, beautiful," he called back, crossing his arms over his chest and shifting his weight from one foot to the other as she approached.

She looked gorgeous in painted-on jeans, steel-blue-and-black "Team Brandt" racing tee shirt, and high-heeled boots. She had tied the shirt at her waist, showing off more than a little skin above her low-cut jeans. Fed up with her leisurely pace, he took two quick strides to meet her and leaned in to give her a quick peck on the cheek.

"We gotta run, babe, come on." He took her hand and turned toward the pit area.

"Whoa." She pulled her hand away. "I gotta' use the little girl's room."

"You'll have plenty of time to do that in the pit area. We have to go now."

"I don't want to use the public restrooms. They're so—"

"I'm late." He dropped her hand and started walking away.

"Luke Brandt." She ran to catch up with him. "Slow down," she whined, "Please, Luke."

He slowed his pace near the pit area when he saw they hadn't started pulling the cars out; he was okay. He waited for her, scowling as she neared. "What happened?"

She feigned innocence. "Whatever do you mean?"

"Why were you so late? I told you no later than eleven o'clock. It's after noon."

"I got a late start and the traffic was horrible."

"I warned you it would be."

"*Okay.* I'm sorry already."

It was a lame apology, but probably the best she was capable of. He leaned in close to her. "Cassandra, this is not a night at the movies or a picnic in the park. It's a NASCAR race and I'm a driver. I can't be late. See all those folks in the stands? They came to watch a race. Paid a lot of money. Most of them drove a long way to get here. The race doesn't wait for a guy's girlfriend who's late. And I won't either. Is that clear?"

She pulled back, flipped her hair over her shoulder and looked away, refusing to answer.

He hustled the last few yards to his car and crew. "Hey, guys. Sorry I'm late."

Several minutes later, as the national anthem was being sung, he stood, hat in hand, and glanced back at Cassandra. She was always late, had no respect for anyone else's time, and little regard for what was important to him.

They'd been seeing each other for a couple of months, and every time he picked her up for a date, she'd made him wait at least twenty minutes. The one time he'd agreed to meet her for a picnic lunch in a park near his garage she'd been a half hour late, then pouted when he had to leave after thirty minutes. He only took an hour for lunch, like his crew, and he wasn't going to make an exception because she was late.

When the anthem ended, he turned to his crew, but caught Cassandra's gaze. Standing behind them, she waved and blew him a kiss. He forced a smile and waved back. She sure was a sight for sore eyes but … that was where it ended. She was more high-maintenance than an old Harley. And *needy.* The most demanding woman he'd ever gone out with. What little time he had to spare between racing every weekend and working on the car, she didn't appreciate enough to be on time. In fact, every aspect of their relationship was about as one-sided as her regard for him.

So why was he wasting his time and effort on her?

An image of Rachel up on stage invaded unbidden and his mood brightened. That's who he should be going out with, not Cassandra. He resolved to make changes on that front real soon.

Luke turned to his car and the race to be run, letting everything else empty out of his head. He needed a good finish today. After last week's win at Talladega and their amazing season, he was, for the first time since he'd started racing Cup Series, in "The Chase"—the top ten for total points in a season. Still far from the top three, out of more than forty drivers, to be in the top ten was a huge accomplishment. He was thoroughly pleased, but more importantly, so were his sponsors.

He began on a real good run. He'd qualified fourteenth in the field and had moved up steadily, consistently gaining position as the laps ticked off.

His #11 Pacific Oil Dodge was an awesome machine that day. He'd started out running a little too tight in the center of the turns, but his crew made a slight tire pressure adjustment and he was dialed in from then on.

At only seventeen laps to go, Luke cut his right front tire and his car suffered suspension damage when it hit the turn one wall. He made it into the pits, but the damage was sufficient to put him out of the race. His first DNF—Did Not Finish—of the season was sure to drop him further back in the standings.

He was furious. With only four races remaining in the season, there was virtually no way to break into the championship hunt again.

The Gift

"We're getting rid of the Thunderbolt today," Luke told his crew. "Jimmy Ray, Cam, I need you guys to deliver it to this address. It's a home out toward Cannonsburg. Park it out of the way, but where it'll be seen if no one's home. I put a note on the dash. Make sure it stays there, understand?"

Jimmy Ray and Cam nodded. "When do you want it done?" Jimmy Ray asked.

"Now would be good. When you get back here we can get to work."

His men opened the overhead door, and the early December chill whipped in, sucking out what little heat they'd coaxed from the small electric heater. Jimmy Ray backed the Thunderbolt out and Cam got into his own truck to follow and give him a ride back.

Alone in the shop, Luke started up the Galaxie. It sounded good. Powerful. The rumble of the huge engine rattled the shop doors. He thought of Rachel and smiled. Surely she'd be pleasantly surprised when she got home and found the Thunderbolt in her driveway. He'd debated which car to give her, settling on the Thunderbolt for two reasons. First, it was a much rarer car to find and it would be worth more than the relatively commonplace Galaxie if she restored it to sell. Second, his crew had worked hard to get the Galaxie running smoothly, and he didn't want to pull it out from under them.

He shut off the engine and closed the overhead door. He had a few more things to fix, then he wanted to run some baseline test laps before he added his new carburetor. The next few weeks were going to be intense, and he looked forward to testing his newly designed carburetor.

When Rachel pulled into her driveway that evening, she immediately noticed the Thunderbolt at the side of the barn. Her heart raced with excitement. Was Luke here? She parked and went to check it out. Slipping behind the wheel, she saw the note on the dash:

> *It runs. And so does the Galaxie, so this one's all yours.*
> *Enjoy.*
> *Your friend, Luke.*

Rachel started it up as her dad came out of the house. She jumped out, popped the hood, and looked the engine over.

Her dad said, "Saw the note. A gift, huh?"

"I reckon it is." She shivered in the cold December air. "I can't accept it though."

"What do you mean? Of course you can."

She shook her head. "I can't. Not from this guy." She looked at him, then turned off the engine.

"Why not? It's from Luke Brandt, ain't it?"

"Yes, but you don't understand. He's trouble with a capital T, and I can't accept a gift like this from him without consequences."

"Sweet pea, you've been waiting on this engine for months now and the chances of another one coming along are, I don't know, slim to none?" He put his arm around her shoulder. "Come on now, honey, you've got to keep it."

Part of her wanted to jump with joy at the opportunity before her. But her sensible side warned her of the inevitable implications if she kept it. So close and yet ... out of reach.

She waffled over it. She shouldn't accept it. She *couldn't*. Every instinct told her it was a bad move. But maybe if she paid him for it, he wouldn't ... what? Have any expectations? What was she afraid of?

She looked at her father and bit the corner of her lower lip. She wanted to take his advice, but he had no idea what Luke Brandt was like. Not the kind of man a woman wanted to be beholden to, that was for sure. "I think I should return it. I'll find another one."

"I think you should keep it. Pay him if you must, but definitely keep it. But do what you think is right, sweet pea." He gave her a reassuring hug before going back into the house.

She stared at the engine for a long time before she finally slammed the hood, opened a shop door stall, and pulled the car inside. When she glanced back at it before she closed the door, her pulse quickened. She looked forward to the coming weekend when she'd have a chance to start working on it.

Working beneath the Galaxie, Luke heard the shop door open and close, the click-click of footsteps on the hard concrete. High heels?

"Hey."

Rachel?

"Anybody here?"

He rolled from under the car, struggling to control his grin. He stood and stretched his long frame. "Hey, beautiful." Whew, she looked pretty. She was obviously dressed for work. She wore a slim-fitted khaki skirt, white sweater, and heels, her long hair clipped at the base of her neck.

The overhead doors were down and the place was empty except for the cars, the steel blue and black #11 Pacific Oil Dodge off to the side, the Galaxie front and center, its hood raised. Behind her, pulled up in front of the shop door, was her Vette. It suited her perfectly—petite, elegant, but full of fire, with plenty of power under the hood. A force that belied the beautiful exterior. Like her, it was all curves, style, and strength.

"How's it running?" She nodded to the Galaxie.

Luke stretched his shoulders, raising his elbows and pressing them backward. He was wearing old jeans and a tight, sleeveless black tee shirt. His dark-brown hair fell into his eyes so he had to tilt his head sideways as he looked at her. "Want to hear it?" He went around and reached in the window to start it up.

It was loud, the rumble of the engine reverberating against the close walls of the shop. "How's it sound to you?" he called over the noise.

She stared into space as she listened for a few moments then shouted, "I think you're losing compression somewhere. There's a hissing sound."

Really? He tried to hear it. "Anything else?"

"Besides the belts?" She listened a bit longer and shook her head.

Luke turned off the engine.

"Dual exhaust, right?" she asked as she walked to the back to have a look. "I think you need to tighten down the pipes too. It shakes more than it should."

She was amazing. The worn belts were obvious; anyone would have heard those. But the hissing from a loss of compression and the loose pipes? He couldn't wait to run a compression test to see if she was right. He picked up a rag from the workbench as he walked toward her.

"I came to thank you for the Thunderbolt—"

"You're welcome."

"And while I do truly appreciate the grand gesture on your part, I shouldn't accept it."

"Aw, come on now—"

"But I want it," she laughed at herself, "so I'd like to pay you for it." She held out an envelope.

Luke glanced at it, finished wiping his hands, and tossed the rag back onto the workbench. "What's this?"

"I'd like to pay you."

"I'm not taking your money. It's a gift." He shook his head.

"Well, I can't accept a gift like that from you, so take the money. Please."

"Rachel." She looked so pretty, he couldn't think straight.

She reached around him and set the envelope on the workbench.

He felt her closeness as she leaned around him, as if in slow-motion. He seized the opportunity and put a hand on either side of her neck, tilting her face up to meet his. He looked into her eyes for several heartbeats, then slowly leaned in to kiss her, hard and demanding at first, and then more tenderly, savoring the softness of her lips as he touched them ever so lightly, over and over.

She relaxed into him and he continued, wanting more, licking her lips, and when her mouth opened against his, his tongue hungrily explored the sweet wet warmth within.

When he finally pulled back, his heart was racing wildly, his head spinning, his knees and every muscle in his whole body felt weak, and he had to focus to breathe. He laughed softly, thrilled with the way she made him feel and the obvious passion on her beautiful face.

"Don't," she whispered, pushing against his chest.

"Rachel," he began, desperate to hold on to her.

She shook her head, "Don't." She broke free and backed away, wide-eyed, finally turning to leave.

What? He couldn't believe she was pushing him away. Not after that. And now walking away? "You're such a tease, little girl. You know you want it. You want me; admit it." He cringed at the anger and arrogance in his words.

Rachel whirled around, eyes narrowed, teeth clenched, and took a step back toward him. "Why do you always do that?"

"Do what?"

"Always ruin it by acting like such a—"

"Such a what?" His voice was harsh, ugly. "Finish it, little girl. Like a jerk? Is that what you were going to say?"

She turned and continued walking away. "Walks like a duck, talks like a duck," she called back over her shoulder as she yanked open the door. She didn't look back.

"Argh." He hated that saying. He whirled, kicked the nearest tool chest, and swore. He walked to the door and watched her pull away as he ran his fingers through his hair in frustration.

Luke was still fuming several minutes later when his guys returned from lunch. Jimmy Ray threw him a bag with his sandwich in it. "You wouldn't believe the '66 Vette we saw sitting down the street. It was a real beauty."

Luke shook his head. "That was her; the girl I told you about who wanted the 427."

"Well I don't know what you said to her, but—" Cam broke off abruptly when Jimmy Ray hit him hard in the shoulder.

"But what?" Luke demanded.

Cam shook his head. "Nothin'."

"*What?*" Luke raised his voice, "Tell me."

Jimmy Ray spoke up. "Pretty sure she was cryin'."

"Argh." Luke ran both hands through his hair. "She drives me crazy." He whirled around, looking for something else he could kick, hit, or throw. He was a complete jerk and he hated himself, knowing he'd made her cry. He inhaled as he tried to calm himself before turning back to the guys. "Jimmy Ray, check the compression on that thing. And Cam, when you finish the belts, tighten down those pipes. They're shaking. I'll be in my office." He stomped to the other room and slammed the door behind him.

Falling into the chair behind his desk, Luke tried not to think about how he'd blown up in front of his guys like an out-of-control top-fuel dragster. Instead, he turned his focus to paperwork. After a couple of minutes, he completely lost it and cleared the desk with his arm in one angry sweep, sending all the papers along with everything else that was there, including his lunch, sailing across the room.

He leaned back in his chair and ran his hands through his hair again. That was the most amazing kiss. What went wrong? He let his mind go back to the beginning of her visit. It had started out fine. He was so happy to see her. She looked gorgeous in that slim-fitting skirt of hers and he'd been excited to show her the Galaxie.

Where did it go wrong? What did he do? The kiss? No, that was amazing. The timing and everything about it could not have been more perfect. She kissed him back, even melted into him. He could still feel her warmth against his chest. She'd kissed like a woman who wanted to be loved; there was no mistaking that. When he pulled back to look at her, before she pushed him away, what was it? What was in the depths of her beautiful eyes? He closed his eyes and relived the moment, focusing on her reaction at the end. When he reopened his eyes, he thought he knew. At first it was passion, unabashed desire, but then it was fear. But why was she so afraid of him?

What was he going to say to her? Was he going to tell her how he felt? Whew, that would've been something new for him. Maybe he'd wanted to. But why didn't he?

How *did* he feel about her? He wanted her. Of that much he was sure. She set his world on fire and now she was mad at him … *again*.

He should've let her go, not said a thing. Let her leave and think about it for a while. She would've realized she wanted him as much as he wanted her. Wouldn't she? But, instead, he was insensitive and arrogant.

Luke brought his mind back to the present and looked at the mess he'd made. He rubbed his hand across his forehead several times. *Now* what was he supposed to do? Clean up, for starters. Then he had to figure out what to do about that little girl who'd burrowed into his heart and soul to taunt him so mercilessly.

He was still on his knees collecting papers when Jimmy Ray knocked on the door. "Come in," he barked.

Jimmy Ray opened the door slowly, pushing debris aside as he did. He stuck his head in and looked down at Luke. "Hey, boss, the compression analysis says there's a leak somewhere. I'm going to start with the head gasket unless you got other ideas."

"Nope. That's where I'd start. Let me know if that's not it."

Jimmy Ray paused. "Everything all right?"

"No, everything's not all right. It's about as screwed up as it can be. Go on now." Before Jimmy Ray closed the door, Luke added, "I'm sorry, Jimmy Ray. Thanks for askin', man, but there's nothing you can do to help me with this one."

At five-twenty Luke was still in his office. The guys had cleaned up, put away all the tools, and had all the doors locked down, ready to call it a day. Jimmy Ray knocked again.

"Yeah," Luke answered.

Jimmy Ray poked his head in far enough to ask, "Hey, boss. Cam and I are gonna stop at Ike's for a beer if you want to join us."

Luke looked at the piles of papers on his desk. "I have a lot to catch up on here and I'm just getting started. Maybe I'll stop by on my way home."

"All right, well, we'll be there."

Luke didn't look back up, but waved instead. "Have a good night."

Several hours and quite a few beers later, Jimmy Ray and Cam were trying to talk Luke into leaving Ike's. "Come on, boss, you've had enough, don't you think?" Cam asked.

When the image of Rachel's passion-filled eyes swam before him, he found his answer and shook his head. "Nope." Luke looked from Cam to the waitress. "April, sweetheart, another round please."

Jimmy Ray shook his head at the waitress, and she collected the empties.

"Go on now, Luke. Go home," she said gently.

Luke stared. She was real pretty and petite like Rachel, but with blond hair and blue eyes. Yeah, she could help him forget. She was exactly what he needed. "Will you give me a ride home, darlin'?"

"Sure, Luke, I'll give you a ride. Sit tight for five minutes while I finish cleaning up, and we'll be out of here."

The next morning, Luke woke, as usual, before dawn, and lay unmoving for several minutes, a happy grin curving his lips as he recalled the dream he'd been having. Rachel was there with him, curled up at his side. She had been amazing, sweet and soft and passionate, like he knew she would be. He stretched lazily, glancing to his side to see the woman sharing his bed. He saw the blond hair first.

He swore under his breath. It had been the most amazing dream, and he was sure it was Rachel he'd made love to all night, not ... April? He closed his eyes again and struggled to remember. Right. April was her name, and she was the waitress from Ike's.

He eased out of bed and dressed, planning to go for a walk in the woods before heading to the garage. He desperately needed to clear his head. He sat beside her and gently woke her. "Hey, sweetheart," he whispered, "I have to take off, but sleep in as long as you like." He brushed her long blond hair away from her pretty face. "And leave me your number, okay?" He knew he wouldn't call but felt he should at least ask for it.

"Mmm," she murmured, smiling up at him. He kissed her on the forehead and left.

Out in the woods, trekking alone through the cool, early-morning mist, Luke tried desperately to get Rachel out of his head. It was no use. She was all he could think about. Why did he act like such a jerk every time he saw her? It was obvious she wanted nothing to do with him. And yet she kissed him back like a woman who wanted to be kissed, like a woman who wanted to be loved. How could she do that, then turn on him and think so little of him? It was his fault. He was the one who was pushing her away. Whenever they'd started to get close, he'd slammed the door with a rude comment. Why did he keep doing that? And how was he going to set things right?

He sat beneath a huge sycamore tree near the creek to watch the sun come up, and thought about the kiss. He relived each nuance of it, from the slow, hard, needy beginning to the soft and tender moments in the middle, to their passionate gaze at the end. He had to get her back. That was the best kiss he'd ever had. His heart raced thinking about it. He needed her ... like nothing he'd ever needed.

But how could he get her to look his way again? He could send her tickets to Daytona, find her in the stands, talk to her then. But that was two months away and then some, and he needed time alone with her to prove he was a good guy.

He was, wasn't he?

All of a sudden, he wasn't so sure. He thought about some of the things he'd done and said that had made her angry since the first time they'd met. No, he hadn't been a good guy at all, not where she was concerned. He'd been a complete jerk.

But a man could change, couldn't he? For something worthwhile, something this important, a man could be anything he set his mind to. For the love of a woman he could be whatever she needed him to be, couldn't he? For her, he *could* be a nice guy. What he wouldn't give for her to kiss him like that again.

As he watched the glorious sunrise over the sleepy meadow and the slumbering hills beyond, he pondered what he knew about her. It wasn't nearly enough, but there was one thing he knew—that kiss was the start of something special. And he had to somehow convince her to go out with him.

When the sun was full up, he made his way to the garage, feeling like a new man. A man with a purpose. He went straight to his office and finished all the paperwork he'd made a mess of the day before, then checked on the Galaxie. The guys fired it up and it sounded great—a whole lot better than the day before—but the hissing was still there.

"Find the leak, Jimmy Ray," Luke said.

Luke spent the rest of the day helping him change out the exhaust valve on the Galaxie.

At home, on his way to shower, he noticed April's note on his nightstand:

She's a mighty lucky girl.
"Rachel."

He picked it up and swore. She'd signed it "Rachel," in quotes. He cringed, knowing he must have called her Rachel in the night. He ran his hands through his hair and let his head fall back to bang against the wall. Oh, man, what kind of guy does that? She was a real sweet girl too. She deserved better.

Luke knew what he had to do.

He walked into Ike's thirty minutes later, looked around, but didn't see April. He headed to the bar.

"Is April working tonight?"

"Nope. She's not in until tomorrow night," the bartender said.

"Okay, thanks." Luke left, but he resolved to stop in the next night to apologize and try to explain. He had no idea what he'd say. What *could* he say? He wasn't exactly sure, but he knew he had to tell her how sorry he was. She deserved at least that much.

He spent the rest of the evening flipping through TV channels as he kicked himself for being such an insensitive jerk and wondered how he could get a fresh start with Rachel.

The next night, he walked into Ike's after work and sat at the same table he and the guys had shared a few nights before. Within minutes, April came over. "What can I get you, Luke?" she asked. Her tone was all business.

"I want to talk to you."

She looked around at the nearby tables. It was still early, and only a few tables had customers at them. She slid into the chair across from him and crossed her arms, unsmiling. "What is it, Luke?" she asked, tapping her red-painted fingernails on the table.

He reached for her hand. "I want to apologize."

She pulled her hand back. "For calling me your girlfriend's name?" Her voice was much harsher than he'd expected.

"I feel downright awful about that. You're a sweet girl and you deserve better." He reached for her hand again. This time she didn't pull away. "I'm so sorry," he said, his voice soft, sincere.

She shook her head and gave him a sad smile as she stared down at his hand covering hers. "She must really be somethin'."

He let out a bitter laugh. "She's not even my girlfriend. She's just someone I met who ... sort of looks like you." They actually didn't look anything alike, but they were both petite and pretty.

She studied him closely. "Well, she's in your head, and she's got your heart all wrapped up too. If she's not your girlfriend, maybe she oughta be." She stared into his eyes. "Maybe you need to tell her how you feel."

If only he could. "I'm not good at that sort of thing. In fact, every time I see her, I say something awful and ..." He looked away and shook his head. "... I end up pushing her away."

A bell rang at the counter, signaling an order was ready.

She stood. "Well, you gotta figure that out, hon."

"I know." He rose with her and gazed down into her face. "You're a beautiful woman, April," he said, genuinely meaning it.

"Go on now, Luke. You're gonna make me cry." She pushed him gently on the shoulder then looked away, hiding the sadness in her misty-blue eyes.

He kissed her on the cheek and left.

Embers

Rachel woke early Saturday morning, planning to work on the Thunderbolt, but as she lay contemplating how she'd spend the day, she wasn't thinking about the old muscle car. It was Luke's kiss that dominated her thoughts.

She closed her eyes, savoring the warm glow she'd felt in that all-too-brief moment. Her heart beat faster as she relived the gentle way he'd held her face in his hands, the tenderness in the way he'd kissed her—hard and hungry at first, then ever so softly—and the intensity of the way he'd made her feel. Deep longing escaped her lips.

She wanted to be loved more than anything. But why him? He was flat-out wrong for her on so many levels. He was absolutely *not* the type of guy to wait for sex, nor was he probably remotely interested in things like love or commitment. Not to mention marriage. Oh God, why would You have me fall for him?

She rolled to her side and pulled her hands together beneath her cheek to pray.

"God, please guide me today and every day. Help me to know Your will and to act on it ... bravely. And thank You for the gift of another beautiful day. Please help me to live it fully as a loving daughter and good Christian. In Jesus' name, forever and always, every day. Amen."

Rachel got up and dressed in her old work jeans and a tee shirt, then joined her father in the kitchen. "Morning, Daddy." She poured a cup of coffee.

"Morning, sweet pea." He set down his newspaper.

"I'm going to start rebuilding the Thunderbolt today. Want to help?" She sat across from him at the small kitchen table.

"Can't today. Mr. Tandy needs my help pulling down some hay for his animals, then I'm putting a gutter back on at Mrs. Libby's place. She'll more'n likely send me home with a four-course dinner, if you're going to be around later."

"I'll be here." Her father regularly helped many of their elderly neighbors. Some paid him a small hourly handyman wage. Others, like Mrs. Libby, paid him in home-cooked meals and baked goods. Her father was a neighborly, good man. She admired how he cared for those around him, even the ones he barely knew.

She had the engine broken down to the head by late afternoon. As she surveyed the parts laid out neatly on the floor beside the car, she wondered if this was ever going to pay off. She believed in her carburetor idea and so did her father, but putting it into this engine was going to be the final test of its viability. There would be no *almost* or *just about*. It would either work, or it wouldn't. If it didn't, she'd be back to the drawing board, square one again, and out seventy-two hundred bucks.

Actually, she could recoup her money on this car. It was in rough shape, but with a completely rebuilt engine and a little body work, it could be worth a pretty penny to the right collector. Muscle cars were a good investment if you were willing to put in the time and effort to restore them yourself. And this was a hard-to-find model, making it even more valuable with a good restoration. And she would do it right, using only original parts.

She glanced at the carburetor on the workbench. It hadn't taken long to rebuild. Not nearly as long as the original prototype she'd blown up earlier. She felt giddy with anticipation as she thought about installing it in the Thunderbolt. A flutter in her belly belied how nervous she was about that final step. "Don't think about it yet," she told herself. "You've got plenty of work to do before you're ready."

She checked the interior to see if she needed to order any materials to restore it. As she slid behind the wheel, she saw Luke's note still taped to the dash. The signature at the bottom read: *Your friend, Luke*. As if they could ever be friends.

It seemed like every time they ran into each other, he said something mean or acted like a complete jerk, and at least one of them left angry. Was it her? Did she bring out the worst in him, or was he like that naturally? He wouldn't have the reputation he did for attracting women if he treated them all like he treated her. Maybe it *was* her. But what about her got him all riled up? What was she doing wrong?

Rachel thought back to their first meeting at the auto auction. She'd been downright rude, but he'd deserved it for selfishly buying both engines she'd wanted. She laughed as she pictured him standing in her cloud of dust. The next time she saw him was at The Old Hickory downtown, and he'd tried to apologize, even offered her race tickets. And what did she say? She'd been okay that time—not with the original apology, she'd made him work at that—but she accepted the tickets and told him she'd go. She even told him she liked his song.

The one he'd sung for her. It was amazing. He had the deepest, sexiest voice. His music had affected her something fierce. She'd even given him her phone number. But he hadn't called.

Maybe he was one of those guys who was out for one thing and one thing only. And sensing she wasn't the type to put out, he decided she wasn't worth his time. But the kiss—he couldn't possibly kiss like that all the time, could he? Special, like kissing someone who was kissing for the first time. The way he had looked at her in the afterglow of the moment ... that was real. Despite her limited experience, she knew it was. It had to be.

But then, the next instant he was rude again, taunting her. And for what? For pushing him away? He probably wasn't used to a woman telling him no. Maybe that was it. He'd gotten excited and didn't like not getting what he wanted. Rachel leaned back to rest her head against the seatback. *Well, too bad, you arrogant jerk, because I am not sleeping with you.*

Rachel forced him out of her head and made a mental list of repairs. The front bench seat needed to be reupholstered, but the backseat was fine and the dashboard and sidewalls were in pretty good shape too. It needed a good cleaning and new carpeting, but that was an easy one. Maybe a new shifter and housing. Those nice little touches, small as they were, went a long way toward making the interior look new again. It was missing a door lock on one of the back doors, but that should be easy to find online.

Rachel took Luke's note from the dash, went to the workbench, and grabbed a pen. She wrote a list on the back, then pinned it to the upper cabinet door in front of her.

She studied the pile of parts on the floor and the almost-empty engine compartment. How cool would it be if he were there helping her, working at her side, only the two of them? She loved doing this. Being a NASCAR driver-owner, he must love it too. She'd never met anyone like him before. And he was so hot. Tall and lean, hard and strong, with those gorgeous baby blues that made her smile for no good reason. And the kiss. Oh, why couldn't he be a *nice* guy?

Rachel berated herself for still thinking about him. She turned the music way up, hoping it would help. It didn't.

Luke walked into the shop early Saturday morning, going straight to the electric heater to plug it in. While he waited for the coffee to brew, he looked across the workbench that ran the length of the back wall, his gaze landing on the white envelope Rachel had left earlier in the week. Inside he found a check for seventy-two-hundred dollars, exactly what he'd paid for the Thunderbolt. He threw it down and stared at it. This was the very spot where he'd kissed her. He closed his eyes and relived it, his heartbeat quickening. "How did you do that to me, little girl?"

Suddenly weak, he leaned against the workbench, took a long, deep breath, then released it. He couldn't believe how much he wanted her, how hard it was to keep her out of his head.

He'd stayed in the night before, on a Friday, too exhausted to do anything because he hadn't had a good night's sleep since she'd walked into his shop that day. Night after sleepless night, he lay awake thinking about her, imagining her lying in bed beside him, kissing him like she had that day, imagining how it would be to make love to her.

Racing was his life and he loved it, but he thoroughly enjoyed the short off-season too. At least he used to. Normally it was a time to relax, unwind, party until all hours, meet new people. Women mostly. But not the last few days. He couldn't get Rachel out of his head, and he couldn't be with anyone else either. A brief image of April flitted before him, followed by self-disgust slapping him in the face.

Luke poured coffee, sipped it, and then set it on the workbench while he pulled out his phone. He stared at Rachel's number, wishing he had a photo to go with it. All he had to do was tap the green call button and he'd be talking to her in seconds. But what would he say? Would she want to talk to him after the last time?

He pictured her sitting at the four-way stop down the street, wiping away tears. Maybe she's not quite so tough, after all.

Oh, I'm so sorry, little girl.

What could he say to set things right? He could pretend it never happened. *How's it going with the Thunderbolt?* She'd probably hang up on him or tell him not to call again. He owed her an apology. *I'm sorry I'm such a jerk. Will you go out with me?* Yeah, right.

No, he couldn't call her.

Maybe he could drop into that little bar downtown, wait for her to show up, then give her a straight-from-the-heart apology. That might do it. Be open and honest and let the chips fall where they may. She'd appreciate that if he did it right.

Walks like a duck, talks like a duck ... Her words rang in his head. He'd have to be careful not to give her an opportunity to use that line again. He'd come to loathe it. So what should he say to her? What was in his heart?

She was.

She'd gotten to him with a single kiss. How could he want someone so bad, ache for her with every fiber of his being, after one kiss?

Luke ran his hands through his hair and leaned back against the workbench. First he'd have to apologize, sincerely and explicitly. A simple "I'm sorry" wouldn't do this time. It had to be like, "You scare me, little girl, and I don't know how to handle that. It makes me want to push you away, but ..." But what? What else? How could he possibly tell her how she affected him? Should he tell her how much she meant to him? Definitely. "Rachel, I think I'm falling in love with you, and it scares me." He couldn't tell her that. Was he falling in love with her? After one kiss?

Luke reached for his coffee, remembering why he was there on a Saturday. He'd come in to change out the carburetor in the Galaxie with his newly designed one, to make sure it would fit and make any modifications if it didn't. He still hadn't run the baseline test laps. The weather had been far too wet and icy, but he wanted the car to be ready when the weather cleared.

He popped the hood, reached for a wrench, and began pulling off the old carburetor. He set it on the workbench beside his coffee cup. As he reached to pick up the new one, he heard a car door close and his heart skipped a beat. For a fleeting second, he hoped it would be Rachel, but his face fell when he saw his father.

"Hey, Daddy." He walked back to the Galaxie. His father, a bear of a man, owned several large companies in Nashville, from manufacturing to heating and cooling to real estate holdings, as well as serving on the boards of other private companies. Luke didn't see him often, but it was typical for him to show up now and again.

"What are you up to here on a Saturday morning?" He faced Luke from the opposite side of the Galaxie.

"Replacing a carburetor."

"This your new car? You going to race it?"

"New in September. Remember the auto auction I told you about? Picked it up there. Don't plan to race it. It's a test car."

His father nodded as he looked over the engine then at the part Luke was holding. "That looks ... different."

Luke appreciated his father's perceptiveness. He was no mechanic, but often surprised Luke with his understanding of the basics. "It is a little different. It's my own design. It's got an Ozonator—an O3 injector—on the bottom that should make it a lot more fuel efficient."

His father raised his brows as he studied the component, then looked back to Luke. "More fuel efficient, huh? You think Pacific Oil is going to like that?"

His father, always the businessman, considered the interests of all the parties involved. "Don't matter to me if they like it or not. Fuel efficiency is key to winning races. You can't log laps when you're in the pits fueling up. And besides, if this works like I think it will, it could be a real breakthrough in more fuel-efficient engines. And if I lose an oil company sponsor, I may pick up an automaker." He gave his father an optimistic grin.

His father watched Luke start to put the new unit into the engine and tighten things down. "Got plans later? Let's go hunting this afternoon."

Luke looked up. "Okay, sounds good."

His father smiled, clearly pleased. "Come by the house around three and we'll head up together, okay?"

"Three o'clock." For the first time he noticed the dimple in his father's cheek. A few of Luke's girlfriends had commented on his own dimple, but how odd that his adoptive father had one too.

"I'll see you then." With that he left Luke to his work.

Luke enjoyed hunting with his father, a sport they both loved. It gave them a chance to reconnect and spend quality time together relaxing, sharing hunting strategies and secrets, trying to outwit the lower species. Anytime Luke could sit in the woods, alone with nature, he was a happy man.

It took several hours to get the unit installed and working properly. Then Luke took the car out for a test run around the block. It was smooth, even when he gunned it. He couldn't wait to run test laps and see how it performed against the original stock four-barrel carb.

He pulled it back into its stall in the shop and popped the hood to let it cool, leaving the overhead door open for the cold air to help do the job. He wondered how it would compare with the standard fuel-injection engines. Next season, for the first time, NASCAR was going to allow fuel-injected engines, which basically meant a computer controlled the flow of air and fuel to the engine instead of an antiquated carburetor. They'd still allow carbureted engines, but the high-tech fuel-injection engines were so much more efficient that running without one would be a significant disadvantage.

He wondered if NASCAR would allow his modified carburetor, assuming it did test out well. Each car was required to undergo a thorough inspection before every qualification and before every race. He'd have to get their approval up front.

Man, he could use an engineer on his team next year. In fact, it would be a prerequisite if he used a fuel-injected engine. He'd have to find someone tech savvy; someone who knew how to use a computer to connect to the car, make mapping adjustments. Someone who could collect and interpret the massive amount of information and provide it to the crew in a meaningful way. Yep, it was going to be an absolute necessity next year, even if he *was* able to run with his new high-efficiency carburetor.

Rachel.

Computer systems analyst, mechanical engineer, beautiful, seductive in the most innocent and yet provocative way—he needed her in more ways than one.

Luke pulled up in front of The Old Hickory Inn where he'd seen Rachel several months before. Her car wasn't at the curb or in the side lot, but he wasn't surprised. It was a cold and rainy night, typical for mid-December, and it could easily turn to ice with another ten-degree drop in temperature. She more than likely didn't drive her Vette in bad weather. He wondered what her other vehicle was. A truck, maybe? He smiled. Chicks in trucks; now that was country cool. He parked and turned off the engine, sitting there for several minutes as he stared out the front windshield.

Be open and honest.

Luke paused to think. All of a sudden he had second thoughts about what he'd planned to say. What if seeing him made her angry? What if she didn't want to talk to him? He couldn't spend another two weeks like the last two. He had to get on her good side somehow. But how could he disarm her so she didn't make him feel like a jerk again right from the get-go, before he had a chance to apologize? He had to make a good impression this time. Had to.

Luke placed his cowboy hat on his head out of habit. She'd called him a cowboy the last time he was there, like it was a bad thing. Maybe she didn't like men in hats. He took it off and tossed it back to the passenger seat, glancing at his reflection in the rearview mirror. His stomach felt full of bees, and he took another deep breath to settle it before he picked up his phone and headed into the bar.

Luke looked around as he walked in. He didn't spot her, or any of her friends, but he caught sight of Gil behind the bar. Pulling up a stool, he ordered a beer. When Gil went to wait on other customers Luke turned back toward the tables and scanned the place more carefully.

"She ain't been in here in quite a while," Gil offered.

"How's that?" Luke asked.

"Rachel, the girl you sang to? That's who you're lookin' for, ain't it?"

Luke chuckled. Gil had a good memory. "Yeah, I was hopin' I might run into her again."

Gil shook his head, "Sorry, dude. Like I said, I ain't seen her in quite a while. Since maybe … since the last time you were in here."

"Is that right?" It was still early. He'd hang around a while, have a few beers, and see if she showed up. A couple of hours and several beers later, he gave up, and said goodnight to Gil.

For the next several weeks, Luke made a habit of dropping in at the little downtown bar, hoping she would be there, but, time after time, he left disappointed. He even stopped in on New Year's Eve on his way home from a party. He didn't stay for a beer that night, though. He felt too pathetic sitting there drinking alone on New Year's Eve.

It was only eleven o'clock when he left, and not wanting to go home, he stopped in at Ike's to see if his guys were there. They weren't, but April was working and he sat down at a table to talk with her.

For a brief instant, he toyed with the idea of taking her home again, but thoughts of Rachel and the last time he'd tried to forget about her haunted him, and he pushed that idea far from his mind.

"Hey, Luke. What can I get ya?" April asked.

She returned a few minutes later with his beer and he invited her to sit for a spell. The place was fairly quiet, so after checking on her other tables, she came back and sat across from him.

"What's up? You look like you lost your best friend."

He gave her a wry smile, "Reckon I mighta'."

April's head tilted, questioning, "Rachel?"

He nodded, feeling like a lost pup.

"Did you tell her how you feel?"

Luke shook his head. "I haven't had the chance."

Sadness filled her pale blue eyes. "You gotta' tell her, hon."

"I know, and I want to. But I need to apologize first and I can't do it over the phone."

"Apologize for what?"

"For being a total jerk I don't know what it is, but every time I see her I say and do the worst things. It's like I'm trying to make her hate me. And I'm afraid …" He swallowed hard. "I'm afraid now she does."

April gave him a compassionate smile. "You couldn't possibly have been that bad."

73

"Oh, trust me, I could. And I was."

Her brows shot up and she studied him. "Why do you think you do that?"

Luke leaned back in his chair and ran his fingers through his hair. "I have no idea. It's like I'm trying to push her away. And that's the last thing I want to do. I think I'm falling in love with her."

Her silence spoke volumes and, when her eyes went misty, Luke realized he'd hurt her. He'd wondered why she stayed that night, even after he called her the wrong name. Now he knew. She had feelings for him. He felt like a total jerk. This wasn't a conversation he should be having with her, of all people. "April, I'm so sorry."

She blinked back the tears and touched his arm. "Luke, honey, who did this to you?"

His brows knit together as he looked at her, totally confused. "Did what?"

"Hurt you so bad you can't let yourself fall in love again."

Who did this to him? No one. He'd never even been in love before. Then it hit him like a concrete wall on the outside track.

His parents.

His parents left him as a little boy, and now, he was too afraid to love. Afraid to get hurt. To get left again. That was it. If you let someone love you, they could hurt you.

He took a drink of beer, set it down hard on the table, and stared at her.

"Luke?" Her face was etched with concern.

"Thank you, darlin'," he said, saddened by his realization, but grateful to her for helping him see it.

"You okay?"

"I will be." He stood and kissed her on the forehead. "Thank you, sweetheart."

The next morning Luke woke before dawn, dressed in his warmest hunting clothes, and headed up to his property. The rain had turned to sleet and ice overnight, and his truck slipped along the wintery country roads. It was slow going, but he reached his favorite hill overlooking the creek well before the sun appeared on the horizon.

He broke out his Thermos and poured a steaming cup of coffee, savoring its strong aroma and rich flavor as well as its warmth against his palms. He let his mind drift freely from one thing to the next as he so often did, but he soon realized that almost every thought was of Rachel or of his life with her in it. He had to figure out a way to make that happen. He was sure of it. Fate intended for their paths to cross that day, and they were supposed to be together. Deep in his soul he knew she was meant for him.

As the sun began to make its appearance, the landscape was bathed in an eerie white glow, daylight reflecting off every ice-covered branch, twig, and blade of grass. The effect was magical, instantly transporting him to an enchanted world of crystalline shapes, wet and dripping. A cacophony of creaking, breaking wood, drips, and things falling to the ground followed. Luke looked up into the tree he was sitting under and jumped up to move to a nearby clearing.

Would Rachel enjoy the unbelievable wonder of the mornings as much as he did? Was she the type of person who would wake early to catch a sunrise? Or would she think he was crazy for doing it, like most of the women he'd dated? No, she'd appreciate the beauty of it, especially that morning. For some reason he couldn't explain, he felt certain of it.

White surrounded him. All around him, the landscape shone brightly, every inch covered in white and silvery dripping ice. There was something so pure about the color white, the absence of all color, the absence of all things dark. Angels wore white, had white halos, white wings. Doves—the bird of peace and promises—were white. Diamonds, the sign of love and purity—white. Good guys always wore white hats, rode white horses, drove white cars. Luke smiled, remembering Gil's words—*Rachel and her knight in the shining white Charger.*

He could be that guy. He could go out and buy a brand-new Charger today. Well, tomorrow, when the car lots would be open. That was the easy part. Then what? Maybe he could drive it out to see her. He knew what he was going to say to her. He'd been prepared for weeks.

His heart was lighter as he turned to head home, crunching through the ice-crusted earth. He chuckled as the sound assaulted his ears. Good thing he wasn't hunting; the animals would hear him coming for miles.

By the time he got back to his truck, the roads were clear, and he went home and spent the next several hours online, looking at the new Dodge Charger.

It came in an all-wheel-drive V6 version, but, fuel economy aside, he wanted the extra power of the high-performance V8. Excited about buying a new car, he left a message at each of the local Dodge dealerships letting them know exactly what he was looking for—a white, V8 Hemi, sunroof, loaded with all the extras—and the first one to call him back in the morning would earn his business. He loved the looks of the two-toned interior and couldn't wait to get in and drive one.

Luke had driven his old truck so long it felt like a right thumb. And if he could make a good impression with Rachel, if this could be a small part of what she needed from him, he'd be on his way. It was the other part, being a nice guy, not saying mean and stupid things to push her away that worried him.

If only he could buy those things—the honest sincerity and sensitivity that he lacked—then he'd have it made.

"Dude, the rest is gonna have to come from within," he told himself. He resolved he would do his best to bring it out for her.

The Bet

Luke continued to stop in at The Old Hickory in the hopes of finding Rachel there, and, finally, on a Friday evening in mid-January, his persistence paid off.

As usual, when he stopped into the little music cafe, he glanced around the place, didn't see her or her friends, so he bellied up to the bar and talked to his friend Gil.

"She's here," Gil said as he slid him a beer. "Playing foosball in the back."

Luke's eyes lit up. "Foosball, huh?" He hadn't played since college. He wondered if she was any good. Because it was a man's game, and she seemed to like those kinds of things, he suspected she was.

"She's been winning for a while, so she might be ready to take a break."

"How much is a game these days?"

"Seventy-five cents."

"How about some quarters then?" Luke slid a dollar bill across the bar.

Gil made change for him. "Good luck."

He slipped the quarters into his pocket, grabbed his beer, and headed toward the back.

Okay, man, this is it. Be cool, be nice, be honest and forthright. Be everything she needs.

Luke paused at the entrance to the game area and leaned his shoulder against the doorjamb. Rachel and Cole were partners, their backs to him, and she was into the game. She was cool and controlled, not a spinner. Luke chuckled when he saw her kick up her back leg when she took a shot. It must have scored because she paused to glance up at her opponents, and the guys looked back, shaking their heads. He couldn't see the score, but based on the tension in her opponents' faces as they dropped the next ball, he guessed they were losing.

Luke steeled himself, took a long pull from his beer, and sauntered up to the table. Standing near the corner behind her, he confirmed the score was in her favor. When Cole scored a nice bank shot from the back and the play paused, Luke reached around and placed his quarters on the end of the table.

Rachel glanced up, then did a double take when she recognized him. She gave him a shy smile.

"Hey, Rachel," he said. "Hey, Cole."

"Hey, Luke." She dropped the next ball.

She and Cole won, and it was finally Luke's turn. He didn't have a partner, so he challenged her to a one-on-one. She grinned and glanced at Cole, who gave her a knowing smile. "Are you sure?" she asked Luke.

"I'm sure, if you're okay with it."

"Oh, I'm okay," She stepped back to take a little break and finish the last of her beer.

He'd waited more than a month for this moment, and she looked even prettier than he remembered. Cole offered to get Rachel another beer and left to fetch it. "What should we play for?" Luke asked, taking the side opposite her.

She laughed and rolled her eyes. "Stakes, you mean?"

"Yeah. I messed up the last time we spoke. I want to start over. If I win, I want a fresh start."

Rachel opened her mouth, but no words came out. She gave the rod a spin. "A fresh start?"

"Yup. That's it. I want a do-over." He looked into her beautiful green eyes and their gaze lingered.

Rachel looked away, but nodded, "Okay. And if I win?"

"Name it."

She shrugged. "I can't think of anything."

Luke thought he might know what she'd like. "You win, and I'll let you drive my race car."

Rachel's brows shot up and she laughed. "Drive it? Your NASCAR race car? The #11 Pacific Oil Dodge? Seriously?"

"You bet." This was good. Either way he won. Either he got a fresh start—whatever that entailed—or he got to spend the day with her when he took her to the track to drive his car. His head tilted and his eyes flashed with challenge. "You think you're that good?"

"We'll see, I guess, won't we?" Rachel shot him a confident grin and set her empty beer down. She put his quarters into the machine, pushed the lever, and the balls dropped down into the slot. She reached in and handed one across to him, then adjusted her goalies and placed her hands at the ready on her three- and five-man rods.

Luke smiled across at her as he took the ball. Win or lose, this was going to be fun. He scored first, a clean and quick five-man shot from the drop. He took the point while she adjusted her goalies, then reached down for the next ball. "You look mighty pretty tonight."

"Thank you." She dropped the next ball.

"I've missed you."

She glanced up for a split second, then scored the next goal with a nicely finessed five-man pass followed by a dead-on hard shot from her three-man. One to one. Rachel handed him the ball and their eyes met. She gave him a gentle smile.

Rachel scored again with the same exact shot. As he dropped the next ball he said, "I was hoping I'd run into you here sooner or later."

"So you've been stalking me? Waiting for me to come back here?"

"I've stopped in a few times is all, hoping you'd be here." His goalies were on the defensive as she continued to shoot against him. She was quick. "I felt downright bad about the way we left it last time."

She scored again, a dink, a fake that squeezed right between his goalies. Three to one. He looked into her eyes as she handed him the next ball, hoping she could see his sincerity.

She glanced around the game room and his gaze followed hers. No one was watching. Her focus returned to the table and he dropped the ball into play. She immediately pinched it with her three-man, stopping the action, and looked up at him. "Why do you do that? Kiss a girl like that and then yell at her, make her feel like a ... a fool?"

"Rachel, I'm sorry." He paused, wanting to make her understand how awful he felt about that day. "I think you're amazing and ... and that kiss scared me. Being with you ... scares me." He hoped she appreciated his honesty.

A glimmer of surprise lit up her eyes before she looked away, then resumed play, scoring again with a stuff off his attempted goalie shot. Four to one.

"Nice," he said. She glanced up at him and smiled nervously. Taking advantage of the eye contact, he continued, "You've been in my head these last few weeks and I can't stop thinking about you. I want to start over ..." He paused for effect, and then as he dropped the next ball he added, "please." His eyes were on her, not on the game, as he waited for her response.

"Why me, Luke? You could have any pretty little fluff in this town. Why me?" She took a shot, but he blocked it. He scored the next goal, a bank shot from his forward goalie. Four to two.

The next ball seemed to last forever, back and forth. Cole returned, carrying two beers, and stood at the end of the table. Rachel eventually scored the final goal, and it was a solid wrist shot, so hard that it almost popped back out of the goal. She pushed the fifth counter across and reached for the beer Cole held out. "Thanks," she said, shooting him an easy smile.

Luke relaxed, dropping his hands from the rods, unconcerned about losing the game. "I don't know why, but I sure would like to find out."

She smiled back at him and he lost himself in the depths of her dark-green eyes.

The smile he'd been waiting for. "Soon as the weather clears up, we'll get that car out and run a few laps, okay? Maybe this Saturday or next."

Her smile grew even wider. "I look forward to it."

"I'll call you. Y'all have a good night." He tipped his hat to include Cole, then turned to leave.

His heart skipped a beat as he made his way back to the bar. That could not have gone better. He'd apologized from the heart, she'd given him a smile that would stay with him for days, and he was going to spend a day at the track with her. He didn't even care that a woman he barely knew was going to be driving his race car mere weeks before Daytona and the start of the new season. She could crash it into the wall and he'd still be smiling.

She wouldn't, though. She knew cars and he was sure she'd know how to handle the power of his race car. Luke emptied his beer and set it on the bar. As he walked out, bracing himself against the cold January rain, he wished for it to end so they'd have a dry Saturday.

Test Laps with a Little Girl

A pleasant Saturday finally dawned bright, clear, and relatively warm for early February in Nashville. Luke was as anxious as a first-year rookie at Daytona as he pulled up in front of Rachel's church in his truck, his race car on a flatbed trailer behind. There was no place to park his rig, so he waited in the street, hoping he would be all right for the few minutes it would take to pick her up. She'd volunteered to work the women's auxiliary bake sale that morning, but was supposed to be done by noon. It was eleven fifty-five.

Within seconds he saw her rush through the doors, waving goodbye to someone inside. Her eyes lit up when she caught sight of the race car on his trailer, and he jumped out and dashed around to open her door. "Hey, beautiful."

"Good timing," she said as she climbed up into his truck.

He closed her door and ran to his side and hopped in. He looked at her. "You ready for this?"

"Absolutely. I've been waiting all week. Are *you* ready for this? Or do you normally let women drive your race car?"

Luke laughed as he shifted into gear. "I can honestly say this is a first. I've never let *anyone* drive my race car before, male or female. You'll be the first."

"I'm flattered. I'll try not to crash it."

"Please." He glanced across to see her mischievous grin. "Daytona's only two weeks away. You'd put me out of the race for sure."

"I promise I'll be careful. I brought you some cookies and muffins from the bake sale." She showed him a small white bakery bag, then twisted to set it on the back seat.

He thanked her and they chatted easily for the rest of the drive to the track. He'd reserved it for the afternoon so they could spend as much time there as they wanted, undisturbed. He described the small one-mile oval where he often ran test laps and asked her if she'd ever driven a car with over 700 horsepower before. She hadn't. Her Corvette, with its 390 horse, 427 Turbo Jet V8 was the most powerful engine she'd run. But at least she knew how to drive a manual transmission.

They arrived at the track and pulled into the pit area. Luke parked and then backed the car off the trailer. He pulled it onto the track, shut it off, and came back to the truck. Rachel had gotten out, put her hair into a ponytail, and stood beside the truck.

"Anything I can do to help?"

He pulled a jumpsuit from the back seat and handed to her. "Put this on."

She held it up to her shoulders and looked down at it, then back at him, surprise lighting her eyes. It looked like her size.

"I raced go-carts in that when I was twelve."

Rachel laughed. "Nice. Well, I'm glad you kept it."

"My mom kept it." He slipped on his own race suit.

He'd stopped by the house earlier that morning to ask his mom to help him find it. She and his dad had both inundated him with a million questions about the woman he was going to let drive his race car. His father found it hard to believe.

Luke retrieved helmets from the backseat, set one on the trailer, and held the other while Rachel finished pulling on her suit. He handed her the helmet and fastened the hook and loop strips at her wrists and ankles. Then he added a neck pad under the collar and closed it up. "I think you're all set. You ready?"

Her smile was huge, her eyes wide with excitement. "I am."

"Okay, let me go over a couple of things." He explained the basics as they walked toward the car. He gave her instruction on getting in, adjusting the seat and the safety harness, and explained that the gas, clutch, and brakes would all feel quite a bit different than her Corvette. "Any questions?"

Rachel shook her head.

"Good."

"How many laps can I take?"

Luke laughed. This was going to be fun. She was going to love driving his car. "As many as you want. I think you've got about a half tank of gas, and we've got all afternoon. Go ahead and put that on." He pointed to her helmet. "It's wired so we can talk to each other while you're out there." He showed her the headset then put it on his ear and hooked the receiver onto his belt. "There's nothing to press. Talk and I'll hear you. Want to give it a try?"

"Hey there, cowboy," she said, looking at him as she spoke.

He cocked his head and gave her a crooked grin. "You look beautiful."

She responded with a smile that cut right to Luke's heart, and he had to look away to break free. He regained his focus and went around to the passenger side of the car, unhooked the mesh screen, and reached through to move the driver seat up, making sure it locked into place before he came back to the driver's side to help her get in.

Once Rachel was in, it was all he could do to not burst out laughing. She looked so little in the seat custom made for him. "Can you see?" He leaned in beside her to evaluate her line of sight.

She laughed. "Not very well."

"Hold on there, darlin'." He ran back to the truck, grabbed a seat cushion, and then slipped it beneath her. "How's that?"

"Much better. It's good."

She still looked downright tiny. He refastened the mesh screen and went back around to the driver's side. "First time around go nice and slow. Get a good look at the track. Make sure it's clear, clean, and dry and get a feel for it, okay?"

"Okay."

"Go ahead and fire it up."

Rachel looked down, found the ignition switch, and pressed it. The engine roared to life, loud and powerful, and she laughed as it rumbled beneath her.

"Hey," he hollered over the noise, his face dead serious as he leaned around to peer at her from the windshield. "Don't wreck my race car." Then he laughed and slapped the hood. "Have fun."

"I'll be careful."

He hooked the mesh screen on the driver's side and, looking back through the windshield, gave her a thumbs up.

She started out nice and slow and Luke relaxed, pleased, as he heard her back off when she hit second gear. "This is great," she shouted.

His hand flew instinctively to his earpiece as her voice blasted in his ear. "You don't have to yell. Talk normal. I can hear you."

"Okay. Sorry."

He stepped back as he lost sight of her around the second turn and leaned back against the concrete half-wall that separated the pit area from the track.

A few minutes later she came out of turn three, around turn four, and into the straightaway in front of him.

"Is the track good?" he asked.

"Perfectly clear and dry."

"You can speed up a little if you're comfortable."

"Okay."

She took several more laps, speeding up in the straightaways then downshifting into the turns. He breathed a sigh of relief every time he watched her come out of turn four with plenty of room between her and the outside wall. She was playing it safe, and he was thankful for it. After the fifteenth lap, as he wondered when she'd get tired of it, she slowed way down coming out of turn four. She downshifted several times, then hit the brakes to stop in front of him.

Luke sliced his hand across his throat, signaling her to cut the engine, and walked up to unhook the mesh screen. He helped her out, and she removed her helmet, shaking out her hair and pulling it free of the ponytail. He was mesmerized by that simple act, as her hair tumbled across her shoulders, the lighter parts of it catching and reflecting the rays of sunlight.

"That was so amazing." Her smile was barely this side of laughter. She practically bounced up and down. "Thank you."

"You're welcome. How did it feel?"

"Powerful!" She eyed the stopwatch in his hand. "How fast did I go?"

"I didn't clock all of your laps but you had one at ninety-five miles an hour. I'm impressed." That was a lot faster than he thought she'd be comfortable with on such a small track. "And you didn't crash it. Thank you."

"Are you going to drive?" She pointed to his race suit.

"No, this is a safety thing. It's a fire suit, so if you caught on fire I'd be able to help you get out."

Her eyebrows shot up and her earlier excitement vanished. She obviously hadn't thought catching on fire was a possibility. "Right."

"But I did want to run some test laps in the Galaxie today and you could help me if you've got time."

"Test laps? In the Galaxie?"

"I developed a new carburetor for it, a bit of a different design. I want to run some baseline laps with the old carb then switch it out and run some more laps with the new one."

"What are your metrics?"

He admired her use of the apt terminology. "Fuel consumption."

Her eyes went wide and her mouth fell open. "Oh."

"What? Did I say something wrong?"

"Um, no. I mean, I can help. I'd love to."

"Great."

This was turning out to be an awesome day. Luke was thrilled to be spending time with Rachel and getting to know her better. And he was impressed. She was smart and knew her stuff when it came to cars. He thought again for a brief moment about how great it would be to have her working as part of his race team, then remembered why he'd tossed that idea out the window.

"Let's go to my shop and get the Galaxie. You can throw all that back into the truck if you want while I load up the car."

With everything packed and ready to go, Luke noticed how pretty she looked sitting on the passenger side of his truck. A dozen different country music songs about girls in trucks flitted through his mind. He wondered if she had pink toenails.

"What?"

He hesitated. "You look so good sittin' over there in my truck."

She laughed and rolled her eyes. "You are so country."

"Why, thank ya, darlin'," he said in his best southern drawl.

On the way to his shop, Rachel asked about his carburetor design. He described what he'd been working on, why he'd wanted the Galaxie, and how important fuel usage was to winning a race. She asked some great questions, impressing him again with her frame of reference and insights.

At the shop, Rachel helped him collect the tools they'd need while he put the race car back into the hauler and loaded up the Galaxie. He showed her his newly fabricated carburetor and was thrilled by her reaction. She seemed to understand and appreciate the ingenuity of it and seemed almost as excited to test it out as he was.

He put the carburetor into a box and did a quick once-over on the tools she'd collected, threw in a couple of shop rags and some gloves, and loaded it into the back of his pickup, adding several full cans of gasoline. He closed up the shop and they were on their way back to the track.

"Here's how I was thinking we'd do this. First we'll run all the gas out of the car. There's not much in it right now, so it shouldn't take long. Then we'll put five gallons into it and count how many laps we can get out of it. I figure this engine probably doesn't get much over ten miles to the gallon, so we're looking at maybe fifty laps or less. Then we'll switch out the carburetor and do it again, seeing how many laps we get with the new carb. And we'll time each lap to ensure we keep the speed consistent on each run."

Rachel listened and nodded.

"I know it's not exactly scientific, but it'll get the job done. You want to drive or log laps?"

Rachel agreed to do the first set of laps to run the car out of gas then let him run the rest of them, while she timed and logged each one. When she took off in the car, he unhooked the trailer from the truck so she could use the truck to deliver the next tank of fuel to wherever the car ran out.

She stopped twenty yards shy of where she'd started, so Luke carried the first of the five-gallon cans down the track. He poured it into the gas tank, set the can aside, and waited for Rachel to get the timer and clipboard ready. Then he ran laps with the Galaxie's old carburetor. They used the headsets to talk to each other.

"Forty-five," she told him. He glimpsed her looking down at the clipboard and writing as he passed by.

"Are you sure?" he questioned, sounding serious but being totally facetious.

"Um."

He grinned as he imagined her looking down at her sheet in a panic, worried she'd somehow lost count and messed it up.

"Yes, I'm sure. Why? Do you think it's not?"

"Nope, you're right on, darlin'. Just testing you." He laughed into the microphone.

"Funny."

The car ran out on the forty-seventh lap, shy of the third turn. Luke got out and popped the hood to let the engine cool down so they could work on it, while

Rachel drove the truck around to meet him. They sat on the back of the car while they waited. After a few minutes, he remembered the cookies and muffins she'd brought and got the white bakery sack from the backseat.

"This is delicious," he said, holding out a muffin. "Did you make these?"

"No, cooking's not my thing, remember?" She touched the arm she'd burned. "I helped organize the sale."

"Looked like it was fairly well attended."

"We do pretty well. It's not quite the hospital fundraisers my mother hosts, but it brings in enough."

"Well, it's nice of you to give up your Saturday morning to make it happen. And mighty nice of you to bring me some. Thank you." Luke popped the remainder of the muffin into his mouth as he hopped down. He went to the front of the Galaxie and held his hand above the engine to check the temperature. It was a cool day, but not as cold as it could be for early February. He guessed it was near fifty degrees—cold enough for a jacket but not so cold that you needed gloves. And the bright sunshine made it feel much warmer than it was. He couldn't think of a better way to spend a gorgeous day than at the track with a beautiful woman.

Luke retrieved the tool chest from the back of the truck, then went back for the box with the carburetor in it, setting them both beside the front of the car. Then he pulled out one of the gas cans and began to pour its contents into the Galaxie's tank. He watched as Rachel approached the engine and held her hand above it before she tapped the top of the carburetor.

"Don't burn yourself."

"Don't worry, I won't. I think it's cool enough to switch out. Want me to start taking this one off?"

"Sure, if you don't mind getting your hands dirty. Actually, I threw in some gloves." Luke nodded toward the tool chest. "In there."

She opened the tool chest, put the gloves on, and within minutes had the old carburetor off. Luke finished with the gas and stood watching her with a wide grin while she finished up the last few bolts and lifted the part off. She knew exactly what she was doing. He appreciated how meticulous she was, seeing her spread out a shop rag on the ground off to the side for the bolts and linkages she was pulling off. When she'd removed the last bolt and lifted off the old component, she straightened and turned to him, giving him a smile that shot right through his heart.

Luke shook his head. "Look at you. You're gonna make me wanna marry you." He rubbed his chin, thinking. Now, that might be a right fine notion there.

Rachel laughed. She stood holding the old carburetor in the oversized gloves. "You want to open that so I can set this down?" She nodded at the box.

Luke took out his new carburetor and she put the old one in its place. He started to put the new carburetor into place, and Rachel handed him the wrench as he turned to reach for it. "Okay, so I'll take that as a 'not quite yet.'" He caught her stare and shot her a warm smile. "Then how about having dinner with me tonight instead?" He held her gaze for several lingering moments, brows raised.

Rachel bit her lower lip. "Um ... I uh ..."

"Got plans?" He turned back to wrench on the engine.

"Sort of."

"A date?" he asked, still focused on what he was doing under the hood.

"No. I'd planned to meet up with my friends later, but ..."

"But you could maybe ditch your friends to go out with me instead?"

"Maybe," she said, drawing out the word.

Luke straightened and leaned back against the car to look at her. "Come on. I'd like to take you out tonight."

Rachel smiled back at him, a giving-in smile. "I'd love to."

"Perfect." He turned back to the engine. "Almost done."

She picked up the last few bolts and held them out to him.

"Thanks." When he was done, he had her get in and start the car up. She gunned it a few times. Satisfied, he closed the hood. "Sure you don't want to do the laps this time?"

"No, that's okay. I'll count. You could use the practice anyway," she said with a playful grin. She picked up the clipboard and pen and started a new set of columns for the second iteration of test laps.

"Yeah, right." He got in, waited for her to pick up her timer, then took off as she clicked it on.

At lap fifty-five when the car finally ran out of gas again, Luke's excitement rang loud and clear as he whooped and cheered over the headset. Rachel drove the truck around to where the car had stopped, beyond the fourth turn. As she got out of the vehicle, he ran to greet her and, picking her up, swung her around in a big circle before setting her back on her feet.

"It worked, baby. It worked."

"Wow. It did. That's great." She grabbed the clipboard from the front seat and he looked over her shoulder as she quickly did the math. "An eighteen percent efficiency improvement. That's amazing."

He was ecstatic. The results were even better than he'd hoped. He popped the hood and looked it over, seeing nothing out of the ordinary. He glanced at Rachel, dizzy with excitement, and she gave him an encouraging smile that melted his heart. What a day.

He put more gas in the car so he could get it up onto the trailer while she collected everything else. He climbed into the truck and started it up, but paused before putting it in gear. He looked at Rachel on the passenger side, picked up the clipboard and pen she'd set on the seat between them, and tossed them onto the dash. "Come over here." She bit her lip, and slid closer as he faced her.

He took her hands in his. Her delicate grace reminded him beauty was everywhere, even beneath dirty fingernails. "Thank you." He pulled his gaze away from her hands. "This was a huge day for me, and I'm so glad you were a part of it."

She shot him her cut-to-the-heart smile. "You're welcome. I'm so happy for you. What an incredible accomplishment."

"Yeah." He wanted to kiss her, but was afraid of scaring her away again. He licked his lips, swallowed the lump in his throat, and gazed into her eyes with an unmasked longing. "Can I ... kiss you?" He couldn't ever remember asking a woman first, but with her, it felt like the right thing to do.

The corners of her mouth curved upward as she slowly nodded.

Luke looked from her eyes to her lips and then back to her eyes before he leaned over to kiss her ever so gently several times, savoring the sweet softness of her lips as he wrapped his hands in her hair.

After the kiss, instead of pulling back, he held his cheek next to hers and closed his eyes. Reveling in the feel of her soft skin against his. Breathing in the subtle, sweet scent of her. Just like he remembered—fresh, ripe peaches over homemade ice cream.

He sat back. "Mmm," he murmured. He once read that you never know the value of a moment until it's a memory, but somehow he knew this one was going to be one worth remembering.

He dropped Rachel at the church with plans to pick her up at her house at seven.

As Luke drove away, he couldn't help the adrenaline rush that made him want to dance in his seat. What a fantastic, incredible, unbelievable day. Rachel was amazing. It was like having one of his most trusted crew there. She knew exactly what she was doing. And she was so pretty. He recalled watching her pull off the old carburetor, standing on her tiptoes as she leaned over the side of the car, her long ponytail hanging down her back while she worked. And when she turned to him with that sweet smile. She was *something*, all right.

He knew where he'd take her for dinner—a quiet little steak and seafood place on the river. But what could they do after dinner? It would be too cold to walk in Riverside Park. A buggy ride, maybe? If it were any other woman, he'd invite her back to his place after dinner. But with her, he wasn't so sure. He needed to tread lightly. He didn't want to mess things up again. He'd gotten a second chance, and the last thing he wanted to do was ruin it. No, he'd be the perfect gentleman tonight, make a lasting impression, and she'd be worth the wait.

He had no doubt.

As Rachel drove home, she replayed their afternoon. She'd thoroughly enjoyed herself. He was thoughtful and sweet, nothing like she'd expected. She still couldn't believe he'd actually let her drive his race car. What an experience. She couldn't wait to tell her father.

And he was a lot more than another gearhead. He was smart. She couldn't believe he was working on a fuel efficiency innovation, like she was. What were the chances?

It had to be a God thing.

Aside from the time he'd looked as though he wanted to gobble her up, she felt comfortable with him, even when he asked if he could kiss her. How sweet was that? She could see his passion and desire plain as day. And, while it frightened her a little, it wasn't at all like the overwhelming fear she'd felt the first time they'd kissed in his garage. This time was different. She felt safe, protected even, as though the last thing in the world he would ever do was hurt her.

She beamed as she watched him turn off. Maybe he was worth a second chance, after all.

Dinner with a Woman

Rachel had spent over an hour deciding what dress to wear, and strewn across her bed were the choices she'd cast aside. She wanted to convey pretty, sophisticated, and mature, but still maintain her conservative nature. She landed on a nicely tailored sheath dress, true red. The cut wasn't revealing, but it fit her curves perfectly, and the overall effect was classic and feminine without being brash or provocative.

She'd curled her hair and pulled it to one side, the long, loose waves cascading gently down her right shoulder. Slipping on a pair of strappy black heels, she added earrings and a small gold cross necklace, then gazed critically at her reflection in the mirror. Her burn had healed nicely; only a faint pink shadow remained.

Pleased with the overall effect, she giggled. Mama would like it. Of course she would. She'd bought her both the dress and the shoes. Rachel tucked a few things into a little black evening bag and called it good, as she heard a car pull into the drive. She glanced at the clock. He was five minutes early.

"I'll be right out." she called to her father as she heard him get up to answer the door.

Luke suddenly felt nervous. He loosened his tie then straightened it, wiped his sweaty palms on his dress pants, then almost stumbled as he made his way up the sidewalk. In fact, he couldn't remember ever fretting about a date like he had about this one. Hesitating on the front porch, he rubbed the back of his neck, looked back at his new car and grinned. She was going to be surprised. He couldn't wait to see the look on her face when she saw it. Should he let on he knew about her fairytale hopes and dreams and that he had only bought the car a few weeks ago because of it? He squared his shoulders and turned back to the door. Nah, why ruin a perfectly good dream come true?

A sturdy-looking man, with graying hair at his temples, wearing jeans and a flannel shirt, opened the door. Rachel's father.

"Howdy, come on in," he said, stepping aside to allow Luke entry, then closing the door behind him.

Luke entered a quaint country kitchen, complete with red-checked café curtains, and turned to greet Rachel's father. "Luke Brandt," he said, extending his hand.

"William Tate," her father replied, shaking it firmly. "It's a pleasure," he added with a warm smile.

"Pleasure's all mine."

Rachel enter the room with a long dark coat draped over her arm. "Hi," she said, shooting Luke a tentative glance.

He swallowed his surprise at her appearance, cleared his throat, and returned the greeting, "Hi." His voice sounded distant and even deeper than usual, as his gaze took in the length of her.

William Tate stifled a laugh, causing Luke's cheeks to redden. Taking Rachel's coat, her father helped her slip into it. "Have fun, baby girl," he said, then kissed her on the cheek. Luke could barely make out his whisper. "You look real pretty tonight."

She smiled at her father and returned the kiss. "Thanks, Daddy." Then turned to Luke. "Ready?"

He cleared his throat again as he broke out of his daze. "You bet. Mr. Tate, it was a pleasure to meet you."

"Same here. You kids have fun."

"Thanks," Rachel said as she and Luke moved to the door.

"And be safe," he reminded them.

"You can count on it," Luke said, holding the door for Rachel.

Luke watched her face as they stepped out onto the porch, and she looked toward the driveway. It was dark, but between the faint moonlight and the yard light from the barn, the driveway was illuminated well enough for her to see the car.

From the look on her face, he knew she recognized it instantly—Dodge Charger. A white one.

Rachel paused at the car's passenger side to allow him to open the door for her. "Nice car."

He reached for the door, "You like it?"

"Love it." She slipped into the soft leather seat, glanced at the interior, then back up at him.

He closed her door and chuckled to himself, thoroughly pleased with his decision to splurge on it. He slid into the driver's seat and faced her. "You look beautiful tonight."

"Thank you." When he continued staring at her, she gave him a questioning look.

"Sorry," he said, shaking his head as he looked her over, "I can't believe you're the same little girl who helped me swap out my carburetor today."

She laughed at his effusive compliment. "I'm *not* a little girl, you know."

"Oh, I know," he said with a mischievous grin. "I can see that now."

She bit her lip and looked away, fidgeting in her seat.

Sensing he'd made her feel uncomfortable, he touched her arm. "Don't worry, the dress is perfect. Definitely says 'Rachel Tate: beautiful young Nashville debutante.' It's so different than the 'Rachel Tate: country-girl mechanic' I was expecting. But I love this other side of you." He gave her an encouraging smile.

She giggled. "You get on, Luke Brandt."

He turned forward and started the car. "What kind of music do you like?" he asked, pressing the screen a few times to bring up the satellite radio options.

"Country's good."

Rachel told him she loved the two-tone leather interior, the display screen, and the ambient lighting. He saw her glance across at the driver's displays and wondered if she was trying to see the mileage. She could probably tell it was brand-new based on the smell and lack of fingerprints.

"You got it." He pressed the screen a few times and adjusted the volume so they could talk.

Rachel played with the onscreen controls while he asked about her father and the farm. She described her father as a hard-working, honest man, up before the sun, in bed by ten, and always willing to help a neighbor. He asked about the barn and she described her workshop there, and they talked about her progress on the Thunderbolt. She evaded his question when he asked why she'd wanted a 427 engine, but he got the feeling that she'd wanted a vintage muscle car she could restore and sell.

They entered one of the nicest places in downtown Nashville. He helped her remove her coat and handed it to the maître d'. Turning back to her, his gaze slowly wandered from her beautiful long curls to her strappy black heels, finally returning to rest on her eyes. They watched him nervously. He whispered in her ear, "I'm sorry if I'm making you uncomfortable. But you look so dang pretty. Like a movie star." He straightened and gave her a reassuring smile.

"You clean up right nice yourself," she said, giving him a quick once-over.

Dinner was as free and easy as their conversation. Luke made her laugh with funny stories about the race circuit, racing nearly every weekend, and living out of a bus for the better part of the year. When he asked about her job, she told him all about the company she worked for. She shared her recent promotion to a systems analyst, the great team of people she worked with, and how she hoped her next promotion would be to the engineering side of the company so she could use her college education.

When they discussed his carburetor design, she asked him if he'd filed for a patent. He hadn't even considered it. He'd been focused on simply trying to improve the performance of his race engine to gain a competitive advantage that would help him win more races. She insisted he file, convinced he'd made a remarkable discovery that could have significant impact on modern-day engines, and be worth a lot of money to automakers who sought to produce more fuel-efficient cars. He considered it and agreed to contact his attorney to start working on it.

Luke watched Rachel when she wasn't looking—as she talked with the waitress or browsed the menu—and thought it was real sweet when she said a quick silent prayer before eating. She was the perfect dinner companion. She laughed easily at his jokes, and he loved the sound of her laughter and the way it made her eyes sparkle. She had a quick mind and surprised him with her witty responses and insightfulness. And she was genuinely excited about his carburetor design and encouraging about its prospects and marketability. He was so glad he hadn't given up on running into her again.

"Rachel, there's something on my mind that I've wanted to ask you. I hope you don't mind."

"What's that?"

"The guy you decked at the bar that night …" he paused as her happiness faded and he wished he hadn't brought it up.

"It's okay, ask." She set her fork on her plate and folded her hands in her lap.

"Was he an old boyfriend?"

"Yes," she nodded, then looked away, all remnants of the easy laughter that had been there minutes before gone.

His heart went out to her as he watched her eyes dart around the room, her sadness becoming anxiety.

"Did he hurt you?"

She leaned back, her body language distancing herself from him, and stared at him as though weighing whether she should be afraid of him too. She bit her lower lip before finally answering. "I don't want to talk about him. Please?" She gave him a weak smile then reached for her wine glass, but set it down right away when her trembling hand betrayed her.

"That's fine. I'm sorry." What was that? Best save it for another day. "How about you and Cole? You two ever date?" Images of the two of them singing that romantic song together at The Old Hickory flitted through his mind, and he wanted to make sure there wasn't anything there.

She relaxed, obviously relieved to change to a safer subject. "Me and Critter?" She laughed. "Cole Ritter. His email address at work is CRritter and the nickname stuck. But, no, to answer your question, he's just a good friend." She took a sip of wine, watching him over the top of the glass. "What about you? Tell me about your girlfriends. Do you really have one in every race town? Are you still dating Cassie, uh … Cassandra?"

"Mmm." Luke looked away. *One in every race town?* Was that what she thought of him? He shook his head. "Cassandra and I—" he paused remembering Cassandra was a friend of hers. "She was sweet, but not what I was looking for."

"No?" She leaned forward. "What are you looking for, Luke?"

He hesitated and grinned as he shook his head again. "Nothin'. I ain't looking for nothin' now," he said, slipping comfortably into his country slang. "I think I found her a couple of months back at an auto auction. And, after today, I'm fairly certain."

Rachel laughed, and looked down, a bright pink lighting up her cheeks.

"Seriously." He reached across the table for her hand. When she glanced up, his eyes captured and held hers.

"After one date?"

While his hand held on, his heart was letting go. "After one kiss."

"You probably say that to all the girls."

"I don't. I've never said that before in my life."

She stared at him for several heartbeats, no doubt weighing his sincerity. When she spoke, her pillow-soft voice tipped the scales in his favor. "That's real nice."

He leaned back, relieved. He might have a chance this go 'round, despite her "one in every town" comment. "Yeah, it is. Thank you for giving me another shot." Warmth returned in her gaze. He must be doing something right. "What are you doing tomorrow morning? There's something I want to show you, but you have to get up early. You up for it?"

"Tomorrow's Sunday."

He raised his brows, questioning.

"I go to church with my dad."

"Oh, right." There went that idea.

"Maybe next Saturday morning?"

Next weekend was the last weekend before Daytona, and he and his crew would be at the track making final adjustments and running test laps on his race car. "How about tomorrow afternoon? It won't be quite as good, but it'll still be worth it."

"What'll be worth it?"

"Can it be a surprise?" he asked.

She seemed to have to think about it. "Sure … I suppose. Tell me what to wear."

"Warm clothes. Comfortable shoes. Dress for the outdoors."

"Okay." She looked down at her plate and pushed at her food.

"What?" Something bothered her. Maybe she didn't like surprises.

"So, you don't go to church, I take it?"

He looked at her. This was obviously important to her, and he wished he had a better answer. "I don't. I haven't since I was a kid, and only then because my parents made me." She looked disappointed so he tried to explain, "Me and God, well, we're not on speaking terms."

Silence. More food pushing. "So you don't pray either? Do you believe in God?"

"I do ... well, I think I do. I don't know anymore," he stammered, unsure how to tell her what he thought when it came to God. "How's your steak?" he asked, desperate to change the subject to a lighter one, one that made him feel not quite so deficient.

"It's good ... perfect."

He wished he could take her home with him tonight. He watched her and let his thoughts wander as he imagined himself dancing with her in the firelight of his living room, unzipping her pretty little red dress, and watching it fall silently to land in a puddle on the floor around her strappy little heels ... He wrenched himself back to the present, steeling himself to not give in to it.

Luke took her hand in his again, thinking for a moment he'd tell her everything, the way she affected him and all the feelings and desires she aroused in him. But as he opened his mouth to speak, something held him back. Was it too much too soon? The last thing he wanted to do was scare her away again. But he wanted her more than anything he'd ever wanted. But no. He needed to slow down, be patient, do it right this time.

Rachel looked at him with a curious stare, "You okay?"

He laughed softly. "I ... uh," he started, and shook his head to clear it. "You ... affect me, Rachel," he told her with a raw honesty, his voice hoarse with emotion.

She gave him the sweetest look: half satisfied, half pity. "Good. I'm glad."

On the ride home Rachel's mind replayed their dinner conversation. He'd been so attentive and made her feel like she was the only thing that mattered. And as she'd looked across the table at him, she couldn't help but think how incredibly sweet and smart he was. She felt special that he'd wanted to have dinner with her. Maybe he was a good one. She wondered what happened to the selfish, arrogant guy she'd been so rude to the first few times they'd met.

But the Sunday thing gnawed at her. She'd tried not to sound judgmental, but it was important to her. God was a huge part of her life, and she'd hoped to find a nice guy who was a Christian.

Me and God, well, we're not on speaking terms.

What an odd way to put it. Was he angry at God for some reason? She tried to ignore the warning lights going off in her head and bit the corner of her lip, hiding her concern. But he was such a great guy. How could he not have faith? She glanced over at him. Maybe God had put him in her life for that reason, to help him find his way back to Him.

As they pulled into the drive Luke saw the barn and asked to see her workshop, thankful to have a reason to prolong their time together. She agreed and, leading him inside, flipped on the bright overhead lights. He looked around, taking it all in. It was definitely not a man's garage. Aside from the melee of farm equipment at the far end, it was clean, neat, and tidy; everything in its place. Even the workbench was free of clutter.

He walked over to the Thunderbolt and inspected her progress under the hood. On the far side of it, he noticed a long kraft paper strip taped to the floor upon which rested quite a few of the parts, nuts, and bolts she'd pulled off. He looked up to the workbench and saw the three-foot-wide paper roll dispenser and shook his head, chuckling to himself. That was definitely something only a woman would do.

"Hey, don't knock it." she said. "It keeps the grease off the floor and prevents tracking into the house."

"Right." A handful of black-and-white photos and news articles, each carefully encased in a sheet protector and tacked to the pegboard between the workbench and the upper cabinets caught his eye, and he leaned closer to check them out. Most didn't surprise him: Edison, Franklin, Bell, Whitney. But when he saw the two that were front and center, he stopped short and looked back at her. "You know about these guys? Charles Nelson Pogue? Tom Ogle?"

"Oh, yeah. They're my inspiration. Amazing inventors. I assume, since you're into fuel efficiency, you know about their work too, right?"

"Yeah, I'm surprised *you* know of them."

She shrugged her shoulders. "I'm a mechanical engineer. I'm into cars. They impress me."

"Right." *She* impressed *him.*

"And I want to invent something someday."

"You do?" He leaned back against the workbench.

"I do."

"Like what?" An engine that runs on vapor? That was Ogle's idea. Supposedly he nailed it, but he sold his patent then turned up dead, and the patent was never found.

"Oh, I don't know." She looked away and Luke got the feeling she was already working on something, if not physically, then at least in her head. He wondered what it was and if it had anything to do with fuel efficiency.

He noticed the speakers mounted up in the corners. "Got music?"

"Absolutely. What do you want to hear?" She walked over to the stereo and started to plug her phone into it.

"Here, hold on," he said. "Put this on." He brought up the song he'd been thinking about on his own phone and handed it to her.

She looked at the screen, smiled up at him, and turned to put it on.

While she was busy with the music, Luke reached to the end of the workbench and flipped a switch that turned out to be the under-cabinet lights. He walked to the door and turned off the bright overheads. When he faced her again, she was watching him, lovely in the soft ambient light. Pleased with the much-improved atmosphere, he marveled at the incredibly sexy woman staring back at him.

The music started to play as he walked back to her. He held out his hand, "Dance with me?"

She took his hand and he pulled her into his arms. They danced to "Cowboys and Angels," the song he had sung to her months before.

He leaned down to breathe in the scent of her, losing his soul in the simple pleasures of the moment. He pulled her closer and she relaxed her cheek against his chest, sighing as he enfolded her in his arms. She felt unbelievably good, so soft against him.

She's not afraid of me now.

When she pulled back to look up at him, he was astounded at the warmth and emotion in her eyes. He gently brushed her cheek with his fingertips, drinking in the way she looked at him and the perfection of her skin.

When the song ended, he leaned down to kiss her, tenderly caressing her lips with his own. And when she smiled he kissed her again, and again, and in that moment, he knew he was losing himself. It was even better than before; she wasn't pulling away. She was kissing him back, parting her lips, welcoming him, her little sighs telling him clearly how much she was enjoying it.

He pulled back and in one fluid motion lifted her up onto the workbench, bringing her to eye level with him.

She laughed softly, no doubt startled by how effortlessly he'd lifted her. She gazed at him intently, breathless from his kisses. She pressed her palms against his chest. "Luke," she started.

Oh no, baby, don't be afraid.

He cupped her face between his hands, gently caressing her cheeks with his thumbs as his gaze traveled from her eyes to her lips then back to her eyes. Her lips parted instinctively as his thumb traced them. "You are so beautiful," he whispered. He buried his hands in her hair at the back of her neck and kissed her again.

When he pulled back, a fleeting moment of disappointment clouded her features, and he smiled, satisfied. She didn't want it to end either. She was as lost in it as he was.

"Rachel," he said, his voice husky with passion, "come home with me."

She shook her head, "I ... I have to tell you something."

"I know. We should take it slow, right? I'm sorry." He paused and choked back his frustration. "You do things to me, darlin'. Things I don't know how to handle." He searched for a calm that eluded him. How could he even begin to explain the way she made him feel when she kissed him?

He was spinning out of control on a crazy carnival ride, enjoying the thrill, the excitement, the exhilaration of it, unlike any ride he'd ever been on. It was way too intense to even think of jumping off. And slowing down? Stopping? Not a chance. There were no brakes on this ride, and he'd be out of his mind to try.

Her eyes sparkled. She was obviously pleased by her effect on him, but she shook her head. "I can't go home with you, but kiss me one more time and we'll call it good night, okay?"

Luke willed his heart to still. "What if I can't stop?" he asked, unsure if he had it in him to let her go. He wanted her something fierce. With every breath of life in him he wanted her. All of her.

She touched his cheek. "I have faith in you."

He liked her choice of words. Maybe she didn't consider him deficient after all. He could stop this ride if she wanted him to. He could wait for her. He'd do almost anything for her. He knew it was the right thing, and he'd be thankful tomorrow.

She placed her hands around his neck, and he leaned in to kiss her, taking his time, savoring each gentle touch as their lips came together, then their mouths, as they freely toyed with their shared hunger.

Rachel stood at the kitchen window and watched his car disappear down the drive, her heart still racing while her fingertips touched her lips. Maybe she shouldn't have let him kiss her like that. Was she being a tease? She had enjoyed kissing him. Was that bad? Was she going too far? But she felt she could trust him. She'd told him no and he'd been okay with it; he didn't even try to pressure her.

But she'd once thought she could trust Austin and look where that landed her.

Green Pastures, Still Waters

Sunday dawned bright and sunny, promising a perfect day for a leisurely trek through the rolling wooded hills and misty hollers of north-central Tennessee. Luke arrived at noon to pick up Rachel, and ten minutes later his truck pulled onto the two-track that led back to his land. He pulled to a stop as they came into a small clearing.

"This is it," he said, looking over at her excitedly.

"Pretty. Are we going for a hike?"

"Sound okay?"

She hesitated and bit her lower lip. "Um … it's a beautiful day for it."

"But?"

She glanced at him sideways. "Should I be worried? Walking off into the woods with a man I barely know?"

He gave her a reassuring grin and shook his head. "No, darlin'. You don't ever need to worry when you're with me. I could never hurt you." Luke hoped she could see the sincerity in his eyes. When she smiled back at him, he knew she trusted him.

He threw a backpack over his shoulder, and, taking her hand, they started walking side by side across an open meadow. Then he led the way along a narrow path through the woods. He pointed out tree stands he hunted from and described how much he loved the unspoiled wide-open spaces.

They continued along a thin path through a densely wooded area until he abruptly stopped. She ran into him and giggled.

"Shh." He put a finger to his lips, trying hard not to laugh at her. "Look there, do you see it?" he whispered, pointing into the trees ahead.

A family of red foxes scurried over a log into the deeper foliage, a mother with three little ones following closely behind. Rachel turned to Luke, excitement lighting up her face. "Oh, how cool."

Further on, at the edge of a creek, she stopped to stare across the water toward a giant willow.

"What is it, babe?"

"I just … have an odd sense I've been here before. Are we—?"

"Look at that." Luke pointed down the creek to a doe and her fawn drinking at the water's edge. "I'm surprised they're out. This time of day they're usually bedded down deep in the woods."

He put his arm around her and they watched until the doe winded them and disappeared back into the woods, her fawn darting after her.

"It's a little farther." He took her hand again.

They stopped beneath a huge sycamore tree atop a small ridge that looked out over a rolling meadow, an undulating stretch of green and gold. A large pond to one side was bordered by cattails, tall wild grasses, and a stand of willow trees. Rachel spun around, taking it all in.

"This is my favorite spot in the whole world." His voice betrayed the depth of his feelings for the raw beauty of the captivating landscape.

"It's beautiful," she said, letting her gaze linger on the magnificence spread out before her.

"Imagine it at sunrise."

"That's why you wanted to come early?"

"Yeah. It's amazing, Rachel. You wouldn't believe it." After several minutes, standing at her side, taking in the beauty of the land, he knelt down and pulled things out of his backpack, beginning with a roll of fabric that he spread out into a large mat beneath the tree.

"Maybe another time."

"Yeah." He sat in the middle of the mat and patted the spot next to him. "Have a seat."

"You come out here a lot?" she asked, sitting beside him.

"Every chance I get." The new race season was around the corner, and although he was excited, he knew he would miss these visits. "Daytona's only two weeks away. Will you come watch me race? I'll get you tickets."

"Daytona? That'd be fun. Thank you."

"It'll be great to have you there." He wanted to say something about winning if she was there, but remembered the last time he'd said something like that.

"Hungry?" he asked. He put cheese, crackers, and grapes on a paper plate and set it between them. He pulled out a bottle of wine, an opener, and two short plastic cups. He opened the wine and she held the cups while he poured.

"A toast." He raised his glass to hers, his eyes holding her gaze captive. "If you're ever lonely or afraid, remember this weekend and know how much you mean to me."

They touched glasses and took a sip. "That was real nice, Luke. This is all … so nice." Her gaze wandered, almost wistful as she looked out across the meadow.

He inhaled the fresh, clean air. "It's the closest to heaven I'll ever get. I've hunted this land for years with my father but … I've never brought a woman out here before."

"No?"

"It's always been my own private place, my refuge from the craziness of life. A place where I can come to clear my head and feel closer to … "

"To God?"

"To nature, to a tranquil place where I can relax and where everything seems … right. It's refreshing. Know what I mean?"

"Like the Twenty-third Psalm?" She quoted, "'He makes me lie down in green pastures, he leads me beside quiet waters, he refreshes my soul.'"

He was enchanted to hear her quoting the Bible. "Maybe. I suppose it does refresh my soul. It's a sense of peace that I feel being here. Not sure what God's got to do with it."

She remained quiet for several minutes before turning to him. "How can you love this as much as you do and not know God made all of it for you? And He's here with you?" She searched his eyes. Was she looking for some small dormant seed of faith?

Luke tore his gaze away to stare toward the meadow as she talked about God. She seemed perfectly at ease as she reached out to his soul, intent on finding something hidden deep within, something he wasn't sure he had. He'd never met a woman like her or even suspected someone like her existed. She was pure goodness and grace, wholesome and full of conviction, yet normal and sweet-hot sexy in an innocent way.

"I admire your faith, but I don't think God likes me as much as He does you." He hoped she wouldn't be disappointed when she didn't find in him what she was searching for.

"He loves us all the same. He gives us different things—different trials, different blessings—to lead us where He wants us to go." When he remained silent, she continued, "You've been blessed with a great life. You're healthy and strong, a successful race car driver. You haven't had any bad accidents, have you?" He shook his head. "And you're smart and handsome with parents who love you, right?"

He grinned. "Yeah."

"So why do you think God doesn't like you?"

"You have no idea what I've had to go through to get where I am. I feel like I've gotten here in *spite* of Him, not because of Him." He wasn't comfortable letting her see his insecurities. Not yet. Maybe never. He'd let her in too far already.

After several minutes with only the sounds of the birds flitting in the meadow, she touched his arm. "Maybe one day you'll tell me about it."

He covered her hand with his. "Maybe someday."

Southern Lights

Rachel panicked when she glanced at the clock on the workbench. She had less than an hour to get ready for her date with Luke. They were going to hear a hot new local band at a country music hall. She quickly tidied the shop and, minutes later, was freshly showered. Rummaging through her closet, she came across the dress she'd worn on her last date with Austin. She'd never gotten around to mending the tear. When she pulled it out, the terror of that night flooded back. Her shaking hands dropped it to the floor of the closet as if it burned.

She paired a skirt and tank top with a short leather jacket that matched her boots—the perfect combination of feminine, fun, and conservative. She curled her hair, added a little makeup, then studied her reflection.

The dress on the closet floor caught her eye in the mirror and she whirled around, glaring at it. Snatching it up, she held it in front of her and faced the mirror. Her head tilted and her teeth clenched. Was it the dress? She shuddered, then wadded it up and hurled it into the closet and slammed the door.

Luke was pleased when Rachel greeted him at the door, ready to go. Accustomed to waiting on women, he marveled that it was the fourth time he'd picked her up, and she'd been ready every time.

"Hey, Luke." Her eyes sparkled.

He stepped inside and admired her. "Sweetheart, you look too pretty."

"Too pretty for what?" She laughed at his over-the-top compliment.

He resisted saying, "Too pretty to leave the bedroom." Struggling to make up something, he pulled her out the door, closed it, and embraced her. "Too pretty not to kiss," and lingered over a kiss.

As they drove into town, he told her about the music hall and the band he wanted to check out, distracted every time he glanced at her. When their conversation lulled, he wondered if he could persuade her to come home with him. He loved kissing her and imagined making love to her. No, it was still too soon. Relax. Enjoy her company. Be a gentleman.

"Hey, Luke." An attractive waitress greeted him as they walked into the rocking country music hall. "I got your favorite table for you." She led them to an out-of-the-way table at the front of a raised section at the back of the bar. "What can I get y'all to drink?"

She was back minutes later and set a beer down for each of them. "Dirk's here tonight. Said he's gonna be playin' later."

"If you see him would you tell him to come find me, please? I need to talk to him." He looked forward to seeing his old buddy again.

When the waitress left, Luke described his good friend and old college roommate, Dirk Jansen, a songwriter. Seemed like half the town was in the music business, the other half into racing. And Luke was into both. He considered telling her about his record company but thought better of it. He wanted her to like him for who he was, not for what he had or what he did.

The music was great. Each band did about three or four songs. Then, after a short break, another band took their place. When a band called Southern Lights was introduced, Luke nudged Rachel's arm. "This is the one."

After the first song, as the thundering applause faded, Luke leaned toward her. "What do you think?"

"They're amazing."

The band did four fantastic songs. As the applause resounded through the bar, Luke decided Wes wasn't lying—this was a band worth signing. He was mighty lucky to have a capable man like Wesley Maddox running his record company. He had an uncanny sense for sniffing out fresh new talent, and the skyrocketing success of their label and its artists over the past five years was proof. He wondered if Wes had talked to them about coming into the studio to lay down some tracks.

Luke saw Wes waiting in the wings as the band left the stage. Of course he would be here; he'd wanted to sign them on the spot. "Hey, darlin', would it be all right if I leave you for a few minutes? There's someone I need to talk to real quick."

"No problem."

He kissed her. "I'll be right back."

Rachel watched Luke walk away, then sat back and listened to the next band. They weren't half as good as the last one, but they still had a nice sound. Maybe the owner of the club set the lineup with the good ones early and the not-so-good ones later, when the crowd would be less discerning.

"Well, howdy, Rachel."

Rachel jumped. Her ex-boyfriend, Austin, stood arm-in-arm with her former best friend, Holly, who seemed as anxious as a long-tailed cat in a room full of rocking chairs. She had been engrossed in the music and hadn't noticed them approach. What could she say to make them leave?

"What? Not happy to see us?" Austin sneered, placing his arm around Holly's shoulders and giving her a little squeeze.

Rachel focused on breathing normally. *Stay cool. Don't let him under your skin.* "Go away."

He whispered in Rachel's ear. "She likes it rough, begs me for it. In fact, she can't get enough most times." He stood and snickered.

Holly's eyes were wide with fear. *What's happened to you?* Suddenly the hurt and anger from Holly's betrayal melted away, replaced with pity and sadness and … what? Regret? Overwhelming regret. Rachel should have warned her about him. She should have filed assault charges and put him in jail where he belonged.

"Can we please go, Austin?" Holly refused to look at Rachel.

Austin glared at Holly as if she'd slapped him, "No way." He pulled out a chair. "I want to meet her friend."

"I'm leaving." Holly pushed through the crowd toward the exit.

Austin darted after her, catching up before she reached the door. Rachel stood, stunned by Austin's quick anger. When he raised his fist and Holly instinctively turned her face away, Rachel gasped. Her hand flew to her mouth to stifle a cry as tears pooled. She felt helpless as she watched from across the room. *I should have done something to stop this.* Austin took Holly's arm and practically dragged her out the door.

Rachel collapsed into her seat and leaned forward to hold her head with her hands. There was no way Holly liked that kind of treatment. Austin was a cruel man, plain and simple. And Holly was trapped. Somehow he'd instilled a fear so strong she was afraid to leave him; Rachel was sure of it. She sent Holly a text: PLEASE TELL ME YOU'RE ALL RIGHT.

She jumped again when Luke slipped into the chair beside her. He put his arm around her, felt her trembling, and pulled back to study her. "Are you all right?"

Rachel simply stared.

He waited, unsmiling, his brows knit together in worry. "What happened?"

"Nothing." Rachel tried to smile and avoided his look of concern.

"It's not nothing. It's definitely something. You're shaking. What are you afraid of?"

"I'm not afraid." She pulled away and his arm fell from her shoulder.

"Okay." He studied her and then took her hand. "What happened? Please tell me."

She whispered, "Austin."

His stare was blank, his brows raised.

"The old boyfriend that you sort of met at The Hickory."

"I shouldn't have left you alone. Is he still here?" His gaze searched the bar.

She shook her head. "They left."

"They?"

"Austin and Holly. My best friend."

He tried to lighten the mood. "Your ex-boyfriend out with your best friend. Yeah, that could kill a good time."

She forced a smile. "I'll be right back, okay?"

"Where are you going?"

"To the little girls' room." She stood. "Don't worry. I won't be a half hour." She lingered, put a hand to his cheek, and gave him a long kiss.

What was that? It felt like goodbye. "Rachel."

"It's okay."

He watched her all the way to the hallway that led to the restrooms, his gaze rooted there as he waited for her to come back out. True to her word, she emerged a few minutes later, and he breathed out relief as she made her way back to the table, admiring her little skirt and cowboy boots. She appeared distracted and upset, but she smiled when she met his stare.

He pulled out her chair. "You going to be okay?" He sat beside her.

"I'll be fine. I'm not so sure about my friend." She tried to shake off her concern. "Did you find your buddy Dirk?"

"There was someone else I needed to talk to. I haven't seen Dirk." He searched the crowd for him.

The next band started and the waitress brought them another round. Luke scooted Rachel's chair closer and stretched his arm around her as they enjoyed the music. He was pleased. He and Wes had spoken with the guys in the band, and they were thrilled about coming into the studio next week. Wes had suggested to Luke they might be a great opening act for the upcoming tour they had set for their newest artist, Emma Grace. He hoped they had enough material, which was one of the things he wanted to talk to Dirk about—new songs.

A portly young man with a pretty blonde appeared at their table and greeted Rachel like a long-lost friend. Rachel introduced Luke to Bryson Davies. He introduced his date, and Luke invited them to share their table. When they left an hour later, Luke whispered, "Nice guy. Another old beau of yours?"

"Not exactly. My mother introduced us. She had high hopes. Critter was impressed too; thought I should go out with him. What do you think?"

"Not your type. I see you with someone ..." he cocked his head to eye her, "taller, more of a ... cowboy." He kissed her playfully on the cheek.

"A cowboy, huh?" She gave him a sweet, sultry look.

"Luke Brandt." Dirk clapped Luke on the shoulder and slid into the chair next to him. "What's going on? And who is this pretty woman next to you?"

"Where have you been? Dirk Jansen, Rachel Tate."

"Howdy, darlin'." Dirk shook her hand.

"It's a pleasure." Rachel dazzled him with her easy smile.

"Dirk, what do you think of Southern Lights?" Luke asked.

Dirk agreed that they were going to be hot.

"Wes thought they might need some new material." Luke hoped Dirk would catch on that he didn't want to talk business, but wanted to let him know he needed more songs.

"Is that so?" Dirk said, "Well, I'll give Wes a call. Thanks for the tip."

"Anytime, buddy." Luke patted Dirk on the shoulder.

"Where's your hat, dude?" Dirk smacked Luke upside the head. "You always wear a hat."

Luke playfully swatted back. "Rachel doesn't like cowboys." He grinned at her.

Rachel's mouth fell open, "I never said that." She eyed Dirk's hat and shrank back in her chair.

"You sorta' did, babe. 'Does it look like I need a cowboy hero? Well, I don't, just so you know.' Remember saying that?" He gave her an expectant grin.

Her cheeks colored. "Okay. Well to set the record straight, I *do* like cowboys *and* guys who wear cowboy hats. You caught me at a bad time."

"Whew." Dirk adjusted his Stetson.

Rachel changed the subject. "So tell me some of the songs you've written. Any I might know?"

"How about 'Am I the Only One?' Or—"

"That wants to have fun?" Rachel said, completing the line in the song. "I absolutely *love* that song. It's one of the greatest ever. My friends and I karaoke to it all the time. Honestly. What else?"

Dirk laughed at her gush of praise. "How about 'Beer is Good,' 'Cowboys and Angels'—"

"You wrote 'Cowboys and Angels'?" she asked, glancing over to smile at Luke.

Dirk glanced at Luke, then turned his attention back to Rachel, "You love that one too?"

Luke expected she'd say he'd sung the song to her, knowing he'd never hear the end of it from Dirk.

"I do." Again, she glanced at Luke.

Dirk looked between them. "Aw, is that y'all's song?"

"I sang it to her the night we met," Luke sheepishly admitted.

Dirk doubled over with laughter, and after a moment wiped at tears in his eyes. "You? Seriously? Dude, in all the years I've known you, I have *never* heard you sing."

"I had to do something. She decked the guy who talked to her right before me."

Dirk looked surprised. "Well, it must've worked 'cause she's sittin' here now. I'd have given a million bucks to see that."

Dirk stayed quite a while, and they all laughed and talked. Luke was thrilled that Rachel and Dirk got on so well. She was fitting into his life with an ease that felt like she could've been there all along.

When he took her home, he stopped in front of the house, looking forward to a few minutes of having her all to himself. Truth be told, he wouldn't mind at all kissing her goodnight for the next couple of hours.

She faced him. "I had a great time. Thank you, Luke."

"Me too." He leaned toward her over the center console. "Come here," he whispered.

She caressed his cheek, unafraid. His breath caught at the petal-soft touch of her fingertips, and when she leaned closer his hands touched her long hair. He kissed her, softly, then with unexpected urgency and passion. When he pulled away he was stunned. He couldn't believe the effect she had on him. He leaned back in his seat and closed his eyes. He wanted so much more—all of her, in his head, in his heart, in his life.

He wanted it all.

When he looked at her, he could feel his smile a country mile wide.

"What?"

"You," he said, incapable of finding words to tell her how he felt. "Will you have dinner with me tomorrow night?"

She smiled.

"At my place. We'll throw some steaks on the grill. I'm a pretty good cook."

Worry creased her brow, "Luke—"

"Afraid of being alone with me?"

She bit her lower lip, then nodded, "Yes."

At least she was honest. "Are you afraid of all men or just me?"

She glared, her lips pressed tight, then let herself out of the car.

That sure didn't go as he'd hoped. He caught up to her at the front step. "Rachel, wait, please." He gently turned her to face him. "I'm sorry. I want to be with you, baby."

She shook her head. "I can't, Luke."

"What are you so afraid of? What did that guy do to you?"

"I'm not afraid of anything. I'm simply not ready and if you can't accept that then … leave and … and stop calling me."

"Whoa. I'm sorry. It's okay. I can wait." He took a deep breath. "I can wait, Rachel, as long as it takes."

She relaxed and lowered her eyes.

He tipped her chin up. "I mean it. You don't ever have to be afraid with me. I will never take more than you're willing to give. Ever."

She stood on her tiptoes and hugged him.

He breathed deeply, filling his soul with her sweet essence, wishing with all his might he'd never have to let go.

When she released him, she stood back and looked up at him. "Thank you."

"We'll go out, okay?"

"We could have dinner here."

He gave her a sideways nod, "With your father? No offense; he seems like a great guy, but I want to be with you. Let's go out, okay?"

She nodded.

"Pick you up at seven?"

"Sounds good."

"Great." He hugged and kissed her quickly, forcing himself to stop before it became too intense. "Good night, baby," he whispered.

"Good night, Luke. Thank you for understanding."

Damage Done

When Rachel went inside she saw the text from Holly's phone, but it wasn't from Holly. It was from Austin—a crude message that told her Holly couldn't text back because she was busy with him. It was so cruel and filthy it made Rachel want to throw up. She went to bed, but remained awake, haunted by his ugly words, increasingly fearful for her friend.

The next morning she called Holly several times, but it always went to voice mail. More thought about the scene the night before led to more worry for Holly's well-being. She decided to go to her apartment. She hoped she still lived there.

Rachel knocked several times. When Holly didn't answer, she wondered if her friend had stayed at Austin's. Then she heard movement inside.

Fear shot through her. *What if he's here?* She gripped the Taser in her coat pocket, comforted that she wouldn't be afraid to use it.

"Holly, I know you're in there. I heard you. It's Rachel. Please let me in."

It remained quiet. Rachel wondered if she'd imagined the sound. "Holly, I'm worried about you. I want to talk. I can help you. Please." She let her forehead rest against the closed door.

"You can't help me, Rachel." Holly's voice was weak. "Go away."

She's here. She hadn't said *I don't need any help; rather, you can't help me.* She did need help. Tears filled her eyes. "Holly, if our friendship ever meant anything to you, please let me in."

"Go away. You can't do anything to help me." Holly's voice broke.

"Then I'm calling your mom." Rachel faked tapping buttons on her phone then held it to her ear, standing back to stare at the peephole.

"Don't you dare."

Rachel spoke into her silent phone, "Hello, Mrs. James. It's Rachel Tate." She paused. "I know it's been a long time," and then, "Great, how have you been?"

When the door opened a crack, Rachel pushed it wide enough to let herself in and pocketed her phone. Her heartbeat quickened as her eyes adjusted to the dim interior. The apartment was trashed, furniture overturned, wall hangings askew, broken lamps and papers strewn everywhere. Holly limped down the short hall to her bedroom. Rachel closed the door, locked it, and followed Holly.

Holly had retreated to bed and faced the wall. The room was as disarrayed as the rest of the place. Rachel sat on the edge of the bed and touched Holly's shoulder. "Please talk to me. Are you all right?"

Holly whimpered. "You should hate me."

Tears rushed to Rachel's eyes and she sniffed. "I don't hate you."

Holly turned to face her. "Don't cry for me, Rach."

Rachel's tears ran down her cheeks at the sight of Holly's face. One eye was swollen almost shut. Her lips were broken and bloody. A huge bruise colored one cheek, and blood was caked beneath her swollen nose. "Oh, my God," Rachel cried out. She hugged her close.

Holly moaned.

Rachel let go and sat back. "He did this to you?"

Holly cried and turned away.

Rachel choked back fresh tears and squared her shoulders. Be strong; she needs you. "I'm taking you to the hospital."

"No. It'll clear up in a few days. Please."

"I swear, if you don't let me take you to the hospital I *will* call your mom for real this time."

"Oh, Rach, let it go. He'll be so mad—"

"Why do you even care what he thinks after what he's done to you?"

"He's not always like this. Most of the time he's a great guy and I love him."

"Are you kidding? How could you possibly—"

"When he saw you last night, he went ballistic. *You're* the one he wanted. But he's a good man most of the time." Holly tried to sound convincing, "It's my fault. I couldn't bear to look you in the eye last night. I had to get out of there."

How could she think any of this was her fault? She didn't deserve to be treated like this. No woman did. Rachel pushed down her anger and got her phone. "You should call your mom and tell her anyway," she said calmly as she found the number in her contacts. She showed it to Holly then held her finger over the call button.

"I'll let you take me to the hospital. But not Mercy General, all right? And you have to promise not to call my parents."

"Deal." Rachel gave her an encouraging nod. Holly was an x-ray technician, and of course she wouldn't want her coworkers at her hospital to see her like this. "Can I help you get dressed?"

"I think I can manage."

"I'll get ice." Rachel went to the kitchen and put ice in a bag. She wrapped it in a clean dish towel as Holly limped out of the bedroom.

On the way to the hospital, Rachel broached the subject of filing charges against Austin, and Holly adamantly refused. "If you don't, he'll continue to do this to you, to other women." Her guilt rose like a tsunami. Had she filed charges herself over a year ago, maybe it wouldn't have come to this. "I'll file charges with you. Remember, he hit me too." She swallowed her rising fear. "And he tried to rape me." She'd never told anyone. Her heart beat frantically as she thought about how differently that night might have ended. "Please, Holl, you have to do this with me," she begged, glancing toward her friend's puffy, bloodshot eyes.

Holly shook her head so slightly it was almost indiscernible. "He'll kill me, Rach," she whispered, tears running freely down her cheeks, her one good eye wide with fear.

Rachel pulled to a stop in front of the emergency room and faced Holly. "Come live with me. I'll protect you and teach you how to protect yourself. We'll learn together. Please, Holl, it's the right thing to do."

Holly trembled.

"If I could do it over, I would've filed charges before, and maybe this wouldn't have happened to you. Please, Holl, think about it."

Holly turned away from Rachel's unrelenting gaze, resting her head against the window.

Rachel helped her into a wheelchair, and an orderly pushed her inside while Rachel parked. As she walked back in, she called the police. Even if Holly wouldn't file charges, she would, even if it was too late for it to make a difference.

Rachel sat beside Holly in the crowded emergency room, holding her hand while they waited. She'd missed her something fierce. She looked down at their intertwined hands, and a hint of a smile curved her lips even as her throat tightened and tears pooled on her lowered lids.

She stared at the ring on her finger, haunted by her own memories of a night not so long ago, the dark ugly images coming unbidden and unwelcome, flitting through her mind with frightening clarity.

She and Austin had been dating for several months and had grown close. She'd liked him. He was fun and sweet, everything a boyfriend was supposed to be. Until that night. As she sat there absently twisting her ring, she wondered again what she'd done wrong.

She'd been clear from the beginning that she was saving herself for marriage. She thought he respected, even admired her. But that night, as she started to leave, something changed, something unexpected and frightening.

"Come on, Rachel. It's my birthday. Stay with me tonight, please, babe? I want to hold you." Austin had taken her hand and pulled her down beside him on the couch.

She faced him. "I can't, Austin. You know I can't."

He scowled. "Why not?"

She looked at his hand holding hers. "Daddy's expecting me home tonight."

"That's ridiculous. You're twenty-three. A grown woman. Entitled to stay out late if you want to." When she stiffened and scooted away, his tone softened. "Your father will understand." He threaded his fingers through her hair, lightly brushing against the bare skin of her shoulder.

The desire in his eyes was intense. She wished she hadn't gotten a new dress and curled her hair. But they'd been dating for almost four months, and she felt comfortable with him, wanted to look pretty for him. It was a special night.

Rachel shivered and straightened. "I'm sorry, Austin. I can't spend the night."

"I know you like me." His greedy stare boldly undressed her. "What's up with you? Don't you want to be with me?"

"Of course I like you. You know I do. But I don't want to be with you that way." She swallowed the lump in her throat. "I'm not ready for anything more right now. You know I want to wait."

"I know." Austin rubbed the back of his neck, and gave her an encouraging smile, but it did little to reassure her. "Come on, babe, nothing will happen. I want to hold you." His voice was soft and gentle as he tried to persuade her.

She considered it for a long minute. He was so sweet, and it would be nice to be held. He obviously cared about her. But could she trust him? She shook her head.

"Stay for a little while longer then, okay? I'll try on my new shirt." He picked up her gift from the coffee table and gave her an easy grin.

She'd bought him a nice dress shirt for his birthday and was thrilled he liked it so much. "All right," she said, still unncomfortable with her decision.

When he came out of his bedroom he had the shirt on, still unbuttoned, showing off a muscular chest with a light covering of dark hair that tapered to a thin line at the waist of his jeans. He moseyed up to her, his dark brown bedroom eyes never leaving hers. "Do you like it?" He licked his lips. "Help me button it?"

She tried to swallow, but her mouth had gone dry. She forced a smile and nodded as he stopped before her. She began a couple buttons from the top, her fingers trembling as they fumbled with the tiny buttons. She glanced up to find him staring at her, and she bit her lower lip to stop it from quivering.

He buried his hands in her hair at the back of her neck as he leaned down to kiss her, barely brushing her lips with his several times. Her breath caught and she trembled in his arms.

She pulled away and pushed against his chest with both hands. "I should go," she said, her voice shaky, her eyes wide, her heart hammering wildly in her chest. She'd let it go too far. She took a step back.

"No. Rachel, please," he said. "Let me love you, babe." He held onto her arms, pulling her into him.

Rachel shook her head and took another step backward. She turned toward the door, and he tightened his grip.

"Austin, stop. You're hurting me." She tried to wiggle free but was trapped in his strong grasp. "Please let me go."

His gaze wandered from her eyes down to her mouth, then lower. He swallowed hard and shook his head. "I can't let you go. Don't you think it's time?" He pulled her to him and wrapped his arms around her as his mouth sought hers again.

"No, Austin, please," Rachel pleaded as she tried again to free herself.

He lunged for her and caught her around her waist. She continued to struggle with him and his anger erupted. "You *will* stay." He held her tight while he leaned down to kiss her neck, her shoulder.

"Austin, please. No," she whispered, terrified.

"Yes."

Rachel tried again to pull away, and he backhanded her across the cheek. Then his other hand wrapped tightly in her hair, holding her fast. She struggled against him as he forced her to succumb to his kisses.

Panic rose inside her. *No.* Don't *panic. That's exactly what you can't do. Think. Think.*

She leaned her head back, letting him believe she had given up. He loosened his grip on her hair, and she relaxed. He'd freed her arms.

She lured his mouth back to hers, and while he was right there in front of her, she mustered all the strength she had and slammed him on both ears at once. When he reeled back, she used the heel of her hand to punch up into his nose. Blood spurted, and he fell to his knees.

She wrenched free, and she fled the apartment, running as fast and as far away as she could get, her heart racing. Driven blindly by pure, raw fear, sheer panic took over, pushing her on, giving her stamina she didn't even know she had until, finally, several blocks away, she glanced back over her shoulder and, seeing no one, stopped to catch her breath. The cool night air burned her lungs.

Rachel stood there for several minutes, bent over, gasping. Her adrenaline pumped as she tried to come to terms with what had happened. She whipped her head up, gripped with fear as she looked back the way she'd come. She finally breathed a sigh of relief, confident he hadn't followed. How could she have let it go so far?

As her breathing began to return to normal she took in her surroundings and recognized where she was. Her friend Holly's place was around the corner. She started in that direction, desperately hoping Holly would be home. Best friends for as long as she could remember, Rachel and Holly made the abstinence vow together when they were fourteen in their small group at church. Nine years later, at twenty-three, they were both still virgins. At least Rachel thought so.

They'd met Austin together at a New Neighbor party at the clubhouse shortly after Holly moved into the apartment complex. Holly had noticed him first and flirted with him most of the night, but it was Rachel he asked out. Rachel declined because she knew Holly liked him, but when Holly insisted she was fine with it, she and Austin started dating.

As Rachel waited for Holly to answer, she wiped the corner of her mouth with the back of her hand and gasped at the streak of bright red blood on it. Holly opened the door, took one look at her, and immediately pulled her inside. She sat Rachel on the couch and within seconds brought a washcloth and ice for her bloody lip and demanded, "What happened?"

"We broke up. Let me borrow your car to get home."

"I'm your best friend. You can tell me what happened. You need to."

"Not now. I don't want to talk about it."

"I want to help. Stay the night."

Rachel shook her head. She wanted to escape, be alone. "Please understand. I need to go. Can I use your car?"

"Then let me drive. You're too upset."

"I'll be fine."

Holly focused on the rip in Rachel's dress. "You're anything but fine."

"It's not a good time to discuss it. Please let me have your car."

Holly got a sweatshirt for Rachel to wear over her dress and gave her the keys. "Be careful."

Rachel pulled her friend's Grand Prix to a stop at the end of the remote two-track and turned off the engine. The lights illuminated the dense woods until they shut off. After her eyes adjusted to the darkness, she got out, easily finding the path that led to the creek and her favorite spot beneath a huge, old willow tree. No one knew it was her secret place where she often went to think, dream, or cry. She always felt safe beneath the enclosure of long, wispy branches that hung close to the ground. As a little girl, she'd imagined it as a wonderfully enchanted place, the delicate branches sheltering her within their magic.

Located on the far edge of their farm, it was well-posted to keep hunters out. In all the years she'd retreated there, she'd never seen anyone, which was perfect. That night, more than ever, she needed to be alone.

Rachel sat on the creek bank and leaned against the tree trunk, puzzling over the evening's events. They had a nice time at dinner. He was charming and made her feel so special. The dinner she'd cooked turned out perfectly; nothing burned—a first for her. They'd shared a bottle of wine to celebrate his birthday, but hardly enough to get him drunk. How could he lose it like that? He seemed like such a good guy. She shook her head, overwhelmed with disbelief. How could she have been so wrong about him?

When she touched the swollen place at the corner of her mouth, a tear fell. He'd struck her. She shivered. She'd come so close to being raped. Thankful for the college self-defense class, she'd never expected to use it against a boyfriend, someone she'd been dating for almost four months, a man she thought she knew.

Rachel pulled her legs up, wrapped her arms around them, and rested her head on her knees. She longed for home and a shower to remove his scent from her skin, to scrub the memory from her mind. But she couldn't go home. Daddy would still be up, and she couldn't let him see her like this. He would know, even if her lip wasn't swollen and her dress ripped. He'd see it in her eyes. She was sure of it.

Maybe she should tell him, so he could help her deal with it. He'd know what to do. No, he would totally lose it, probably grab a hunting rifle and go after Austin. She couldn't let that happen. When he went to the fields in the morning, she'd sneak in and shower before he saw her. Then she'd decide what to tell him and what to do about it.

Rachel sent him a text: SORRY I'M SO LATE. I MIGHT STAY AT HOLLY'S TONIGHT SO DON'T WAIT UP. LOVE YOU, DADDY. GOOD NIGHT. She hated to lie, so she used vague words. It didn't entirely eliminate the taste of guilt, only made it more palatable, but still better than letting him worry or outright lying.

She leaned her head back against the tree and let her tears fall. Would she ever find a guy who would wait for marriage? Was she worth waiting for?

Rachel stared at her purity ring. It represented her commitment to God to walk in purity and wait until marriage. It reminded her every day to make good decisions about life, love, dating, and sex. Mistakes came from living in the moment, without considering the consequences. The ring prompted her to look where she was going and strive to fulfill her promise to lead a Christ-centered life. She believed God had a plan for her life and trusted Him to guide her.

Her dad texted back. THANKS, SWEET PEA. LOVE YOU TOO. GOOD NIGHT.

Rachel felt guilty, staring at the screen until it went dark. She pulled the hood of Holly's sweatshirt up over her head and lay down on the soft grass. She prayed for a long time, then cried some more, and finally drifted off to sleep.

She woke beneath a cozy old hunting jacket, strangely comforted by its warmth and unafraid of the unknown man who'd placed it there. She'd snuggled into its earthy scent, reassured there were still some good ones out there, not too far away.

Rachel stayed by Holly's side as she was treated for several bruised ribs in addition to multiple facial bruises and contusions. Photos were taken, and a full police report was filed by both Holly and Rachel. They prayed and cried, renewing their friendship with a bond made stronger by their shared nightmare experiences.

It was nearly six o'clock when they got back to Rachel's house. After settling her friend in her bed, Rachel went outside to call Luke.

"Hi, darlin'," he answered. Rachel's heart lifted at the excitement in his voice.

She tried not to sound emotionally exhausted. "Something happened today."

"You okay?"

"I am, but I need to stay in tonight." She hoped she wouldn't have to explain. Silence. *Oh, Luke, don't be upset.*

"What happened?"

"I, um … I can't."

"You sure you're okay?"

"Positive." She knew she was failing to reassure him.

"I can come over. We could go for a walk. You sound like you could use a friend about now."

"I don't think I'll be very good company tonight. It's been an awful day."

"I was looking forward to seeing you."

The disappointment in his voice comforted her. It would be nice to feel his strong arms around her. "Okay, sure."

"Good. I'll be over in a little bit."

"See you then."

Rachel went inside and peeked in on Holly. She was sound asleep. Rachel was relieved Holly was going to be all right. The doctor had assured them everything physical would heal, but how long it would take for Holly to recover emotionally?

How long until she could trust a man again? A year and half later, Rachel still wasn't quite sure she could trust Luke. A slow smile curved her lips as his words echoed in her mind. *I will never take more than you're willing to give. Ever.* She could trust in that, couldn't she?

She sat on the front step and bent her head to thank God for bringing her best friend back into her life, for giving her a chance to forgive, and for blessing them both with the courage and strength to fight back. She begged Him to help Holly survive this horrible experience, with a pure heart that would be able to love again. She begged for forgiveness for being too weak and afraid to report it when it had happened to her.

She steeled herself against the pain and soul-crushing guilt when tears threatened, then prayed for all the other women Austin may have hurt. She vowed to do everything she could to put his evil in its place, then asked for God's help to make the right decisions and do the right things, "… forever and always, every day. Amen."

She tried to push aside the events of the day as she headed to her shop and turned on her music, opening up one of the overhead doors to enjoy the cool night air. Holly had gotten blood on her white leather passenger seat, so she filled a container with cold water, grabbed a clean shop rag, and worked on the stain.

As she dabbed at the blood, memories of Austin flooded back again. She pushed them away, no longer willing to accept their haunting. How long was it going to take? When does *you'll get over it* begin? More importantly, when does it end?

"Hey, beautiful," Luke called as he walked into the garage.

Startled by his voice, Rachel hit her head on the roof of the car and sent a container flying, spilling liquid on the floor. Tears glistened in her panic-filled eyes.

"Sorry." He gently pulled her up into his arms. Her heart raced against his chest. "Hey, it's okay." He held her, wondering what had happened. When her trembling stopped, he looked at her face. "Are you all right?"

She blinked several times and shook her head, "I'm sorry." She retrieved the fallen container, studied the damp car seat, closed the door, and put the container on the workbench. When she turned to him, she seemed more settled, but not totally collected. "Want to go for a walk?"

"Sure." Whatever happened sure ruffled her. Holding hands, they walked to an orchard on the opposite side of the house.

On the way, Rachel relayed the story, starting with Holly and Austin at the music hall the night before and going back to the night a year and a half ago. They sat on a garden bench at the edge of the orchard. She wept describing the damage Austin had inflicted on Holly and the guilt she felt for not filing charges against him.

He held her while she cried. No woman should have to endure that kind of abuse. What kind of man treated a woman that way? "He didn't—" he paused.

"Rape me?"

Luke nodded, his anxiety difficult to mask.

"I got away, but Holly didn't." She wiped her tears and rubbed them off on her jeans. "I brought Holly home to stay for a while. She needs me. We need each other." She put her hand on his and squeezed.

Luke agreed, relieved she hadn't had to go through what her friend had. "I'll kill him if he comes near this place."

Worry etched her face as she searched his. "No. Promise me you won't do anything, Luke. We're pressing charges, and he'll get what's coming to him. We have a good case that'll put him in jail for a long time for sure. Don't get yourself in trouble."

He ran his fingers through his hair. "Rachel—"

"Promise me."

"Okay, okay, I promise. But if I see him out somewhere—"

Rachel shook her head. "He's not worth it."

"Come here." He pulled her onto his lap and held her while she rested her head on his shoulder. He breathed in the scent of her hair, pushing anger out of his heart, replacing it with her warmth and trust.

He savored her fragile sweetness. He needed to take care of her, ensure no one hurt her again. Reigning in his emotions, he whispered, "Hey."

She lifted her head, absently wiping her wet cheeks and looked at him expectantly.

Her damp face glistened in the moonlight, beautiful and vulnerable, gripping his heart with a surge of protectiveness. "Thank you for telling me, trusting me. I know it wasn't easy, but I'm glad you did." He brushed away the remaining moisture. "If there's anything I can do, anything at all, tell me, okay?"

"There is something."

"Name it."

"Would you go with me to Holly's tomorrow afternoon so I can get her clothes and a few things?"

"I'd be happy to." His heart swelled with affection. *God help me, I'm falling in love with this little girl.* He ran a hand through his hair to shake off the feeling he was losing himself in her.

She dominated his thoughts on the drive home. He was surprised, but pleased that she'd trusted him with all she'd been through, though it broke his heart that someone had so mistreated her. It explained her brusque standoffish attitude the first few times they met, her unwillingness to go out with him, and her reluctance to have dinner alone at his place. She was going to be hard to get close to, but now he knew why.

He'd have to take it nice and slow. She was still fragile and healing. Although she refused to admit it, still afraid too. He'd have to earn her trust, her love. He said he'd wait as long as it took, but how long would that be? Could he hang on? For her, he could. She was worth the wait.

Luke followed closely as Rachel unlocked the apartment door, then glanced behind him and down the sidewalk both directions before he locked them in. The interior's upheaval made his blood boil. What kind of man was Austin?

Rachel took boxes from him and pointed down the hall. "I'm going to go pack some of her clothes."

"Anything I can do?"

"You could set things in order if you want."

As she disappeared into the bedroom, he picked up a broken picture frame with a photo of Rachel and a woman he guessed was Holly. The two teenagers stood with their arms around each other, heads tilted together, huge grins shining. What she'd been like before Austin had instilled a fear of men in her. He righted a side table, set the picture on it, and continued to straighten the room.

He glanced up to find Rachel leaning against the wall next to the kitchen, eyeing him. "Hey."

"Can you find a plastic bag in the kitchen for some toiletries?"

"Sure." She turned toward the bedroom, and he headed for the kitchen.

Luke was searching through lower cabinets when the apartment door flew open and slammed against the wall.

"Where are you?" a man's voice bellowed. He stomped down the hallway. "You are dead."

Austin.

Luke rounded the corner of the kitchen as he disappeared into the bedroom. He sprinted after him, pulling up short at the doorway. The guy had stopped just inside the door. Rachel stood on the far side of the room, alert and wary, pointing a Taser at his chest. She shook her head at Luke.

"Where is she?" Austin's gaze searched the room, and Luke ducked back to remain undetected.

"Austin."

"Where is she?" he demanded.

Luke peered around the corner. Rachel's lips pressed into a thin line, her eyes filled with disgust and loathing. "In the hospital," she lied.

"You're responsible for this."

Luke struggled to control his fury. *Good God Almighty, give me strength.* He wanted to beat the living daylights out of him.

"You need to leave," Rachel said, her voice calm and controlled. "There's a restraining order against you. You're not even supposed to be here."

"This is all your fault," he shouted, pointing a finger at her. " She was perfectly happy with me until she saw you last night."

Rachel squared her shoulders and held out her empty hand. "Give me the key, Austin."

Austin moved toward her. "I'll give you something better," he said, reaching for his belt.

That's it. Luke bounded forward, but Rachel was quicker. She squeezed the trigger.

Austin fell to the floor screeching in agony as electricity coursed through his writhing body. When it stopped, Luke placed a boot on his wrist and yanked the key from his fingers. "If I were you I'd take off before she does it again and before I break a promise and lose it completely."

Austin's frantic eyes focused on Rachel, who held the Taser, aimed and ready. "No. Rachel, please." Then he gave her a menacing look as he struggled to his feet, gasping. "You're gonna regret this," he said, yanking the wires from his chest.

Luke picked him up by his shirtfront, and in one swift motion slammed him against the wall. He leaned in close, staring straight into his eyes, "You come within a mile of Rachel or her friend and you'll be dead, 'cause I'll kill you myself." He let go of him as suddenly as he'd picked him up, and, like a ragdoll, Austin slid to the floor.

"Get out," Rachel said through clenched teeth. "Go now or I swear I'll zap you until you pass out, and we'll drag your sorry butt out."

Austin glared at her, struggled up again, then staggered out. Luke followed, locking the door behind him.. He pulled the curtain aside on the front window. Austin heaved himself behind the wheel of a silver Camry and tore away.

Returning to Rachel, he looked her over. "You okay?"

She nodded, disengaged the spent cartridge, and tucked the Taser into her pocket, "I've wanted to do that ever since I bought this thing … I'm so glad you were here, though. Thank you."

"Me too, baby." She fell into his arms, and he held her, marveling at her courage and strength. He would've liked to kick the guy's butt, but a part of him was glad Rachel had gotten the satisfaction of bringing him to his knees.

She put her palms against his chest. "I'm almost done." She went back to the bed and zipped up a large suitcase.

Luke leaned back against the wall while she pulled a drawer open and packed the sweatshirts and jeans in the large box on the bed. "Can I help?"

"Did you find a plastic bag?"

"Oh, yeah." He retrieved it from where he'd dropped it in the hallway and handed it to her. "Is this okay?"

"Perfect. Thanks." She headed into the bathroom. "Check the front closet for jackets and put them in the box."

"You got it." He took the box to the living room.

She finished in the bathroom, and, returning to the living room, added the bag to the box. She went back to the bedroom and returned with the wheeled suitcase from Holly's closet.

Luke picked up the box. When Rachel joined him at the door, he nodded toward the broken picture frame. "Want to take that?"

Her haunted expression made him wonder if they were good memories or bad. "It's shattered." His heart ached for her. The frame wasn't the only thing broken.

"We could get a new frame."

Hope glimmered in her eyes. "Good idea. Holly will love it." As she tucked it the box she put it under a bright-pink sweatshirt that he felt sure he'd seen somewhere before.

Disappointments

Monday evening after work Rachel found her father at the kitchen table, working on a crossword puzzle. "How was your day?" She kissed him hello on the cheek. She'd had the most amazing day and could hardly wait to tell him and Holly about it.

"Pretty good, sweet pea. How was yours?"

"Good. Where's Holly?"

"Sleeping, I reckon. But she was up for quite a while this afternoon. She's doing a heap better today; made me a right nice lunch."

"Great. That's good." She was relieved to hear her friend was healing. "You won't believe it, Daddy. I got the promotion I've been waiting for."

"You did?"

"James, my manager, told me they needed another engineer on a project team to work on a baggage system for a new airport that's going in outside London. And he recommended *me*. I met with the project leader, and they offered me the position. Can you believe it?"

He stood and gave her a big hug. "That's great, sweetheart. I knew it was only a matter of time before those short-sighted nitwits saw your potential."

"I'm so excited. I start next week. I can't wait. I'll be glad to get rid of the boring programming stuff and actually be challenged."

"Congratulations, honey. I'm so proud of you. You deserve it."

"Thank you, Daddy. I have to go tell Holly."

When Rachel eased open the bedroom door, Holly was awake, struggling to sit up in bed. Holly grimaced at the effort and Rachel hurried to help, but there was little she could do except position her pillows.

She sat on the bed next to her and they talked for an hour. Holly assured her she felt much better and repeated how much she appreciated all Rachel had done.

She talked about finding a new place to live and asked if Rachel would take her to get her car and help her look for another apartment.

Rachel was reluctant to let her best friend go so soon, and tried to talk her into waiting. Holly agreed to a few more days, but was adamant about not overstaying her welcome. She pointed out that sharing the one bedroom would be a real challenge when she returned to work. She had irregular hours at the hospital, and they'd constantly be waking each other up.

Rachel shared the news of her promotion, and Holly was thrilled, knowing how hard Rachel had tried to find an engineering position after college, and how disappointed she'd been to have to settle for the programming job.

When Luke called that evening Rachel told him her exciting news. He seemed happy for her, but then an unmistakable disappointment clouded his voice.

"What did you say the project was? A baggage system?"

"At an airport outside of London."

"As in London, England?"

"The London Stansted Airport. Why?"

"So, you'll probably have to go there, right?"

"Yeah. I'm going in about six weeks. Isn't that so cool, Luke? I've never even been out of the country before."

"You sound excited."

"I am."

"Do you have a passport?"

"I got one before I graduated from TSU, just in case."

There was a long silence.

"Luke?"

"I'm happy for you, baby. I really am."

She frowned. He sure didn't sound happy. But why? Surely, he wasn't still hoping she'd go to work for him.

He said little after that, and Rachel wondered if he'd turned on the TV or was checking e-mail. He invited her to dinner the next night to celebrate her promotion, but she had a late meeting with her new project team, so they settled on Wednesday night, even though he'd have to leave for Daytona right afterward. Despite the dinner invitation, when they finally said goodnight, she had the distinct impression he wasn't excited for her at all.

The next morning at work James called a team meeting and announced to the software development group that Rachel would be leaving them for an engineering role. They made plans to transfer her current assignments to others on the team. As the meeting ended and they filed out of the conference room, she overheard someone mutter, "Must be nice to have friends in high places."

She didn't have any friends in high places, so she chalked it up to jealousy. But as the afternoon wore on, she couldn't get her mind off of it. She thought about her friends, some of whom had fairly influential parents, but none would have the means to influence something at BEI International.

By mid-afternoon she succumbed to her curiosity and started digging around on the Internet. She came up with nothing from any of her friends' parents, so she tried another angle.

She went to BEI International's web site and started there. She hadn't been back to it since she'd interviewed with the company two and a half years ago, and was surprised it still looked the same. For a technology company she was disappointed it wasn't more edgy. She did a search on the company name and came across a press release dated nine years ago that announced a merger between Brandt Engineering Incorporated and a small engineering firm in London, the result of which would become BEI International.

BEI. Brandt Engineering Inc. Rachel was stunned. How could she work there for two and a half years and not know what the company's initials stood for? *Brandt*—as in Luke Brandt? She'd told a coworker girlfriend about going out with Luke and driving his race car last weekend. Was he behind her promotion? She hunted further and learned his father had started the company and still owned a controlling interest.

In fact, she discovered his father owned a lot of things in and around Nashville.

She stared at her computer screen, feeling like a plump water balloon with a pinhole. How could he do this to her? He knew how much she wanted to get into engineering, and all he had to do was place a call to make it happen. She wanted it bad, but not like this. Did he think she'd be happy? Why didn't he mention it last night when they spoke on the phone? Did he think she wouldn't find out?

When Luke called she didn't answer, but let the phone vibrate until it stopped and the voice mail indicator lit up. She couldn't talk to him yet. She'd see him tomorrow night at dinner. Maybe she'd feel better about it by then.

Each time Luke called that evening, it went straight to voice mail. He had exciting news and was disappointed she wasn't answering. He finally sent her a text: GOOD NIGHT, ANGEL. I'LL CALL YOU TOMORROW.

The next day he tried several times, but she never picked up. He called her office, but only reached voice mail there too. Late in the afternoon he got a text from her: SOMETHING'S COME UP AND I CAN'T SEE YOU TONIGHT. SORRY FOR THE SHORT NOTICE. He read it several times and waited for a follow-up text, but when nothing else came he responded: PLEASE CALL ME.

The text and unanswered calls unsettled him. Something was wrong, and he hoped it didn't involve Holly. When she didn't call back, he was sure of it. He was supposed to be at the track first thing in the morning and had planned to leave right after dinner with her that evening. He wouldn't see her for another four days, and then only if he saw her at the track, so he drove to her place.

A couple of the shop doors were up, so he walked straight to the barn where she was working under the hood of the Thunderbolt. "Hey, beautiful."

She hesitated before straightening to look at him. "Hey, Luke." Her wrench fell to the floor with a clang.

He took her phone from the stereo mount and saw all of his unanswered calls and unopened voice mails.

"What are you doing?" She picked up the wrench.

"I thought maybe your phone died." He leaned against the front of her car. "What's up?"

Rachel toyed with the wrench, blinked, and rubbed the back of her wrist across her forehead. "I'm sure you had the best intentions in the world, but I don't appreciate you messing with my job, my career."

"What are you talking about?"

She glared. "My promotion? Me getting that engineering job? Tell me you had nothing to do with that."

Seriously? That's what this is about? "Rachel, I had *nothing* to do with it."

"I don't believe you. BEI? Brandt Engineering Incorporated?"

"It wasn't me." At dinner with his parents Sunday evening, he'd told them about Rachel, mentioning her desire for an engineering job while stuck in programming at BEI. He never dreamed his father would do anything about it. "Rachel, baby, it may have been my father, but I'm sure he was only trying to help."

"Well, I don't need his help. And I don't want it."

"I'm sorry. Is it that bad? Can't you accept it as a lucky break? Isn't it something you've wanted for a long time?"

"Yes, I wanted it. But I wanted to *earn* it."

He leaned his hands on the hood of the car across from her. "You're not going to get it on your own merit, babe. You're a woman in a man's profession. Get used to it."

"Ohh!" She oozed frustration, spun around, and stormed back to the workbench.

This wasn't going well. "Rachel—"

Slamming her wrench on the workbench, she whirled back to him. "I know. And that's what makes it so all-fired impossible. Now I have no choice but to accept it. I can't go back to the programming job even if I wanted to. That would be like putting smoke back into the fire, but I didn't want it like this." She turned and her shoulders dropped. "I wanted to earn it."

"I'm sorry, baby."

When she turned back, the fight fell right out of her. "Most people don't like to be handed everything, Luke. A person has to earn things on their own in order to feel worth something."

"Rachel." He closed the distance between them in two long strides. In one swift movement he lifted her to sit on the workbench in front of him like he had before. He needed to talk to her face to face, to keep her from walking away.

"Stop doing that." She wiggled to get around him to get down, but he stood his ground in front of her, holding her in place.

"Doing what?" His teeth clenched. "What?"

"Picking me up and putting me wherever you want. I'm not a rag doll you can put on a shelf. I'm a person, not a puppet you and your father get to play with." She struggled again, but he held her fast. "Let me down."

Luke kissed her fast and hard. When she began to respond, he slowed down. He could feel her relax, melting into him.

"No." She pushed him away. "Please go." She turned, refusing to look at him.

He let go and studied the sad tilt of her head, then lifted her chin to bring her eyes back to him. "I didn't do anything wrong." When she pulled away, he grabbed an envelope from his back pocket, tossed it onto the workbench beside her, and walked out.

She wondered if he had anything to do with it, knowing firsthand how parents can sometimes mess things up despite the best intentions. She picked up the envelope, and looked inside—race tickets. Daytona. She swallowed the lump in her throat and tossed the envelope back on the workbench.

Luke felt the familiar twist in his gut as he pulled his truck into his designated spot in the infield at Daytona Speedway, his crew and equipment trailer coming up right behind him. He shut off the engine and surveyed the area. It was a beautiful track, exciting to run with its super-high banked turns. He felt great about the race. He might even win it this time.

He wondered if Rachel was going to come or if she was still mad. He'd tried to call her Thursday evening to let her know he'd placed fourth in the field after qualifying laps—it was the best he'd ever done at Daytona—but she didn't pick up. He hadn't had the chance to share with her that he'd gotten approval from NASCAR to run his new carburetor. His car was as fine-tuned as ever, and with his new carburetor, it was sure to use much less fuel. As long as the tires held out, that meant fewer pit stops and more time on the track making laps.

He had an excellent chance to win, to get his name on that big championship cup, right there alongside Petty, Allison, the Earnharts, the Waltrips, Stewart, and Gordon. He needed her there something awful. He needed her to see him win.

He was always too excited to eat before a race, and his stomach growled in protest. He plunged into the final preparations alongside his crew. When the car was finally set and ready to go, he headed to the front of the pit area where he stopped inside the short cement wall and looked across the track to the stands.

His gaze honed in on the lower rows of the center section where her tickets were, carefully scanning the faces of the people already seated. He'd given her six tickets again and thought that she and her friends would be easy to spot, but he didn't see them. Maybe they hadn't arrived.

He thought back to the way they'd left things the other night, fully understanding her anger, but the bottom line was, she'd been given a great opportunity. Since there was no way to undo it, she should get over it and make the most of it. He ran his hands through his hair. He probably should have spent more time to help her get past it.

He relived their last kiss. Maybe if he'd kissed her a little longer. He turned back to his car and his race team.

"Hey, son." His father placed his arm affectionately around Luke's shoulder.

"Hey, Daddy. You didn't tell me you were coming today." They embraced in a warm hug.

"I had to come and watch my favorite son in his biggest race of the year."

Luke chuckled. His daddy always called him his favorite son even though he was his only son. "How'd you get in here?"

His father flashed his famously confident smile. "Just had to tell 'em who I was."

Luke wished he had half the confidence his father had. Some people are simply born with a presence, a special quality that makes others want to bend over backward to accommodate them. His father was one of those people. It was his special gift, and he'd honed it to perfection. He could talk a leopard out of his spots with one ask.

His father's grin grew serious. "I need you to come by the office tomorrow afternoon so we can talk."

"Sure." He suspected it was a talk he didn't want to have, but, then again, he had his own grievance he needed to set right with his father.

Minutes before the start of the race, as Luke stood with his hand on his heart listening to the national anthem, he found himself scanning the stands again for

Rachel. He couldn't see her, but that didn't mean she wasn't there. Maybe she was watching from home. He glanced up at a couple of the cameras. Disappointed, he wondered when he would see her again.

He hadn't been able to get her out of his head since he'd met her at the auction. The only time he wasn't thinking about her was in his racecar. When he got in there, nothing else got in with him.

What was it about her that set his world on fire? She was a pretty little thing and full of spunk. And she was into restoring old cars. How cool was that? And a mechanical engineer to boot. Smart, pretty, and a gearhead, like him—that was hot.

At the auto auction where they'd met, she'd wanted a 427 engine. Why? She still hadn't told him. There were other muscle cars in much better shape than the ones she'd bid on, but she'd only bid on the two cars with 427s. He rubbed his chin, analyzing her words. She knew about blown engines. She even knew what kind of engine he ran in his race car, or at least that he didn't run a Ford.

They'd spent a couple of great weeks together. She was amazing help with the Galaxie, timing laps, and pulling off the old carburetor. She didn't seem impressed that he was a NASCAR driver. He was just another guy, and she probably had lots of guys asking her out. Maybe that was part of the reason he was so hot for her. She wasn't throwing herself at him like other women did. She was a challenge and a mystery and he liked that. And she was into cars. He loved that.

After a final disappointing check of the stands, he climbed into his car. Then, leaving all thoughts of her behind, he ran one of the best races of his career. His car was so dialed-in that he had no problem pushing his speed in the turns. His carburetor improved his fuel consumption so much that the only reason he had to pit was for tires, when they'd top off the gas for good measure at the same time. His crew operated with precision—no glitches, no mistakes. His pit stops were executed at lightning speed.

The one thing that kept him from a first-place finish was a bump by Dale Jr. as Luke had tried to pass him down low coming out of turn four on the second to the last lap. It was enough to loosen up his tires and make him slip. That little bump had cost him the race and nearly cost him his car as he'd maneuvered quickly to avoid losing control. In the blink of an eye, a bump like that could send a car flying up into the wall. That's how guys got killed, which Dale Jr., of all people, knew.

Heat

M onday morning Luke marched into BEI International, determined to set things right with Rachel. He was beyond fed up with ignored calls and texts. She hadn't even replied when he'd sent a text asking if she'd seen his spectacular finish.

On the long drive home from Daytona, he had tried to convince himself that it didn't matter. She was just a woman, being totally irrational and overly emotional. He didn't care if she never spoke to him again. He hadn't done anything wrong. But his feelings for her remained. He wanted her to know he was a good guy. And that it wasn't his fault.

"Good morning, Alice," he greeted the professionally dressed auburn-haired receptionist behind the massive front desk. It had been a while since he'd been in the building, and as he looked around the quiet front lobby and the offices and cubicles that spanned beyond, he was thankful he didn't have a desk job. He'd go crazy closed in all day long.

"Good morning, Mr. Brandt. It's good to see you. What an excellent finish yesterday. I thought you had it for sure."

"Thank you. I did too. I reckon it wasn't my day. Is Rachel Tate in today? I wonder if you could tell her someone's here to see her. But don't tell her it's me, okay?" he added with a wink.

"Of course, Mr. Brandt."

"Please, Alice, call me Luke."

"Of course." She placed the call as instructed, and a few minutes later Rachel walked around the corner.

"Hey, beautiful." The dreary overcast day got a little brighter. She looked good in a long, gray, straight skirt and fuzzy, lighter gray sweater. Her hair was twisted into a neat ponytail. She carried a leather-bound notebook. When she saw him, she stopped short.

"Hi," she said, unsmiling.

He closed the distance between them and took her arm to lead her off to the side for privacy. "I was hoping I could take you to lunch today."

"I can't. I'm sorry."

Luke tried not to lose his cool. "Why not?"

She pulled her arm away. "I have plans."

"Then we'll talk now." He took her by the hand and started for the door.

"I can't leave with you." She pulled her hand away. "I have a meeting in ten minutes with my new team."

"Alice," Luke called across the lobby, "please do me a favor and have Rachel's meeting pushed back an hour."

"Yes, Mr. Brandt."

Rachel gaped at him, furious at his clout. But she'd left him no choice.

He took her hand, led her to his car parked out front, and opened the passenger door. She gave him an angry glare as she got in, and he closed the door. He drove to the rear of the business park and stopped at the back of a distant parking lot.

How dare he come into her workplace and pull her out because it suited him? And her coworkers actually knew him. *Yes, Mr. Brandt.* Seriously.

There was nothing to discuss. His family was powerful. She got that. And she wanted no part of it. She'd live her own life, and as soon as she was able, quit this place and find a better job. At least having the engineering position would help her get another job as an engineer. It's always easier to find a job when you have a job.

She was almost taken in by his serious expression as he shut off the car and faced her. She had to blink and look away. No. She would not be controlled.

"Rachel, we need to talk about this." He searched for a trace of warmth in her cold, angry glare.

She crossed her arms, staring out the window. "There's nothing to talk about."

"Yes, there is. You know I wasn't behind your promotion, right?" He wanted assurance she didn't hold him responsible.

She whirled to face him, her fire reignited. "You *were* behind it. Your daddy may have made the call, but you told him about me. You *are* to blame. You knew he'd make the call. You probably asked him to."

"You can't possibly believe that."

"Can't I?"

"That's crazy." Luke banged his hands on the steering wheel then stopped. With a semblance of calm, he faced her. "Trust me. If I had anything to do with it, I'd have done it a lot differently than this."

"Oh."

"I'd have gotten you fired."

"What?"

"Then you'd need a job and might reconsider joining my race team." He softened his tone at her shocked expression. "I certainly wouldn't have given you a promotion that would take you halfway across the world and away from me."

Rachel sagged in the seat. He hadn't planned to admit that he wasn't thrilled about her promotion because it would take her away from him, but seeing her reaction, he was glad he had. Silence settled between them.

Swallowing frustration and anger, he brushed her cheek with his knuckles. "Rachel." What else could he say? He wanted to tell her how he felt about her, but he didn't even know himself. How could he possibly put it into words?

She leaned her head into his hand. "It's okay. I believe you."

Relieved, he reached across to hug her, holding her in his arms for several minutes. "I missed you something fierce this weekend."

"I'm sorry, but Holly left this weekend. Moved to California."

She said it like it didn't matter, but her eyes betrayed her pain. "Oh, baby, I'm sorry. You just got your friend back, and now she's gone again."

"It's for the best." She sounded like she was trying to convince herself. "She's going to stay with her sister until she gets a job and can find her own place. She needed to get away from here, from him, but she'll be back for the trial."

Luke's heart went out to her, and he wondered if she'd thought about going with her. He didn't want to lose her, not now, when he was starting to get close to her. "Are you going to be okay?"

"I will be. I have so much hatred in my heart for that man. For all the pain he's caused us, all the things he's taken from us, and I know it's horrible to think some of the things I do, but I … I can't help it. I wish we'd never met him."

"Me too."

"Will you take me back now, please?" She sounded deflated and tired.

When they pulled up in front of her office, she faced him. "I am sorry I missed your race, Luke. I heard you had an amazing finish, and I would've loved to see it."

"It's okay. You can make it up to me. Come to Phoenix with me next weekend." Having her beside him on the ride would be great. On a twenty-some hour drive he could get to know her, not to mention having her in his bed for two or three nights.

When she didn't answer right away, he wondered if she was trying to think of a way to say no. "Come on."

"I can't, Luke. I'm sorry. But the week after is Bristol, right? I promise I'll come to that one."

Maybe she wasn't ready to spend a whole weekend with him. "All right, Bristol then. I'll get you tickets. And pit passes. I want you right there beside me." He squeezed her hand then brought it to his lips for a kiss.

"Sounds fun." Rachel reached for the door handle.

He put his hand on her arm, "What are you doing tonight?"

"Working on the Thunderbolt."

"Want some help?"

She smiled the first real smile he'd seen that day. "Sure."

"Great then. I'll see you at seven or so?"

"Seven's perfect."

"See you then." He released her arm, and she kissed his cheek before getting out. When she disappeared through the front doors, his head fell back against the headrest. Things were okay between them again.

The office of Mr. Brandt Sr. was off the grand foyer of his multimillion-dollar estate home outside of Nashville, where he comfortably called neighbors many of the top country music legends. It was the same house Luke had grown up in, and in all the years he'd lived there, his daddy had been making deals from that plush home office.

Behind the solid oak six-panel double doors, it was furnished with the same high quality furniture as the rest of the home. A walnut desk with its high-back leather chair and comfortable seating area dominated the office. The room had a well-stocked bar, a massive hand-carved fireplace, and one-of-a-kind original oil paintings depicting beautiful landscapes filled with wild game. Floor-to-ceiling windows framed by luxurious drapes overlooked the front circle drive, fountain, and meticulously maintained gardens. Ornate built-in bookcases provided a break in the rich wainscoted walls.

When Luke arrived, the double doors stood open, welcoming. As he walked in, his father rose from behind his desk and hugged him.

"Thanks for stopping by. How about a drink?"

"No, thank you. I'm good."

"Coffee?"

"No, thank you."

"Well, come on in and sit down."

Luke chose a comfortable buckskin armchair while his father sat opposite on the matching leather sofa.

They talked about the race for a good twenty minutes, his father ecstatic about how well he had done. He was proud of Luke and mindful to remind him of it often. "And how's that girlfriend of yours? Rachel, is it?"

"You know her name. She was an agenda item for you a few days ago when you made that call to get her the promotion you thought she wanted."

"She didn't want it?" His father acted surprised, but unfazed by his son's accusatory tone.

"Oh, she wanted it all right. But she wanted to *earn* it. She wasn't happy at all when she found out you were behind it. In fact, it took me a passel of talking to convince her I had nothing to do with it. I almost lost her because of your meddling."

"Well, she doesn't know a gift horse when she sees it."

"You don't know her. She's not the kind of person who takes kindly to handouts. She's worked hard for everything she has. People don't always like to be handed everything." He repeated Rachel's words. "A person needs to earn things on their own in order to feel worth something."

"Is that so?" His father studied him.

"Yeah, Daddy, that's so. Please don't mess with her again." He was polite, but crystal clear.

"Maybe I should meet this girl. Bring her by for dinner one night."

"Right now might not be good. She's gonna need some time to cool her fire."

His father laughed. "She sounds like a woman who knows her own mind."

"And then some," Luke agreed with a wide grin.

His father went to the bar, poured himself a short glass of scotch, and came back to sit across from Luke, taking a hearty swallow before setting the drink on the table between them.

"Luke, I'm going to come right to the point here. I need you to come and work with me." His father leaned forward to look into his eyes. "Now before you go and say no again, I want you to know I'm going to make you work for it. I'm not turning my company over to you until you've earned it, flat out. You'll have plenty of time to learn the ropes. And I sure could use your help, son. I need someone I can trust."

Luke felt the all-too-familiar pang of guilt about turning down his father's offers to join him, but he had no desire to spend his days closed up in an office, even one as nice as his father's. He'd be miserable, and he'd be terrible at it. His father had a way with people, but Luke hadn't picked up the knack for getting folks to see things his way. "Daddy," Luke started in his usual apologetic tone.

"Hold on before you say no. I want to encourage you to keep your NASCAR team. You're making good money, and you and your team are performing better than most of the guys out there. Your landscaping business and record company too. They won't make millions, but they're plenty profitable. We'd roll them all into Brandt & Son Holdings; how's that sound?" His intense gaze beseeched Luke. "It kind of has a ring to it, don't you think?"

"So, hire a driver for my car? Not race it myself anymore?"

"There're plenty of great drivers out there looking for a good ride."

Luke walked to the windows. His Charger parked in front of the house made him think of Rachel. What kind of life did she want? Would she want to be on the road in a motor home nine months of the year during the race season?

She might prefer a home in the country with her own workshop. And if they had kids, what kind of life would that be for them? Maybe he was getting way ahead of himself, but he was certain that his future had to have her in it. It was too soon to know what kind of life she wanted.

Luke turned back to his father, who had stood and was watching him from across the room. "Daddy, I'm not saying no, never, but I'm not ready to give up my racing. It's what I love." He paused to let that sink in. "And I know you got a lot of things going on, but you need to stop expanding, stop buying more companies to run."

"You don't make money sitting still." His father repeated one of his favorite quotes.

"You and I both know you are not sitting still, not by a long stretch. And besides, how much more money do you need to make?" He stretched out his arms to indicate the room they stood in and all that surrounded it. "What else do you want that you don't have?" What *did* drive his father to work so hard?

He chuckled, then scanned the room thoughtfully. "A man wants to leave something behind, something he's built up with his own sweat and blood. Something he can pass on to the next generation."

Luke came back to stand before his father. In that moment, he'd never loved him more. "You've already given me more than I could ever possibly want or need."

His father's eyes began to fill. He had been wonderfully blessed to have been adopted and loved by the kind man who gazed at him with such affection. "I love you, Daddy, and I know you want to give me the whole world, but I don't know what I ever did to deserve it."

"You've been my favorite son your whole life."

Luke laughed and they hugged.

"Can you stay for dinner?"

"Not tonight. I'm going to Rachel's to help her with a project."

"A car?"

"She's working on that old Thunderbolt."

"The one you gave her?"

"She insisted on buying it from me."

"She sounds real special: pretty, works on cars, must be smart as a whip to be a mechanical engineer. A woman only God would've known you'd love."

Luke laughed. "Right."

"I look forward to meeting her. Promise to bring her by real soon."

"I promise, but no more meddling or you'll ruin this for sure."

"On my honor."

Luke and Rachel spent the evening working on the Thunderbolt. They put it back together, and added a new water pump, radiator, and alternator that Rachel had picked up at her favorite place to shop: the junkyard. The enjoyment made it unlike any date she'd ever had. She caught him watching her, approving her expertise.

"You know I meant it when I asked you to join my race team, right?"

She knew he was serious before she looked at him. "I appreciate the offer, but they say you should never date someone you work with. Well, it goes double the other way around—never work for someone you're dating." She giggled at her own joke.

He threw a shop rag at her. "I'd be a great boss."

She dodged the rag, then picked it up. "Yeah, until we broke up."

"What makes you think we'd break up? We've got something special, Rachel, don't you think?"

His warm blue eyes questioned her. She had no idea where their relationship was going, but she was having a good time finding out. He was so different from what she'd expected. "Maybe."

"Come over here," he said in his I-want-to-kiss-you voice.

She set down her wrench and walked toward him, stopping short of his reach. "What?" she asked innocently.

He snatched her and pulled her into his arms, laughing as he held her against him and looked down at her. "This is fun."

She nodded. "Thanks for your help."

"You bet." Their long kiss took every whisper of her breath away. When he pulled back he said, "Whew. You're something else."

She moved backward. "And what is that? What am I?" *Please don't say a tease.*

"Something special, that's for sure."

Her insides melted. That was nice.

"I could fall in love with you, Rachel Tate." His eyes conveyed the same sentiment with unspoken intensity.

Her heart skipped a beat, her stomach fluttered, and she whispered, "Yeah?"

"Yeah." He grinned.

She reached up to brush back a stray wisp of her hair and swallowed hard. She could get crazy drunk in those intoxicating blue eyes of his. *Be careful, Rachel. He's earned his reputation.*

"Want something to drink?"

"No, I'd better go, or I might get us both in trouble."

Stolen

A couple of days later when Rachel stopped by Luke's shop to bring him lunch, police cars were parked in front and the place was surrounded by yellow crime scene tape. Luke watched from his perch on the tailgate of his pickup. Inside the building, one man took photos. Several others tiptoed through the tools and auto parts strewn on the floor.

"What's going on?" Rachel asked as she walked up.

He closed the distance between them, his face lighting up despite the chaos around him. "Hey, baby." He kissed her cheek. "I should've called you; I'm sorry."

She took in the activity in and around the building. "What happened?"

"Someone broke in this morning. They trashed the place and took a bunch of tools, but none of the expensive stuff." He dropped his voice to a whisper, glancing around to be sure he wouldn't be overheard. "And they took my carburetor right off the car."

Rachel cringed at the news. "They take anything else off the car?"

"No, just the carb. It's like they knew what they were looking for. You didn't talk to anyone about it, did you?"

"I didn't mention it to anyone. You asked me not to. I told my dad about the test laps, but I didn't tell him which components you were switching out. Oh, Luke, I'm so sorry."

He ran his hands through his hair. "You don't have to stay. I'm afraid I'm not going to be very good company this afternoon."

"It's all right. But you still need to eat." She handed him the bag she'd been holding.

"Thanks, babe." He pulled a sandwich out and sat back on the bed of the pickup, placing the bag beside him. "I sent the guys home. I'm sorry I didn't even think to call you."

"I understand." She sat beside him and took out the other sandwich. "What can I do? I can come back after work and help you clean up the mess."

"You're a real sweetheart, you know that? But I can do it. It won't take long. Rebuilding the carburetor will take some time. And I have a race this weekend." He looked straight ahead for a few minutes, then back to her. "I probably won't see you until I get back."

"It's okay."

He forced a half smile and kissed her cheek.

Luke worked around the clock the next few days to rebuild his carburetor, hoping it would test out the same as the first one. He wouldn't have a chance to put it through the paces until he got to Phoenix and could run some practice laps. He was taking the old four-barrel carb just in case, but anticipating another great finish like Daytona—even one place better.

He couldn't stop thinking about the break-in, certain it was the carburetor they were after. They'd trashed the place, in all likelihood looking for the specifications for it. But if you had the component, why would you need the specs? Who knew about his carburetor besides the NASCAR officials? He hadn't told his sponsors or other drivers or teams. Only Jimmy Ray and Cam knew about it, and they were both as trustworthy as they came. Both had been with him since his dirt-track days.

Luke made phone calls and set up a meeting with his attorney for Monday to start the patent process, and arranged to have a new state-of-the-art security system installed over the weekend.

He took second again at Phoenix. Celebrating afterward with his team, he thought about Rachel, convinced that had she been there he would have won. He looked forward to Bristol with heartfelt anticipation.

Smoke

It was a gorgeous Saturday afternoon, clear and warm with a bright, powder-blue sky the color of her favorite old, faded blue jeans. Rachel and her friends made their way into the pit area at Bristol Motor Speedway. She'd been to the track, several times in fact, but had never gotten into the pits. Their seats were usually high up on the other side.

Seating made no difference at Bristol, or any NASCAR race. Being there was an electrifying experience for every sense: the bright colors and nonstop action, the roar of the engines and the screaming crowd, the smell of fuel, exhaust, and heated rubber, the rumble of the cars shaking your seat and the taste of an ice cold soda or beer on a smoking-hot day. Racing was a unique experience no other sport could come close to for death-defying thrills and high-speed competition. And Bristol offered the best of both.

She and her father loved watching NASCAR on TV every Sunday afternoon. And as far back as she could remember, her daddy had taken her to at least one race a year, usually Bristol or Martinsville, Virginia, since they were the closest tracks. The Bristol night race was the best. Nighttime competition lent a unique thrill to the event, and the half-mile track was so fast and tight it was often compared to racing jet fighters in a gym.

"Hey, Luke," she called as they approached.

He spun around at the sound of her voice and, with a huge grin, scooped her up in a bear hug. Then, setting her back on her feet, he kissed her on the cheek. "You look pretty as a picture. I am so happy to see you."

He greeted her friends, pumping hands with each of the guys—Cole, Jackson, and Reese.

"It's so thrilling to be on this side." Allie gawked at the cars and drivers, the crews and the press people. "There's so much going on."

Luke clapped his hands, then rubbed them together. "I'm going to do well today. I can feel it. You ready for a good race?"

They all agreed.

"Great. Me too." He placed his arm around Rachel's shoulders. "There're seats in the bleachers, or you can stand where you want as long as you stay behind that line." He pointed to a solid yellow line on the pavement behind them. "Pay attention 'cause there aren't any fences back here, and sometimes things come flyin'."

Rachel glanced at her friends with a barely contained excitement. This was going to be an unbelievable day. She looked back to Luke to find him gleaming with anticipation.

He took her hand and pulled her away from her friends. "Thank you for coming," he said, the seriousness in his tone and the intensity in his gaze unsettling.

"Of course. Thank you for the tickets."

"I ... uh," he stared into the distance before turning his attention to her, "I'm going to do well tonight. This is my time. I can feel it. You have no idea what it means to me having you here tonight."

She couldn't help her grin.

"You'll stay after the race, right? Help us celebrate if we win?"

"We can celebrate no matter how you finish," she said. "We reserved a couple of hotel rooms down the street."

"You don't need hotel rooms. My motor home right over there has plenty of space. Stay with me, please." She bit her bottom lip and he sensed her hesitation. "You girls can have my bedroom, and there're at least four other beds for me and the guys."

Her pulse raced as she anticipated sleeping in his bed. "Okay, I'll ask them."

"Great." Taking that as a yes, he beamed at her then glanced at the people milling around his car. "Come meet my crew." He introduced her to Jimmy Ray, Cam, and several other guys whose names she didn't catch and then to Bobby Carmichael, a big shot from Pacific Oil, his primary sponsor and the only one not wearing a fire suit.

The race was more exciting than Rachel could have imagined. Luke had to pit halfway through with an alignment problem, and when his crew finally got it fixed he was a lap down from the leaders. But he had a full tank, and while the others had to pit to refuel, he struggled to come back from behind, finally making it into second position with only two laps to go.

The last few laps had Rachel and the whole crowd of thousands on the edge of their seats as Luke's blue and silver Pacific Oil Dodge was running inches behind Jeff Gordon's black DuPont Chevy, each vying for first place.

God, please don't let him crash.

The announcers shouted with unrestrained excitement over the loudspeakers as they described the action on the back turns. Gordon went a little too wide coming out of turn two on the last lap, and Luke snuck down inside and stole the lead on the backstretch. Everyone was on their feet trying to see the back of the track and the last set of turns. Luke held on to the lead coming through the last two turns, and Rachel and her friends screamed at the top of their lungs as they saw his number eleven Pacific Oil Dodge come out of turn four, still in the lead, then cross the finish line less than a quarter of a car length in front of the black DuPont Chevy.

"He won! He won," Rachel screamed. And her friends all screamed right along with her as they jumped up and down and hugged one another.

In the winner's circle, amid sprays of champagne and beer and the wild cheering of the fans, Luke thanked his fans, his sponsors, and his special guests. He looked right at Rachel and thanked the angel in the stands, the wings beneath his wheels. She turned to hide from the cameras, her cheeks burning bright pink, but Luke snatched her hand and pulled her into the center. He put his arm around her shoulders while he held the trophy up with the other hand. The video rolled and the cameras flashed.

When the excitement faded, Luke went to help his guys roll the car back to the pits, but Jimmy Ray wedged himself in front of him to take hold of the steering wheel. "We got this. You go on."

"Thanks, man." Luke patted Jimmy Ray on the shoulder before he joined Rachel and her friends.

"So you're coming to celebrate with us?" Luke looked expectantly from Rachel to Allie, Becca, and the guys.

"Absolutely," Allie answered for the group. She was always the first one to speak up when it came to making plans. Her fun-loving spirit was one of the things Rachel loved most about her. They'd known each other since high school. On the homecoming court all four years, Allie's good heart attracted people to her. She had an almost exotic appeal with long, wavy dark hair and bright blue eyes, the one who drew men's attention when the three of them went out together. Though wilder than Rachel, with different values, she respected Rachel's conservative side, never pressuring her to do things that made Rachel uncomfortable.

Rachel asked her friends about staying in his motor home, and while the girls were eager, the guys were reluctant, unsure it could house them all, but they agreed to play it by ear.

Luke put his arm around Rachel as they all walked back to the pit area. "I've got about an hour and a half of work to do to load everything up, but y'all are welcome to hang out in the motor home. There's beer in the fridge; help yourself."

"That'd be great," Reese said. "Man, that was an awesome finish. No lie, best race I ever saw." He loved sports—not only racing, but all sports. He could talk about competition and games from football to curling. When he wasn't attending a sporting event, he was watching one on TV. His company had box seats at the Titans and Predators games, and Reese often invited the rest of them along for a great time. Rachel felt good she'd gotten to repay the favor twice now.

"Thanks, Reese. I think that had to be my best race ever too." Luke's voice was still colored by the thrill of his win.

"Especially after getting lapped while your car was broken," Becca said.

Rachel chuckled at her friend's choice of words. Cars broke *down* but they didn't get *broken*. Becca was a chemical research scientist for a pharmaceutical company. They'd met in a freshman chemistry class at TSU and been good friends ever since. Although she knew her chemistry inside and out, she remained stereotypically clueless about cars and racing. They shared an inside joke that had to do with the periodic table, and it never failed to make them laugh. Whenever one of them saw a guy with a cute backside they'd say the word *sodium* and they'd both break out in giggles.

"If you hadn't thrown a rod you would've had that race hands down," Allie said.

"Y'all are going to have to come to all my races," Luke said, exuding a sincere warmth and friendliness.

"Get us tickets like these and we'll be there," Jackson said. Good ole Jackson, always in for a good time. A Notre Dame grad, he was both brilliant and funny.

A little older than the rest of them, he loved classic sitcoms and could sing almost every theme song from the popular shows of the seventies and eighties. They'd met him through Cole. Jackson was a manufacturer's rep and called on the aeronautics company Cole worked for.

"I'll see what I can do," Luke said, "You've got to bring this little angel along though."

"Oh, no doubt," Jackson agreed.

Rachel and her friends hung out in Luke's motor home while he finished loading up. Luke hadn't exaggerated about the amount of room. The master bedroom suite in the back had a king size bed and private bath. The second bedroom held double bunks. A queen size bed nestled over the driving compartment, and a full-size couch in the main area folded out into a sleeper.

Luke entered a little over an hour later, showered, and emerged fresh and ready to party. They walked down the street to a roadside honky-tonk that was already hopping. A country music band played at one end opposite a game room at the other, with a dance floor and tables in between. Booths lined the front wall, and a long bar ran the length of the back wall.

Race fans swarmed Luke to congratulate him. While he was caught up with them, Rachel and her friends headed to the bar. Rachel watched Luke soak up the accolades, excited at seeing him so overjoyed. When she turned around, Cole handed her a beer.

"Thank you," she said.

He followed her gaze. "He may be a while. Want to play a game of foosball?"

Rachel glanced at the game room as she considered it. "Maybe a little later."

"All right. Let me know."

"Hey guys, there's a table," Allie called, and they scurried over to grab it.

When Luke joined them, he apologized for getting pulled away as he grabbed a chair from a nearby table and sat. A pretty blond waitress in way-too-short cutoff jean shorts and a tied-up red gingham blouse was beside him almost instantly, "Hey, Luke," she said in a sugar sweet voice, "what can I get y'all?"

Luke looked at Rachel and her friends.

"I think we're all set for now," Cole answered for the group.

Luke had a beer too, but he asked the waitress for a round of shots. "Tequila or whiskey?" he asked, looking around the table.

"Whiskey," several of them answered at once.

"None for me, thanks," Rachel said before the waitress left.

Luke looked surprised. "You're going to celebrate with me, aren't you?"

"Oh, absolutely, but I don't do shots."

"Trust me, you do not want to see her doing shots," Allie told Luke, looking sideways at Rachel then stretching her arm around her friend.

"Thanks a lot," Rachel shot back, playfully pushing Allie away.

"The last time, she got a tattoo," Allie said.

Rachel's jaw dropped and she turned to Luke, "I did not get a tattoo."

Luke laughed. "Yeah, I definitely couldn't see you with a tattoo." He turned back to the waitress. "Okay, six then."

When the band started to play a rockin' song, Luke's face lit up and he turned to Rachel. "Am I the only one who wants to have fun?" Rachel instantly recognized the song. He held his hand out to her and they hurried to the dance floor.

Rachel sang along as they danced, and it wasn't long before the lead singer held out his hand to her and motioned for her to come up on stage. She shook her head, but Luke pushed her along, and before she knew it she was standing beside the guy, wearing his cowboy hat, sharing a microphone, belting out rowdy lyrics with a contagious enthusiasm that rocked the place.

Luke leaned back against the bar to watch, admiring her sweet voice, her down-home, country-girl charm, and her unmistakable wild streak as she sang her heart out and tapped her boots to the beat of the music.

He took a long, deep breath at the sight of her. The stage lights shimmered off her shiny hair, illuminating the soft curls that tumbled out beneath the cowboy hat. She moved to the music with a seductive innocence, her low-cut faded blue jeans hugging her curves, and while she didn't flaunt them, they were there all the same.

Rachel looked sideways to the lead singer as they sang in unison. She seemed to be having the time of her life.

When the song ended to deafening applause, the lead singer asked Rachel, "What's your name, darlin'?"

"Rachel Tate."

"Ladies and gentlemen, give it up for Rachel Tate," he shouted into the microphone, and the applause increased.

She took a sweeping bow, removed the hat and, standing on her tiptoes, set it back on his head. "Thank you," she said into the microphone, her head turned to beam at him. With that, she left the stage, grasping Luke's hand he extended to help her down the steps.

He scooped her up in a bear hug and set her back on her feet. "That was amazing. You totally rocked that song."

She grinned up at him. "Thanks. That was so much fun. But you're not gonna make me get up on stage every time we dance to a good song, are ya?"

"Sorry about that. No, absolutely not. Once you were up there I didn't have anyone to dance with. But you sure did look like you were having a great time."

"I did."

They danced, drank, and celebrated. When Reese brought another round of shots, Luke told him, "Let me get those next time. In fact, let me buy tonight. I got paid today."

They laughed with him and agreed to let him pick up the tab.

When Rachel and her girlfriends came back from the ladies' room later, and she didn't see Luke, she joined her friends on the dance floor. After several songs they returned to the table, but Luke was still missing. She assumed he'd gotten pulled away by race fans again. Hot from dancing, she asked if anyone wanted to go outside with her to cool off, and Cole jumped up to join her.

Outside, Rachel leaned back against the building and lifted her hair up off the back of her neck. "It's hot in there."

"Sure is."

They heard giggles coming from around the corner, and they glanced knowingly at each other, like they were overhearing something private. Rachel's heart stopped when she recognized Luke's unmistakable deep voice, and she listened more intently. She looked away from Cole, hoping he hadn't glimpsed her painful disappointment.

"I can't tonight, baby. I got company staying with me."

"But you won't be back around here for months," the sugar-sweet female voice whined.

"I could come back sooner," Luke said, his voice seductive and enticing.

"But you won't."

Rachel turned to Cole, trying to hide her embarrassment. "I'm going back in." She yanked the door open. When he didn't move, she hesitated. "You coming?"

"Nope." He didn't even look at her, just took a pull from his beer. He remained nonchalantly leaning against the side of the building, staring out into the parking lot.

"You know you don't have to—"

"I know, but I'm gonna." He gave her a single affirming nod.

"Suit yourself."

Rachel went back to the table, and watched the door, wondering who Luke would walk in with. She looked around the bar and couldn't find their waitress anywhere and guessed it could be her. It sounded like her.

When Cole came back in, he no sooner sat than Rachel asked him to play foosball. It didn't matter who Luke came back in with. It wasn't her, and that was all Rachel needed to know.

Luke found Rachel at the foosball table with Cole in the middle of a close game. As he watched them play and tried to talk to her, he realized something wasn't right. She was cold and distant—one-word answers, not bothering to look his way even when there was a pause in the action. They won the game and she excused herself to go the ladies' room before they took on the next team of challengers.

"What's got her fur all backward?" Luke asked Cole.

Cole took a long pull from his beer and turned to look Luke dead in the eyes. "She went outside a bit ago and overheard you and your little girlfriend."

Luke's gaze darted around the bar and he wished he was anywhere else than right there.

Cole caught his attention. "Look, man, I don't care how you choose to live your life, but, don't you hurt her." Vehemence filled his admonishment.

Luke's guilt flared into anger. "You threatening me?"

"I certainly hope so. She deserves better."

Luke had never felt so uncomfortable. It was one thing to realize he'd screwed up, but another to have her friend—a guy at that—call him out. "I know she does, but I didn't do anything wrong." He finished his beer and set it down.

"That's a load of crap, and you know it. She was all over you like honey on hot biscuits." Cole fought to control his voice and temper.

"There's not much I can do when women throw themselves at me."

"You can duck."

"Duck what?" Rachel asked, joining them and handing each a fresh beer.

Cole and Luke exchanged looks. While Luke struggled for an answer, Rachel took her spot at the table and looked across at them, brows raised, waiting.

Cole took his spot beside her. "You know, when stuff comes flying at you, whether it's expected ... or not," he said with a meaningful glance at Luke.

Luke forced a smile for Rachel's benefit, but he was starting to not like her friend Cole. And while he appreciated his protectiveness of her, he wondered if there was something more there. "Hey, baby, let's go dance," he said, moving to the end of the foosball table and reaching for her free hand.

"Mmm, I'm playing foosball right now and we're winning. After this next game, okay?"

Luke stayed to watch, but it made him seethe seeing how invincible Rachel and Cole were together. As good as she was up front, Cole was rock solid at the back. It wasn't long before a few of Luke's teammates lured him away, and Rachel didn't seem to notice. The night ended, and they never danced again.

On the way back to his motor home, Luke put his arm around Rachel, and she leaned into him. He sensed he was smack dab in the calm before the storm, and wondered how and when she was going to rain down on him.

Luke settled everyone, kissed Rachel good night, then lay there on his sofa bed and gave in to the self-loathing that was his frequent companion where women were concerned.

Cole was right. He was a jerk and she deserved better. He replayed images of her throughout the day beginning when she'd called his name and his first sight of her at the track. Her excitement bubbled when she blew him a kiss and gave him a two-fisted thumbs-up before he rolled out to the starting line. And she'd lit up the place with her country-girl charm as she sang and danced on stage.

So why was he outside with Daisy when he could've been inside with Rachel? *Because you're an idiot. Walks like a duck, talks like a duck. Win as many races as you want, but you'll always be a loser. No one will ever want to stay with you.* He decided he'd had way too much to drink as he tried to push the ugly thoughts away. He rolled over, closed his eyes, and tried to shut them out, but the condemning voices continued to haunt him.

Luke woke with the sun and decided to walk to a nearby coffee shop, so the others could sleep. He went to the back to grab a jacket from his bedroom, glad the girls had left the door open a crack. As he quietly reached for it, he looked down at Rachel sleeping on the side nearest him.

Warmth wrapped around his heart and squeezed ever so gently. She looked like a real-life angel. Lying on her side facing him, her hands were palm-to-palm beneath her cheek as if she'd fallen asleep praying. He'd have given anything to climb into her dreams, wrap her in his arms, and nestle close until she woke.

His insides fluttered. He *had* seen her like that before—a year ago last fall when he was hunting—she was the little girl in the pink hoodie under the willow. He covered his mouth to stifle a laugh, and leaned against the doorframe for several more minutes, amazed that she was the same girl and ecstatic that he'd found her again.

After his coffee run, he pulled up a lawn chair and watched the sun rise over the track as he thought about Rachel, his angel beneath the willow, and how he could explain his actions the night before.

She joined him a little while later, pulling a chair next to his.

"Good morning," he said, handing her a coffee.

"Morning," she said. "Thanks."

After a lengthy silence, he turned to look into her sleepy eyes. "Are we okay?"

She hesitated. "Sure. Why wouldn't we be?"

Luke looked away, afraid she'd see his guilt. "I don't know." He shouldn't have asked. Maybe she was letting him off on this one. She was deep-down sweet and good, with no idea how she touched his heart. He thought about the conversation with his father and remembered the things he wanted to ask her so he could form a plan for his life beyond the next race season. "Will you ride back with me in the motor home?"

Rachel glanced toward it and hesitated.

He touched her arm. "Please. I want to talk to you. I feel like we barely got to spend any time together yesterday."

She finally gave in. "I reckon there are a few things we need to set right."

Guess she wasn't letting him off after all. He gave her a weak smile, but her calm resolve unsettled him. He had a bad feeling about what she meant by *set right*.

Hopes and Dreams

Rachel and Luke said goodbye to her friends. As they pulled out of the track in the motor home, Rachel wondered how best to bring up the subject of the waitress. She was more disappointed than hurt, but she'd survive. "He's just a guy," she'd told Allie. She knew she was playing with fire, and it was only a matter of time before she got burned. So why then was she so upset that he turned out to be exactly the kind of guy she thought he'd be? She watched him maneuver the big rig with an ease that came from experience and pushed away the longing that crept into her heart. *Stay cool; don't let him get to you.*

As they merged onto the interstate, Luke finally broke the uncomfortable silence that hung between them like ninety percent humidity on a hot summer day, "So, tell me, where do you see yourself in say, five years?"

She thought for a moment. "I don't know. I'd like to have an established career as an engineer, invent some cool things, get married, have a baby, or two or four." She grinned. "Someday."

"Yeah? And live in the suburbs?"

"In the country. I like open spaces. I have to have a place to swim and fish and walk in the woods."

He shot her a glance, his intense eyes gleaming. "Perfect."

He kept asking similar probing questions and eventually she began to wonder why. Was it something he did to make a girl think she was the one? *I could fall in love with you, Rachel,* he'd told her in her garage last week, and the way he'd looked at her, she almost believed him. She'd wanted to believe him. But after last night, she didn't know what to think.

Was this a game for him? Was she crazy to think she could be the one? Maybe God had placed him in her life so she could help him find his way back to Him. She twisted a strand of her hair around her finger and stared out the window, wondering what His plan was for her life and whether or not it included Luke.

"Rachel," he said, getting her attention.

"Sorry. What did you say?"

"You okay?"

"I'm fine. Just thinking."

"Tell me."

She shook her head.

"Please."

She looked at him and her heart hurt. Maybe it would be good to put it all out there, let him know she didn't trust him, how she feared liking him too much, how she knew he was trouble, that eventually he'd hurt her. What's to lose? Lose now or lose later; it didn't much matter. It would only be so much worse later. She could break it off right now and be done with him. She swallowed the lump in her throat and realized her heart was racing. She stared at him, thought what a great-looking guy he was, how sweet and tender he was with her. And the way he kissed her.

"Rachel?"

"I don't trust you. I like you; I do. More than I oughta." She struggled for the right words. "But ..." She shook her head and bit her lower lip. "You are incredibly hot, Luke Brandt. And sweet and gentle. I know you could love someone like, like ..." she stammered, finally finding her words. Her voice softened. "Like heaven on earth, like God intended for a man to love a woman. But ... I'm afraid. I know sure as sugar I'm going to get burned. You break hearts, you leave scars, you use women, and I don't want to be used."

Luke laughed nervously. "Don't hold anything back, sweetheart."

She stared at her lap, his callous laughter bringing hot tears to her eyes. How could he not take her seriously?

When he noticed the look on her face, his laughter died.

She regained her fire and faced him. "Answer some questions for me now. Is this your standard operating procedure? Tell a woman you could fall in love with her then ask her all about her hopes and dreams as if you're the one that'll make them all come true? Then what? A month or two down the road, when she falls for you hard, you move on to the next one? Is that how it works? I want to know what to expect here."

His silence said plenty.

"Okay, maybe this one's easier," she said, turning back to him. "Are you going back there to see your little blond Daisy Duke later this week? Next week? When?"

"That's not fair, Rachel. She's a nice girl I went out with a couple of times. I was trying to let her down easy."

The silence disappeared in the roar of a passing semi. "We're all nice girls, Luke." Her voice was soft, her disappointment unmistakable.

He took one look at her face, and when she turned away he banged on the steering wheel. "How do you always do that—cut to the chase so quickly and so brutally? It's maddening. You make me feel like everything I do is plain wrong."

"You think that was okay last night? I thought *I* was your date, and you were outside kissing it up with—"

"You don't know that—"

"Tell me you didn't kiss her last night."

"Rachel." Silence.

Just do it. Break it off with him, like a Band-Aid, one swift yank. Get it over with. She *so* didn't need a guy like him. "I had fun yesterday, the last few weeks, and thank you for the Thunderbolt—"

"Rachel, don't, please."

"Luke—"

"Wait a minute." He pulled into a rest area, parked the motor home, and shut off the engine. "Come here," he said, taking her by the hand and leading her back to the sofa. He stared down at their hands, both of his holding both of hers.

She wondered what he could possibly say that would change her mind. "I know I don't have a right to have any ... expectations. But I want to know where I stand with you. I don't want to be your little Daisy Duke a month from now, or three or six, begging you to stay, heartbroken, knowing you've moved on." Why couldn't she finish it? Why was she even giving him a chance to explain? There was nothing he could say to make it okay. Was there?

Luke stared at her long and hard. His gaze fell to her hand, and he caressed it gently while she waited. "You remember a few weeks ago at dinner when you asked if I had a girl in every race town?"

"Yeah." She winced. That had been a mean thing to say, and she'd surprised herself when she said it.

"Well, I ignored it at the time. It hurt coming from you, but what hurt a whole lot worse was realizing it was true. In some race towns I have several women I've gone out with. But it's because I've been searching for that one special person that can make my life complete, and I never found her." He paused. "Until now."

"And no, baby, I don't operate like that at all. I've never told any girl I could be falling in love with her, and I never cared enough before to ask anyone else the kind of questions I asked you about your hopes and dreams. Take my word as a gentleman."

He squeezed her hands. "Don't be afraid of loving me, Rachel, please. I don't know any more than you do where this is going, but I do know that so far it's beautiful, and I think you're amazing, and I know I want you in my life. And it scares me too, babe, to be honest. I've never felt this way about anyone before, and I'm so afraid I'm going to mess this up. The last thing in the world I would ever want to do is to hurt you."

Rachel thought she could see sincerity in his eyes, but she still wondered if she should trust him. "You're telling me everything you think I want to hear."

He shook his head, "Rachel, this is from my heart, babe. Believe me. I want to be with you, only you."

A flicker of hope softened her resolve. He must have sensed it because he slowly leaned over to kiss her with a gentle tenderness that let her know how he felt about her. On top of his raw honesty, genuine insecurity, and heartfelt words, the kiss sealed it. He was worth another chance.

They talked easily for the next several hours, and she asked him many of the same questions about what he wanted out of life. She liked his answers. They were a lot like hers.

About halfway to Nashville, his phone rang and he glanced at it. "It's Wesley Maddox. He runs my record company. Mind if I take it?"

Record company? "No, it's fine."

"Thanks. He only calls when it's important."

Because he took the call over the wireless, she could hear the conversation. Luke introduced her as a matter of courtesy, so Wes would know they weren't alone on the call. Wes explained that their new singer, Emma Grace, wanted a certain band leader for her tour who was already under contract with another artist, and she refused to settle for anyone else. Wes had called Luke to ask for direction.

"We have her under contact to do this tour, right?" Luke asked.

"Absolutely. There's nothing in there about what band is going with her. I had two lined up. One was Southern Lights. She did a couple of numbers with each one in separate practice sessions and hated them both."

Luke thought for a minute. "Here's what we do. Find another band, a good one that fits her style. One with a good-looking lead guitarist close to her age would be good, but don't let that be a deal breaker, as long as he's hot. Don't even do a practice session. Let her see him perform somewhere and tell her that's her band leader, period, end of story."

"No say at all? She won't like that, Luke. She won't like that at all."

"Well, she doesn't have to like it. But I'm sure you can handle that part," Luke finished with a chuckle.

"Oh yeah. That's what you pay me for, ain't it? Take care now, Luke. And nice to meet you, Rachel."

"Likewise," Rachel said.

"You too, Wes." Luke ended the call.

"You're a music producer too?" She knew of Emma Grace, a huge up-and-coming star on the country music scene.

"I own a small record company. Want to cut a single for me?" he asked, only half kidding.

She giggled at the thought. "For you or with you?"

"You pick."

She laughed. *As if.*

"Come on. It'll be fun. Let's do it sometime, you and me. You know you secretly want to be a rockin' country music superstar."

"It would be fun to sing with you, even have it played on the radio, but in all seriousness, I'm not the diva type."

He glanced over at her. "You're right. You're not and I'm glad. But you sure did rock Richie's Roadside last night."

Her cheeks brightened. "It was fun."

"Next week's race is Fontana, in California. Will you come with me? I could let the guys take the rig, and you and I could fly out."

Rachel considered how to turn him down nicely. "Luke, I um—"

"You don't have to answer right now. Think about it, okay?"

She didn't need to think about it, but when she opened her mouth to say so, his expectant gaze cut her short. Maybe she should at least let him think she'd consider it. She could tell him no later. "Okay, but no promises."

"Great. Let's spend some time together this week. I bet you're getting close on that Thunderbolt. Maybe if I help, we could get it running this week. What do you think?"

"That'd be great."

"I'll pick up dinner. Does your dad like Chinese food?"

"He might, but I don't," she informed him with a giggle. "How about I make dinner? Say, six o'clock?"

"I thought you didn't cook."

"I said I wasn't a very good cook, but there are a few things I can make."

He flashed a mischievous grin. "As long as you don't burn yourself again."

"I'll be careful." Compared to the fire she was already playing with, dinner was the least of her worries.

Dinner Monday night didn't exactly go as she planned. Not wanting to risk her own cooking, she'd arranged for Mrs. Libby, her elderly neighbor, to bring over a simple ready-to-serve meal. But when Mrs. Libby had to leave unexpectedly to be with her daughter who'd gone into labor, she'd simply dropped off the pot roast early with cooking instructions.

Rachel's father put it in the oven at the right time, three hours before they planned to eat, but forgot to add the potatoes, onion, and carrots. When she got home and realized the oversight, she added the vegetables to the roaster pan for the remaining thirty minutes. She baked the biscuits exactly as Mrs. Libby instructed, but when the timer went off they were already burned on the bottom—not to the point of being inedible, but most definitely overdone.

Luke arrived on time. When they sat down to dinner, Rachel served the pot roast on a large platter and set it in the center of the table. It looked wonderful. The biscuits, burned side down, were artfully arranged in a towel-lined basket beside it. After they'd joined hands and her father said the blessing, they filled their plates and began to eat.

She heard a loud crunching noise coming from Luke. He stopped chewing and stifled a chuckle. She hurried to take a bite of the vegetables. They were virtually raw. They looked at each other and burst out laughing. Her father laughed until he cried. When he finally stopped, he offered Luke a roast sandwich.

Luke politely declined, ensuring Rachel that the roast itself was delicious, and with a hopeful nod toward the counter, he added, "And that peach pie over there looks absolutely wonderful."

They all had a good laugh, but Rachel had never felt so embarrassed.

Luke brought takeout from a barbeque rib joint in town the next night.

Working side-by-side, by the end of the second evening they had the car purring like a well-oiled machine. They took it for a drive down the country backroads, and Luke had to laugh as he watched Rachel behind the wheel of the big old muscle car, grinning like a ten-year-old given the keys to the farm truck for the first time.

When she pulled it into the shop and turned it off, she looked over at him with a wide grin. "Thank you so much for all your help. I'm so excited to get it running."

Luke chuckled, surprised by her enthusiasm. "The pleasure is all mine, darlin'." He had a sudden urge to pull her across the front seat and into his arms, but recalling her earlier protests when he'd set her up on the workbench, he thought better of it. "Come here."

When she slid over, he pulled her onto his lap and stared into her sparkling eyes. "You're amazing," he said, his voice choked with emotion. He wiped a smudge from her cheek, and she leaned her head into his hand. "Oh, Rachel." He wanted to tell her he loved her, but was he sure? He didn't want to hurt her. No matter what, he vowed he wouldn't hurt her.

"What?" Her fingertips brushed the hair from his temples.

Luke watched her, waiting, wanting. Then, as though she'd read his mind, Rachel kissed him tenderly, teasing his lips with her tongue, then with a white-hot passion that came out of nowhere, surprising him.

When she finally pulled back, she gave him a shy smile. "Sorry."

She was incredible. He'd never met anyone who made him lose himself like he did with her. "Don't ever apologize for kissing me like that," he said between short gasps.

Rachel laughed and slowly leaned down to kiss him again.

"Rachel …" he stopped her as he leaned his head back against the car seat. "I can't kiss you like that and not want to make love to you. You do things to me, darlin', and I honestly think you have no idea."

Her eyes narrowed, contemplating. The *tick-tick-tick* of the cooling engine filled the silence. Slowly, she moved off his lap, scooted to the driver's side, and got out.

Luke collected himself, then got out and leaned against the workbench, crossing his arms in front of him as he watched her pick up tools, tidying the shop.

"Did you decide yet about Fontana?" he asked.

"Fontana?"

"The California race this weekend?" he reminded her.

"Oh, right. Yeah, I can't, Luke. I'm sorry."

"Can't or don't want to?"

She put away the last of the tools and leaned against the hood of the car, facing him. "Can't," she said. "I can't be with you like that." She frowned. "I'm not ready." She watched his expression.

Was she expecting him to pressure her, like other boyfriends may have done? Instead, he startled her by pulling her into his arms. "It's okay. I can wait for you, Rachel. I can wait as long as it takes." He knew he was grinning like an idiot, but he didn't care one bit. She was incredible, and he was falling in love with her.

She relaxed against him and squeezed. Yeah, he could wait, and she'd be worth it, no doubt about that.

"Let me make dinner for you tomorrow night at my place." When she hesitated, Luke set her back from him and looked at her sideways. Was she still afraid of being alone with him? "Don't worry, baby. You'll be safe with me. I promise, nothing's going to happen if you don't want it to."

Rachel shot him her cut-to-the-heart smile. "I know. And thank you for that. What time?"

Flames

Luke's neighborhood was much nicer than Rachel had expected. She'd never given any thought to how much money NASCAR driver-owners made, but she didn't think it was near enough to warrant the extravagant area she found herself driving through. On the outskirts of town, nestled between rural suburbia and endless farmland, she ambled along winding streets lined with exquisitely landscaped estate homes and widely spaced mansions, some so far from the road they could barely be seen.

Toward the end of a road aptly named Twenty Oaks Lane, Rachel paused at the crossroad to Luke's street to let her gaze travel the rest of the lane ahead of her. It meandered through a shady tunnel of massive ancient oaks that rose to great heights from a mantle of flowering shrubs and dripped Spanish moss. Then it bounded into the sunlight around a vast circular flowerbed with a fountain in the middle. The path led to the wide steps of a stately white antebellum house. Covered porches on multiple levels wrapped the house in cool, welcoming shade. Rachel caught her breath at the home's pure elegance and the setting's natural beauty, like a water-color-painted scene from bygone days when cotton was king.

Reluctantly she tore her gaze away and turned onto Luke's street, Carriage Road, a much narrower tree-lined two-track that wound around to end at his address—a beautiful old carriage house that had been made over into a quaint country home. Situated on the Twenty Oaks property well behind the larger main house, it was separated by a sprawling orchard, and, closer to the main house, a broad expanse of gardens. Rachel wondered who lived beyond the fruit trees and flowers. She admired the private serenity of the place as she made her way to his front door.

He threw steaks and asparagus on the grill, and they ate outdoors on the back porch, overlooking a well-maintained lawn that sloped gently to a small creek. They talked about his upcoming races, her next steps on the Thunderbolt, and how she liked her new project team. He was a perfect host and she enjoyed his company with an ease that settled between them.

As they ate, a dark thunderstorm in the distance rolled closer. By the time they'd finished and collected the dishes, rain fell fast and hard. She helped him rinse the dishes and tidy up the kitchen, and as they made their way to the living room, he asked her if she wanted to watch the Bristol race he'd recorded, rent a movie, or listen to music. She opted for the music.

Luke put on soft country music, then started a fire in the fireplace while Rachel stood in front of a large bay of floor-to-ceiling windows to watch the storm. Thunder boomed and lightning flashed, and Rachel jumped with each clap of thunder.

He went to stand behind her and wrapped his arms around her middle. "Relax, it's a spring storm," he said, his voice soothing to her ears.

She leaned against him. "I know."

"Dance with me?"

She turned in his arms and looked up at him, "What makes you think I want to dance with you?" she teased, using the same phrase she'd used at the hospital fundraiser when he'd cut in on her and Cole.

He gave her a wide grin. "You're here, aren't you?"

She giggled, "I am at that."

Luke pulled her in, and she inhaled his subtle, masculine scent as they slowly danced to the music that filled the room. He held her close, and she savored his warm strength as she rested her cheek against his shirt. His hands caressed her back. As the song ended and another one began, he looked at her, his dark blue eyes burning with a passion that made her shiver. Lifting his hands to bury them deep in her hair, he tilted her face to his while his gaze traveled from her eyes to her mouth and back to her eyes again. Her heart raced, anticipating his kiss.

Leaning down, he brought his lips to hers, soft and tender, consuming her with an unexpected intensity. When his kisses began to travel freely from her lips down to her neck and shoulder, she leaned her head back.

"Rachel, I am so in love with you," he whispered, his voice hoarse with emotion. He gazed at her and saw the effect of his words, his touch, his kisses.

Oh, God, help me. Was she falling in love with him, too? The way he looked at her, she knew he loved her. She could see it. *This is it, God, isn't it?* This is how it's supposed to be. "Luke," she said, not sure what to say to stop what was happening, or even if she wanted it to stop.

His shoulders sagged as he pulled back and set her from him. He cleared a catch in his throat and inhaled sharply, running his fingers through his hair. "Let's turn on the race." He nodded to the television.

She shook her head slowly. "I don't want to watch the race." She gazed up at him, leaning around to recapture his attention.

When he looked back at her, his brows knit together, and he studied her, no doubt trying to figure out what she wanted. He waited patiently, anticipating, watching her. She touched his cheek, tried to give him a reassuring smile and his eyes softened. Her pulse raced. She knew what she wanted, but could she say it?

"Love me, Luke," she whispered, her honey-sweet voice, little more than a breath, sounding foreign to her ears. "Please."

A huge breath fell out of him and he swallowed hard as he stared at her, eyes wide, for a long minute. His hands went up to hold her face, and his mouth found hers again, his kisses consuming her whole heart and mind. Rachel's heart beat madly as his brows raised as if to say, *Are you sure?* When she smiled back, his expression relaxed.

"You are so beautiful," he said, his deep voice soaked with emotion, barely more than a whisper. He stood and in one swift motion scooped her up into his arms.

Luke carried her down the hall, kicked open his bedroom door and set her feet gently on the floor. He had waited so long for this moment, had imagined it, longed for it, and dreamed about it so often it had nearly consumed him. At last she'd admitted she wanted him, and he was glad he'd waited.

This time it would be different. *Like heaven on earth, like God intended for a man to love a woman,* her sweet words echoed in his head. He buried his hands in her hair as he leaned in to kiss her.

Luke resumed what he'd started in the living room. But this time, when he pulled back to look into her eyes and tell her again how much he loved her, he stopped cold, shocked by what he saw there. "Hey, what is it, baby?"

Rachel shook her head and forced a weak smile, her whole body shuddered, and the wild look in her eyes couldn't be masked. "Rachel." What was she so afraid of? Then it dawned on him. "Baby, have you ever been with a man?"

Rachel's eyes grew even wider, and she bit her lower lip like she did when she was thinking or worried.

"Don't lie to me," he warned.

She shook her head.

Luke jumped, the realization stopping him like a black flag at the track.

He spun around, banging his fist against the door as he stormed out of the room. Seconds later, he stomped back in. "Come on. You don't need to be in here."

He went to the kitchen, standing at the sink, fists planted on the countertop. When he finally turned around several minutes later, he found her leaning against the doorway, arms crossed, watching him. He studied her, trying to read her blank expression. He couldn't tell if she was sad, angry, hurt, embarrassed. She was not happy though, that was for sure, standing there in her pretty tiny-flowered dress and cowboy boots, glaring back at him.

Luke reined in his frustration, and went to stand before her. "Rachel," he began patiently, reaching for her hand, "you should've told me, baby."

She simply stood there, looking at him.

He shook his head. "I can't be the one to take that from you, little girl."

She stood straight and stomped her boot, tossing his hand aside, "Dang it, Luke! I am not a little girl. I'm a woman, and I want to be loved like one."

She was so beautiful and strong and good, and he wanted her something fierce. But he couldn't. "I don't deserve you."

She glared at him. "Don't patronize me, Luke Brandt. You're a coward; that's all you are."

He stared at his boots and swallowed the lump in his throat. "You're right. I am a coward. Because I am so afraid I'm going to hurt you." He looked into her angry green eyes. "And, baby, that's the last thing in the world I'd ever want to do."

"Oh." She pushed him aside and stormed off to the front room, snatched up her purse, and headed for the door. Luke caught her as she opened it and pulled her back into his arms, kicking the door closed behind her.

"You're not going anywhere in this storm."

She struggled against him, but he held her tight, and quickly realizing she was no match for his strength, she gave up, sighed heavily, and let her head fall forward, defeated. His heart beat wildly, and he closed his eyes, still trying to wrap his head around her purity.

He loosened his grip and caressed her hair with one hand while the other circled her waist. He glanced down to where her small hand rested against his chest and noticed the ring she always wore was gone. He recalled seeing it there earlier when they'd said the blessing together at dinner. He gently touched her bare finger. "Did you lose your ring?"

She pulled away and looked up at him, but it was a long time before she answered, "No, it's over there." She nodded in the direction of a side table in the living room.

There was such a sad melancholy in her face as she stared across the room, he wondered if the ring held some special meaning for her. Curious, he went to retrieve it, inspecting it closely as he brought it back to her. It was beautiful, a gold band with a cross and a heart interlocked and an inscription: 1 TIMOTHY 4:12.

A Bible verse. Of course.

"Why'd you take it off?"

She stared at it, biting her lip. "It's a purity ring." She shot him a tentative glance. "I wore it as a promise to God that ... that I would wait for marriage," she explained, her voice trailing off to a whisper at the end.

He almost choked on the emotion that ripped through his heart as he thought about what she'd been ready to give up for him. "Here, put it back on. Please." He took her hand and placed it on her finger.

She stared at the ring, her lips curving into a hint of a smile, and when she finally looked up at him, the overpowering tenderness in her eyes made his heart skip a beat. He stood frozen in place while she placed her hands flat on his chest, watching her face as her fingertips moved across his skin, her soft delicate touch slowly caressing, up and over his shoulders and down the length of his arms. Inspecting him?

Testing him?

When she looked back up, her expression was pained, conflicted. She touched his face and he thought she was going to kiss him, but instead she closed her eyes, frowned, and turned away. Returning to the living room, she stood before the large bay windows, wrapped her arms around her middle, and stared out into the stormy black night.

This was probably for the best, Rachel thought, as she struggled to grasp the enormity of what had happened. Luke was not the marrying kind. He'd only break her heart when he moved on. But, oh, she wanted him. She wanted to love him. And he said he loved her. Did she dare trust in that? Should she believe him? Or had he said that to all the others who came before her?

The storm raged. Rain came down in blinding sheets and lightning flashed across the night sky, a perfect match to the overwhelming turbulence inside of her.

Luke picked up his shirt from the living room floor and slipped it on before joining her in front of the windows. Standing behind her, he wrapped her in his arms and pulled her back against him. "Don't be angry with me, baby."

She relaxed against him, basking in the comfort of his strong arms. "I'm not ."

A comfortable silence settled between them as she grappled with her emotions and unmet desires.

"You said you loved me, Luke. You want to be with me, right?"

A small gasp escaped him, and he leaned his head back to stare up at the ceiling. "Oh, Rachel," he turned her around to face him, "how can you even ask me that? This is darn near killing me. I love you, baby, and I want more than anything to make you mine, in every way. With every breath of life in me I want you." The passion in his soft-blue eyes clearly conveyed his sincerity. "You've got to know that, right?"

She looked up into his loving gaze and nodded, suddenly sure of everything. "You're a good man, Luke Brandt, and I'm falling in love with you too." Their eyes lingered and she basked in the perfection of the moment. She hugged him to her, resting her cheek against his shirtfront. "And don't ever think for a minute that you don't deserve me, because you absolutely do. God brought us together for a reason, and who are you to deny Him if I want to love you?"

"Oh, Rachel, baby, you are pure goodness and grace. I'm a lucky man, sure enough. But I'll wait for you, baby. I know your faith is important to you, and I respect that. I love you for that. It's part of what makes you so special."

She relished the safety of his loving embrace while she said a silent prayer: *God, thank you for blessing me with this wonderful man who loves me enough to wait for me.*

She sent her father a text to let him know she was going to wait out the storm and not to worry. They fell asleep together on the sofa. When she woke before dawn to head home, the storm had finally abated, at least the one outside.

Burned

The next day Luke and his crew headed for the Fontana race, and he spent most of the long drive west thinking about Rachel and reliving all their good times the last several weeks, his heart shimmering with pure contentment. His guys couldn't help but notice, and while they were happy for him and enjoyed his good mood, he could tell they were worried about how his relationship with her would affect his racing.

Luke set them at ease as he drove their number eleven Pacific Oil Dodge to another astonishing first-place finish. His team went wild, and it was a long time after the race before he made it back to his motor home to shower and call Rachel.

She'd watched the race from home and shared in his excitement as they talked for a good half hour until he was interrupted by his guys knocking on the door. He let them in and asked them to hold on while he went to the back bedroom to finish the call. When he joined them a few minutes later, they walked down the road to a little sports bar where, as soon as they walked in, he was immediately surrounded by excited race fans waiting to shower him with congratulations and hand him cold beers.

He basked in the accolades, but as the women flirted with him the sound of Cole's voice reverberated in his ears: *You can duck.* He decided early on to call it a night. He walked back to his motor home alone, missing Rachel something awful, and wondered how he could talk her into coming on the road with him the next time.

Aside from watching Luke's race on television, Rachel spent the remainder of the weekend fitting her carburetor and cooling mechanism into the Thunderbolt. She thought she had it figured out and made numerous notes on her spec diagrams, apprehensive about actually trying it.

Monday after work she rushed home to resume working on it. Luke would be back the next day, so she expected she'd have one more night to work on it on her own. She hadn't told him about it, wanting to wait until she'd tested it out. If it actually worked, it would be an astounding innovation with remarkable possibilities, but if it didn't … well then, she figured it was another crazy idea—something only a woman would think up, people would say.

She'd barely started when she heard a man's voice call, "Hey, Rachel."

She was bent over working under the hood, and when she stood up, she was surprised to see Cole coming through the open door. "Hey, Critter. What's up?"

"Another project?" he asked, stopping on the opposite side of the car.

"Yeah, restoring this old muscle car. What do you think?" She proudly stepped back from it.

He inspected it critically. "A little more work to do," he said, glancing to the workbench where her carburetor and cooling mechanism were sitting among pages of engineering diagrams. "And a few parts to put back in, by the looks of it."

"Yeah. What brings you all the way out here? Is everything all right?" She hurried to shift the subject away from the extra components.

His expressions was serious. "Depends. I haven't seen you since last weekend, and I wanted to make sure you were all right."

His concern was endearing. What a nice guy. "I'm all right." She thought about Luke's conversation they'd overheard. "He's not a bad guy, Cole. He's searching for that somethin' special, like we all are."

He gave her a wry smile, moved over beside her, and leaned against the driver's side door.

"What is it?"

"I just," he stammered and swallowed his hesitation, "I wanted to let you know that I found that somethin' special." He shot her a tentative glance.

"You did? Who is she? Do I know her?"

"Oh, yeah. You know her, all right." He wrung his hands as his gaze wandered around the shop. "It's you, Rachel," he said, his expression serious as his pale blue eyes searched hers, anxiously waiting for her reaction.

"Me?" she shot back, taken off guard.

He nodded. "I'm in love with you, Rachel. I have been for a long time now, ever since you went out with Austin. I don't know what he did to hurt you, but if I ever see him around again, I swear I'm going to set the score straight. In fact, every time you go out with a guy who doesn't treat you right it makes me crazy, and I finally figured out why. It's because I love you."

Rachel stared at him. "Oh, Critter. You are too sweet. I don't know what to say." She walked to the workbench, set down her wrench and faced him. "I like you, Cole. You're a great friend and … I'm truly sorry if I ever said or did anything to make you think otherwise, but I don't … I don't …" she paused, hating herself for the pain that clouded his features, "I don't have those kind of feelings for you, Cole. I'm sorry."

He squared his shoulders and stared at her for several long moments, but after an awkward silence, he simply gave her a resigned shrug. "It's all right. I thought this might be as good a time as any to let you know, before you fell too hard for Mr. NASCAR and he hurt you too."

"He might not."

"I hope not; I truly do. You've been hurt way too many times." He stared down at his hands, then looking up, he winced. "I want you to be happy; you know that, right?

Rachel nodded, wishing his pain wasn't her doing.

"Well, I suppose I should go." He turned to leave.

"Cole," she called as he neared the door.

He turned around.

"Are we okay? Still friends, right?" She hoped she hadn't lost one of her best friends.

He walked back to where she stood near the workbench. "Absolutely." He held out his arms, and she gave him a big hug. When he didn't let go for several minutes she knew she'd hurt him, and when he pressed his lips against her hair, she realized how much.

"Well, ain't this just to beat all," Luke barked from the doorway, surprising Rachel with the fury in his voice. Fists clenched and eyes blazing, he stomped toward them.

"Luke," Rachel cried out.

As Luke neared, Cole stepped away from her. Rachel had a bad feeling. From the look on Luke's face it was going to get nasty quick.

"What have you done, Rachel?" Luke hollered, his face colored with rage. "I wouldn't take your virginity, so you turned to your good ol' buddy Cole? Decided you couldn't wait after all, huh?"

Rachel's mouth fell open, and tears instantly filled her eyes as his words slapped her, his ugly accusations knocking her against the workbench.

Cole didn't hesitate to slam Luke with a solid right cross that smashed against his jaw. Fists flew as the two pounded each other, brawling like a couple of country boy heathens. Rachel screamed at them to stop. Fueled by his fury, Luke whaled on Cole, but he got as good he gave. Cole's calm finesse matched Luke's wild anger. But when Luke backed Cole against a wall, Rachel rushed forward. She tried to get between them, and the next thing she knew she was falling against the Thunderbolt and everything went black.

When Rachel tumbled to the concrete floor, Luke's anger vanished as quickly as it had come. He rushed to scoop her up. "Look what you've done, Cole," he yelled, cradling her in his arms.

"You have no idea what you walked in on." Cole wiped at his mouth with the back of his hand.

Luke stood, holding Rachel in his arms. "Get out of here."

Cole looked helplessly at Rachel's limp form, then glared at Luke. "You're going to hurt her, and I'll be there to pick up the pieces. Like I always am. She doesn't know it yet, but I'm going to be the one who loves her for the long haul. Wait and see. You're done." He took another worried look at her unmoving form before he stormed out.

Luke carried her into the house, and as he struggled to close the door behind him without kicking it in, her father rushed into the kitchen.

"Good Lord! What happened?" her father demanded as he hurried forward, his face etched with worry. Seeing his little girl out cold and lying like a ragdoll in Luke's arms, bright red blood staining her cheeks, brought him near to panic.

"She hit her head. Pretty sure the blood's all mine though," he said, hoping to ease the older man's anxiety. He knew he must look rough. Cole had landed some solid punches; he could feel blood trickling from his nose and mouth.

"Bring her in here." Her father raced ahead into her bedroom and yanked down the quilt. He was back in seconds with two hand towels, each half wet with warm water. He pushed Luke out of the way, handed him one of the towels and sat down on the bed beside Rachel. He gently wiped the blood from her face, relieved to discover her only injury was the bump on her forehead. His wrinkled features relaxed.

Luke couldn't pull his gaze away from Rachel's face as her father took care of her. He wiped his nose and mouth with the towel he'd been given as his heart broke for her. *Oh, God, help me. What have I done to you, little girl?*

"Tell me what happened, son," her father demanded.

Luke looked at the lines in the older man's face, deep with worry, and felt pure and utter shame for what he'd done. Swallowing the lump in his throat, Luke looked at Rachel. "I, um … I can't," he said, shaking his head.

"Did she do that to you?"

Luke half smiled, recalling what she'd done to Austin, Sport Coat Guy. "No, Cole was here."

Her father nodded, understanding, "You and Cole? And she got in the middle of it?"

Luke nodded, "Somethin' like that."

"Well, there's nothing more to be done. You go on home now."

"Maybe I should take her to the hospital."

"No, she'll be fine. If she doesn't come around soon I'll take her." When Luke simply stood there, he repeated, "Go on home now, Luke."

He wandered outside, but unable to leave, went back to the barn. Walking in, he relived the unbearable pain in his gut when he'd come around the corner to see Cole holding Rachel in his arms, his eyes closed as he kissed her hair. He knew there was something more there. But how could she pick Cole over him? How could she?

He ran his hands through his hair and tried to shake off the crushing guilt and fear that threatened to bring him to his knees. Not knowing what else to do, Luke glanced around at the mess they'd made. Tools lay strewn across the floor, and papers were scattered everywhere. He set the towel down on the workbench and began picking up tools.

Near the door, several jackets littered the floor. Luke scooped them up and began hanging them on the hooks on the wall. When he noticed a bullet hole in the sleeve of a camouflage hunting jacket, his mouth fell open. It was his coat, the one he'd placed over her that day in the woods. His eyes closed as his mind went back to the image of the sleeping angel beneath the willow. The moment passed and he reopened his eyes to the mess of reality before him. He hung it up with a heavy heart, and turned to see what else remained.

After straightening the papers into a neat pile on the workbench, he glanced at them. They were engineering diagrams for a mechanical component that looked oddly familiar. He recognized the bare bones of a carburetor, but with significant modifications including a component that had water intake. The components from the drawings sat toward the end of the workbench.

"Get out!"

Luke whirled around at Rachel's angry voice. His heart hammered wildly as he strained to find the words to set things right. "Rachel—"

"Get out. I don't want to hear it."

He walked toward her.

"Don't come near me. I hate you. Do you hear me, Luke Brandt? I hate you. How dare you do that to me? Think that of me?"

"I'm sorry, baby. I didn't know what to think, walking in here, finding you in his arms and ..." He struggled with the image in his head, and the fear he may have lost her to someone else. "His eyes were closed. He's in love with you, can't you see that?"

"Were *my* eyes closed? No, they weren't, but you didn't bother to see that. And I know he's in love with me. That's why he was here, to tell me that. But I don't love him. But you couldn't see that, could you? Because you didn't bother to look or to ask."

"Rachel, please." He reached for her, but she jumped back, beyond his grasp.

"No. I will never forgive you for the ugly things you said to me. Never."

He stared at her for several long minutes as his heart bled out.

She walked to her workbench and looked over the carburetor. "Please go," she said, not bothering to turn back to look at him.

After several minutes of silence, while he stared at her back and tried to think of something more to say, he glanced at the components on the workbench in front of her. "Is that a take-off on my idea?"

"No. I had this idea long before you came along. Why do you think I wanted that four-twenty-seven so badly?"

He swallowed. Right, the auto auction. "When were you going to tell me about it?"

"When it worked."

"Look at me, Rachel, please."

She shook her head.

His silent guilt was deafening as he watched her, knowing he'd done exactly what he'd been so afraid of doing. He'd hurt her deeply, and he hated himself for it. "I'm sorry, Rachel." He paused at the door, lifted his hunting jacket from the hook, and glanced back to her, overcome with an intense longing to wrap her up in it again, dispel all the cold, painful things he'd spewed, and resurrect her budding warmth.

When she heard his car pull away, Rachel slid to the floor, letting her head fall forward onto her knees, and wept bitterly—for the almost-was, for the never-gonna-be.

Regrets

L uke woke on the couch well past noon the next day, blurry-eyed and hung over from a lone night of drinking as he'd tried to find comfort in the quiet companionship of his old friend Jack. But even the whiskey wasn't enough to get her out of his head. Pain and regret always outlast the alcohol. He should've learned that much by now.

He groaned as he rolled off and stumbled to the kitchen, picking up his phone from the side table along the way. While he waited on his coffee, he brought up photos of Rachel on his phone and slowly flipped through them, smiling as he relived each of the chronicled events of their short time together. He especially liked the ones he'd taken of her at Bristol and the ones of her on stage at the bar. His fleeting happiness disappeared as his memory slammed back, a cruel reminder that he'd lost her, and his heart broke all over again.

Luke rubbed the sleep from his eyes, collapsed onto a barstool at the counter, and let his head fall on his arms. It hurt. Of all the cuts, scrapes, broken bones, and bodily injuries he'd ever suffered, nothing came close to the unrelenting ache of his shattered heart. By far the most agonizing damage ever inflicted on the human soul, this wound cut deep. And left gaping and unattended, it would take a lifetime to heal, the scar sure to render it incapable of ever functioning right again.

He had to get her back, set things right. He'd never met anyone like her, and he'd never find anyone like her ever again. She was meant for him. It couldn't be over.

He ran his hands through his hair, and looked for a pen and piece of paper. He'd send her flowers along with an apology—something sweet and sincere. A few minutes later, materials in hand, he sat and set his mind to come up with something special.

After an hour, Luke still had no idea where to begin. "I'm sorry" fell so far short. It was enough to make him want to cry. His creativity blocked by the black cloud of his despair, he went over to the stereo and turned on some country music, hoping to find inspiration there.

It took all afternoon to write and he still wasn't sure it was good enough, but decided he'd have to settle so he could get it to her that evening. He found a blank note card and carefully wrote it out, then drove to the florist.

Rachel arrived home from work, kissed her daddy hello, and went to her room to take a nap. When he came in later to ask if she wanted some dinner, she declined and said she was turning in for the night. Not ten minutes later he returned holding a long box. "This came for you."

She got up and took the box from him. She went to the kitchen and set it on the counter. After a brief hesitation, her father returned to his television program in the other room.

She took a deep breath, opened it, and lifted out an envelope. Inside were six race tickets, pit passes for Martinsville, and a folded note card. She put the tickets and the note card aside and lifted the flowers out of the box. Two dozen red roses. She inhaled their sweet scent, but found no pleasure in their beauty or their fragrance, still sunk in her painful heartbreak. She arranged them in a vase and picked up the card. Her father was still in the living room, but she decided to take it to her room to read in private.

She sat on the edge of the bed and steeled herself. She opened the note card to see his carefully handwritten missive.

> *This hurts, Rachel, and if you can never forgive me I understand.*
> *But know that it'll nearly kill me to lose you. I miss you, darling.*
> *I miss your beautiful smile. I miss your sweet kisses. I miss every*
> *beat of your heart. Tell me what I need to do to win you over. I'll*
> *do it! I need you in my life, like the sun needs the moon, like the*

fields need the rain, like a church needs a Sunday. Please, baby, forgive me.

I love you with all my heart,
Luke

Rachel stared at his words, then blinked as they blurred through the tears that pooled on her lower lids. She closed the note and tucked it beneath her pillow. Lying down, she folded her hands beneath her cheek and prayed for the unbearable heartache to be taken away, for guidance in making the right decisions in her life. She begged God to help her heal, help her forgive, help her to love again. Someday. Then she silently cried herself to sleep. Again.

The next day Luke was in his shop early as usual and seated at his desk. His thoughts went back to Rachel, and he drew a sketch of her modified carburetor and realized that it was designed to work on gaseous fuel, liquid gasoline that was heated and turned into a vapor inside the component. He rubbed his chin as he thought through it and realized how ingenious it was. The vaporized fuel, at the right flashpoint, would be able to produce a similar combustibility, but with a fraction of the amount of gas. And the other component, unlike anything he'd ever seen before in a combustion engine, must have been a cooling mechanism.

She was one smart woman. He wondered if it would work. He shook his head, overwhelmed by the admiration he felt for her. He'd give anything to be there for that first test. If only she was still in his life. "Holy smokes, I miss you, Rachel!" he cried aloud to the empty room.

Rachel finished installing her carburetor and cooling mechanism late Saturday night. After church on Sunday, while her father turned on the race, she went out to the shop. She carefully double-checked everything before she was ready to start it up. She looked at it long and hard, wondering if she should push the car out of the shop first, in case the thing exploded again. She could have her father come help her. *No, just do it.* She stood at the front of the car and put her hands together and said a quick prayer. She'd put so much time and sweat into this moment. She prayed it would someday have a positive impact on her world, on God's world. She slipped behind the wheel, took a deep breath, and reached for the key.

From the pit area at the Martinsville Motor Speedway Luke watched, hoped, and waited for Rachel to show up, but she never did. Not surprised, but thoroughly disappointed, he looked forward to a few hours' relief from missing her. When he got into his race car, his wounded heart wouldn't be getting in with him.

Rachel bit her lower lip and slowly turned the key. When the engine fired right up, she listened carefully. It sounded great, normal, like it should. She let it idle for several minutes, then went to look under the hood. It was working. At least it was running and hadn't exploded. That was something.

She closed the hood and got in to take a test drive. She drove into town and filled up the gas tank, then jumped on the interstate and drove forty miles to Franklin, Kentucky, before heading back. In town, she stopped to refill the tank, watching the numbers click by on the pump as the gas flowed. She didn't wait long; it stopped at a half gallon.

Rachel stared at it for a minute and then, thinking something wasn't right, pulled in on the lever again. It instantly shut off. The tank was definitely full. But she'd gone eighty miles. On a half-gallon of fuel? No way. She paid for her gas and drove eighty-two miles before turning around. Again she pulled into a gas station to refill, and this time the pump stopped at just over a gallon. One hundred sixty-four miles on *one* gallon! She laughed out loud as she hung up the hose.

Luke finished fourth in the field of thirty-nine, and his team was ecstatic with another respectable finish. He was leading the season in total points and was the toast of the track as the press sought him out for interviews. He went through the motions with little enthusiasm, and as soon as he was able to break away, retreated to his motor home, adamant about not joining his crew in celebrating.

Rachel returned home wildly excited, eager to tell her daddy about her test run, only to find him sound asleep in his chair, the race over. She sat on the front porch and stared at the freshly tilled fields. She tried to think of someone else she could share her news with, but there was no one. Cole would appreciate it and be genuinely excited for her, she was sure of it. But after what happened the other night, she didn't feel she could call him. Her girlfriends would be clueless, and definitely not her mother; there was no one.

Luke.

He would totally appreciate it and be ecstatic. She wondered how he did at Martinsville but, with a quick shake of her head, forced the thought away.

Alone in his motor home, Luke put in the race tape from Bristol and fast-forwarded through, searching for scenes with Rachel in them, finding several. The best ones were from the winner's circle after his first-place finish when he'd pulled her into the middle of things. He paused the scene and stared at it long and hard, the thunderous cheering of race fans resounding in his ears as the tears ran freely down his unshaven cheeks.

He went to the kitchen, poured a short glass of whiskey, and took a long drink, relishing the pain as it seared his throat. He stared at the warm amber liquid. Getting drunk again wasn't going to get her back. No, the last thing he needed was another whiskey lullaby. He had to think things through, keep a clear head, and get her back. Not having her in his life wasn't an option. She was made for him, sure as rain. He had to figure out a way to be the kind of man she deserved, the kind of man she could love.

Rachel resigned herself to go for a walk in the woods and soon found herself sitting alone beneath her willow tree as the heartache returned. The loneliness and anguish overcame her and her tears fell again.

The next morning, after watching the sun rise from beneath his giant sycamore tree on the hill, Luke trekked over to the willow where he'd first laid eyes on her. It seemed so long ago. Images of her asleep there on the grass lingered in his mind. If only he'd awakened her that day, or waited for her to wake, they could have met under totally different circumstances.

But he'd been in too much of a hurry, needing to find that buck, meet his daddy for breakfast, get to work. There's always something about the busyness of life that gets in the way of living it the way you want.

He'd caused her so much frustration, so much pain, from the moment they first met at the auto auction and all the times since. Would things have turned out any differently if he'd met her that morning beneath the willow? Or would he still have tried to push her away? Would he still have been unable to trust her with his heart? Maybe they were like fire and fuel, no good for one another.

Rachel stared at the personnel form on her desk, trying to absorb the impact it would have for her if she were to go ahead and sign it. The exclusivity contract was a mandatory part of her transition paperwork to her new engineering team, but it would irrevocably give BEI International all rights to anything she developed, whether it was work related or not.

She knew it was a standard practice for engineers, designers, and software developers, but she couldn't sign it, not with being so close to making her vapor fuel carburetor a reality. The sticky note on it indicated it was due back to Human Resources by Friday. It was Monday. That gave her one week. Was that enough time to file for the patent? Maybe she could stall and get two weeks, conveniently forget about it until someone from HR reminded her. Who knew how on top of this paperwork they were?

That evening, she took her laptop to the shop, pulled up her stool, and brought up the U.S. Patent website to start the online process of filing a patent. She discovered she needed detailed engineering specifications, and while she had the scale drawings she'd drafted on paper, she didn't think they were good enough to accompany a patent filing. She'd have to redraw them using her drafting software.

As it began to rain, she turned on her favorite country music playlist. She began on the drawings, but struggled to focus, her thoughts straying to remembered kisses, strong arms, and blue eyes. The sad songs weren't helping. They made her want to cry, so she switched to a Christian music playlist. She turned back to her computer screen. Much better.

By ten o'clock she'd finished most of the carburetor drawing and had the rough outlines for the cooling unit. She was careful to save her work often and not on her work laptop. She created a special folder on an external drive to keep all of her drawings and documents related to her project. Comparing her computer drawing to the one on paper, she was pleased with the new version. It looked professional. She was double-checking all the measurements when someone knocked.

Rachel opened the door to a slightly drenched, but still dashing Luke, leaning against the doorframe. How was it even possible he could be that good-looking? He held his cowboy hat in his hands, and his long hair fell at a rakish angle across his brow. His baby blues sparkled in the bright overhead lights, and his wet jeans and dress shirt hugged his lean frame. Her heart began to race and her gut tightened.

"Howdy." He waited for a long moment as she held the door and looked at him. "Can I come in?" He raised his eyebrows and flashed her his bright smile.

She forced herself to look away. "I'd rather you didn't." Her voice was cold, detached. And she didn't care.

The rain beat a steady rhythm on the barn's metal roof and a gust of wind shook the overhead doors. She shivered, uncomfortable as he stood staring at her. She kept her gaze averted, willing him to go away.

"Please, Rachel?"

She hesitated, considering, but as his ugly words reverberated in her ears, the hurt returned, stiffening her resolve, fortifying the wall around her heart. She dropped her hand from the door and returned to her seat at the workbench.

When she heard the door close and the sound of his boots on the concrete floor, she knew she was going to have to face him. He wasn't going away easily. He leaned against the workbench beside her stool and glanced at what she was working on. "Drawing up your components?"

"Yeah." She kept her focus on the screen.

"Tested it yet?"

She nodded.

"Did it work?" His excitement made her want to cry.

"It worked."

Luke looked down at the papers scattered on the workbench beside her. He picked up a page that had nothing but numbers on it. She snatched it away, but not before he'd seen what was on it. "A hundred and sixty-four miles to one gallon? Seriously?"

Her proud smile confirmed it.

"Holy smokes," he cried. "Can I see it?"

"Yeah, go on." She'd known he would totally appreciate the significance of it.

Luke popped the hood on the Thunderbolt and peered in at the new components she'd added. "Amazing."

She watched from her stool, wishing with all her heart that things were different, that she could share with him the excitement of her accomplishment. Instead, she breathed in a long, slow breath, determined not to let her defenses down. "Why are you here?" She stared into his eyes when he turned her way, hoping, praying she wouldn't get lost in them.

A moment of silence vanished in the thunder that rattled the barn as he simply stared back at her, speechless. "Rachel, baby—"

"You know I don't want to see you, Luke ... I don't want to be with you, right?" She cringed. Her voice sounded cruel and cold, even to her.

He scowled and rubbed his chin. "You told me a few nights ago that you were falling in love with me." He came back to stand in front of her.

"Well, I don't want to love you." She turned back to her computer screen and tried to focus, tried to let her mind and heart escape the confrontation she desperately did not want to be having.

"So," he hesitated, leaning back against the workbench to peer at her, "you don't love me anymore?"

"I didn't say that." Rachel continued to stare at her computer screen. "I said I don't *want* to love you."

From the corner of her eye, she saw the little smile that curved his mouth. He moved closer and leaned back, trying to get her to look his way. "Rachel, you were made for me, and I need you. I need you in my life."

She glanced over to him and quickly looked away, shaking her head, "No, Luke."

"God brought us together for a reason, and who are you to deny Him if I want to love you?"

She whirled to glare at him. Those were her words. She felt the hot tears threaten and had to look away as she blinked them back. "Okay, now you're twisting the knife, Luke."

"Rachel," he started, his deep voice soaked with emotion, "I love you, baby. Please give me a chance ... give us a chance. I'm so sorry I said those awful things. I didn't mean it. I didn't mean any of it. I was in shock. I was jealous and angry. It made me crazy to see you in another man's arms. I didn't know what I was saying. Please, angel." He reached out to touch her face.

"No." Rachel smacked his hand away. Hopping off her stool, she stepped away and turned to face him. How could he think those things about her? "Cole is a friend. That's all he'll ever be, no matter how he feels about me."

"I know that now ... but it killed me seeing him so obviously in love with you. And you were hugging him back."

"As a *friend*."

"I didn't know that." He took a step toward her. "I can't begin to tell you how it felt to think you didn't love me after all, to know that I was losing you to someone else."

She looked away and steeled herself to remain calm. "Okay, but the things you said to me were so ugly and mean. You have so much anger and mistrust and hatred in you. I can't imagine why." She shook her head and spoke softly. "You don't know how to love a woman, Luke."

"Teach me." He took another step.

She retreated and continued to shake her head as she bit her lower lip. Despite her resolve, tears welled up when she looked at him. "That would be like teaching someone how to breathe, and I can't. I don't have it in me to teach you."

He took another step and she backed away, "No. Luke, please." She closed her eyes tight and willed the tears to go away. Opening them, she met his gaze. "Please go," she whispered. When she couldn't hold the tears in any longer, she simply lowered her face so he wouldn't see them fall.

He watched her fragile strength crumble. He struggled for words, while the silence that hung between them disappeared in the raindrops that crashed on the roof, like the tears that rolled off her cheeks splashed on the concrete between her boots.

He slowly closed the distance between them, his heart aching with intense sorrow as he peered at the heartrending tilt of her head. With a gentle fingertip, he lifted her face to look at him. She blinked as she glared, tears streaming down her cheeks, and it broke his heart clear through to know he caused them. He swallowed the lump in his throat. "This is wrong, Rachel. So wrong." His voice broke. "We belong together."

She slowly shook her head, sniffled, and let the tears fall.

He stood there in a panic, watching her cry. He had nothing else. This was it.

His heart raced—he'd actually lost her. He loathed the man he was. He'd tried so hard not to hurt her and look what he'd done. Hot tears stung his eyes as he watched her cry right there in front of him. He nodded and rubbed his chin. Yeah, she was better off without him. He slowly backed away and turned to go, stopping at the door to glance back at her one last time before he walked out.

Hearing the door latch, Rachel fell to her knees and sobbed. *I love him. Oh, God, did I do the right thing? How could he be so unbelievably sweet and tender and then so downright mean and say such ugly things when he's supposed to be in love with me? I'm so confused.*

His plea for her to teach him how to love echoed in her head. Did he mean it? He seemed genuinely disgusted with himself for the way he'd spoken to her, but it wasn't the first time. Was there something beneath the surface preventing him from trusting her, from trusting in love? Was he simply incapable of loving someone, of believing that someone could actually love him back? Why was he always pushing her away with his angry taunting words?

"He needs me," she whispered. "He needs me, doesn't he?" *I'm not strong enough, God. I—please help me to know what to do. What is Your plan for me, Lord? Please show me, and I will trust in it.*

When she cried herself out, she got up, wiped her eyes, and went to the workbench to pack up her things. She saved and closed her files and tucked the small external drive into her pocket, then stowed the paperwork neatly away in the upper cabinet. She shut down her laptop, put it back in her bag, and turned off the music. At the door she turned back to make sure everything was tidied up, and, satisfied, she flicked off the lights and pulled the door closed.

She ran across the drive in the pouring rain and into the house, kissed her daddy good night in the living room, and got ready for bed. As she began to take off her jeans she reached into the pocket and pulled out the external drive and went back to the kitchen to tuck it in her purse.

A movement in the drive caught her eye, and she thought she saw someone heading into the barn. Her heart floated in her chest as hope flooded back. Did he come back for her? Was she being given another chance to forgive him? Is that what God wanted her to do? She ran to the barn, and finding the shop door ajar, gently pushed it open. "Luke?" She crossed the threshold and reached for the light switch.

Suspicion

Strong arms grabbed her from behind while a hand covered her mouth, smothering her cry. She struggled, astounded for a split second that Luke would be so rough with her.

"Be quiet and you won't get hurt," he warned.

Her adrenaline skyrocketed and she stifled a scream as she realized it wasn't Luke. She was no match for the strength of the brawny arms that held her.

She tried to stay calm, but her heart raced and her knees felt weak. Her eyes darted around the dark shop. Was he the only one? What did he want? Was he there to hurt her? Did she dare try to use her self-defense moves? She tried to glance over her shoulder, but he brutally jerked her head forward. He was huge! *Oh, God help me.*

He dragged her to the workbench, fumbled for the switch to the undercabinet lights and began throwing open cabinet doors, searching. He found the stack of papers and crammed them into his dark jacket, then he moved to the hood of the Thunderbolt and popped it open. He bent over, still holding her firmly in one arm as he struggled to make out what he was looking at in the dim light. They were both surprised by the swift blow from behind that dropped him to the floor.

"Rachel, run!"

Luke. *Thank You, God.* She backed away as the intruder regained his feet and turned to take on Luke. Terrified for Luke, she watched as they fought. She told herself not to panic, but knew she had to do something. She ran to the house and shouted to her father as she grabbed his shotgun from over the kitchen door. "Daddy, I need you. Quick. In the shop." And she flew back out the door with the gun.

She ran across the drive to the shop and stopped short inside the open doorway to cock the gun. The men were on the other side of the car. She rounded the vehicle toward them, raised the gun, and took aim. The huge man lunged for the workbench, grabbed a crescent wrench, and swung at Luke, who dodged the first swing, but was thrown off balance. The next one landed against his head with a loud crack.

Horrified, she watched Luke collapse. She aimed at the now-still figure of the intruder, and pulled the trigger. He doubled over with a look of disbelief, grasping his thigh. She cocked the shotgun for another shot, and he bolted, stumbling for the door. As he ran, she gave chase, lowering the gun as he limped down the drive.

She sprinted back into the shop as her father ran out of the house. He raced after her, flipping on the overhead lights to find her kneeling on the floor, holding Luke's head in her lap. He was out cold. "Rachel. What in tarnation? I thought I heard a gunshot."

She cradled Luke's head, sobbing, panic setting in. There was blood, so much blood, everywhere.

Her father dashed to the workbench and pulled paper towels off the roll. Hurrying back to them, he knelt beside her and carefully placed them over Luke's head injury. Then he secured them with a clean shop rag. "Come on, you'd better get this boy to a hospital."

"Someone broke in." Her drawings were scattered everywhere. "And he knew exactly what he was looking for. He wanted the carburetor. How does anyone know about it?" After they loaded Luke into the backseat of the Thunderbolt, Rachel ran around to the driver's side.

"Daddy, I need your help. Collect all these papers and hide them for me, somewhere no one will find them. Then call the police and please, Daddy, be careful. He may come back. I know I shot him, but if he wants it badly enough, he'll be back."

She pressed the overhead door button, pulled her car out of the shop, and within minutes was flying like the wind down the highway in the pouring rain to get Luke to the hospital. *God, please let him be all right. Please, God. Don't take him from me. I want to love him, I do. And I can teach him. With Your help, I can do it. I know I can. I can teach him all about trust and faith and love—if You'll give me another chance. Please don't take him.*

Alone in the hospital's waiting area, Rachel used Luke's cell phone to call his father.

"Hey buddy, it's pretty late, isn't it?" His father's voice was groggy with sleep.

"Mr. Brandt," she began, "this is Rachel Tate—"

"Rachel. Well, hello there, darlin'. I've been looking forward to meeting you."

"Luke's been hurt. I'm at Mercy General in the emergency room with him now. He's got a fairly serious head injury. He was unconscious, but breathing when I brought him in. I'm hopeful he's going to be fine, but you might want to—"

"I'll be right there," he said and hung up.

Rachel called her father to check in. The police had arrived and were still there, going through the shop with a fine-tooth comb. He told her they'd sent an officer to the hospital to get her statement.

Several minutes later Daniel Brandt rushed into the waiting room, his wife in tow, and with a quick glance at the faces of the other people seated around the room, he walked straight to her. "Rachel?"

"Yes, hello, Mr. Brandt." She stood to shake his hand. Daniel Brandt was a huge bear of a man, and she instantly recognized Luke's blue eyes.

He took her hand, thanked her for calling them, then pulled her into a warm embrace. He stepped back to introduce his wife, Jilly, who, despite the late hour and the obvious concern etched in her worried brow, was a beautiful woman. Her blond hair and big, brown doe eyes were striking. As the two of them sat beside her, Rachel thought how much more Luke resembled his father than his mother.

"Tell us what happened," Daniel Brandt said.

She described everything, leaving out the details of their breakup and the carburetor. She let them know how brave Luke was in sneaking back in to surprise the intruder and come to her rescue. She told them how she'd shot the guy after he hit Luke with the crescent wrench.

"Mrs. Tate?" A police officer stood before them.

"Yes … um, Miss Tate," she corrected him.

"I'm Detective Landry. Your father called about a breaking and entering and possible assault."

"Yes." She recounted the story again.

"Any idea what they were looking for?"

"Tools maybe? I restore old cars as a hobby, so we've got a pretty well-equipped garage."

"Anything else you can think of that might offer a motive?"

Rachel thought for a moment. "No, nothing," she lied, shaking her head. She didn't mention her carburetor design. No one knew about it, and she wanted to keep it that way.

"If you think of anything—" he said, handing her his card.

"Of course." She glanced at his card. "Thank you, Detective Landry."

The doctor who'd been tending to Luke came out several minutes later, "Miss Tate?"

"Yes." She stood, her face a mask of anxiety, her heart pounding wildly in her chest. "These are Luke's parents, Jilly and Daniel Brandt."

"I'm Dr. Barrington," she said, nodding to each of them. A smile brightened her face. "I'm happy to tell you, I think he's going to be fine. He has a nasty gash along the side of his head that took quite a few staples to close and a few bruises and minor contusions, but other than that, it doesn't look like there's any permanent damage."

Rachel and the Brandts exchanged relieved glances.

"He's likely going to have a massive headache for at least a day or two."

"Can we see him?" Rachel and Daniel Brandt asked at the same time.

"Of course, but he's still unconscious and may not wake up for a while. And we'd like to keep him here for observation for a couple of hours once he does."

Rachel and the Brandts followed her back to Luke's room. Rachel spent the next several hours beside him while his parents came and went, brought her coffee, and tried to get her to eat. She finally fell asleep in a chair pulled up beside the bed, her head resting on the mattress next to his shoulder.

Rachel was the first thing Luke saw when he opened his eyes. When he touched her hair, she woke with a start, gazing at him with sleepy eyes. "Hey, you," she whispered.

A slow smile spread across his face as he began to remember what happened. He'd lost her in a thunderstorm. He frowned. Was that a dream? More like a nightmare. He stroked her cheek. *Holy smokes, I am so in love with this little girl.*

"Luke?" She looked worried.

He gave her a mischievous grin and cocked his head to the side. "Who are you?" he asked, feigning confusion.

Her eyes grew wide.

He laughed. "Hey, I'm kidding."

Rachel jumped up and backed away from the bed. "You're downright mean to the bone, Luke Brandt. You get on." Tears of relief filled her eyes, and she absently wiped them away.

Luke motioned her to come closer. "You were worried."

She nodded. "Don't do that to me."

He took her hand and brought it to his lips, and, suddenly serious, kissed it. "I can't even tell you how happy I am you're here." He hoped his voice conveyed his sincerity and the depth of his feelings for her.

"Thank you for coming back."

"I couldn't face my life without you in it."

"I'm glad," she said, trying to smile. "I couldn't either."

"So now I'm your cowboy hero?" he teased, wanting more than anything to see her smile shine through again.

She laughed softly. "You got that right." She glanced at the bedside monitors, then looked at his head. "How do you feel?"

He felt the bandage wrapped around his head. "Like I kissed the outside wall at about a hundred and eighty miles an hour."

After a soft knock, his parents peeked in. They hurried forward as Rachel stepped away. His mother took Rachel's place at his side and held her boy's hand. "Oh, Luke. Thank God you're all right."

"I have to go call in at work," Rachel said on her way to the door.

Apprehensive, Luke said, "Don't go."

"I'll be back. Leaving you is the last thing on my mind."

She returned to his room and stopped outside the door. Luke and his father were whispering harsh, angry words.

"Don't give me that. Who'd you tell?" Luke's voice seethed.

"No one. You wanted me to wait until she ... I didn't tell anyone; you have to believe me, son."

"I swear, Daddy," Luke's voice betraying his barely controlled anger, "If I find out you had anything to do with what happened to Rachel tonight ..." He paused. "I will never, ever forgive you."

Her throat went dry. Her heart raced and her hands trembled as she quietly backed away from the door. She leaned against the wall, struggling to grasp the implications of what she'd overheard. Until she what? Got it working? Was his father after the carburetor? Was he behind the break-in at Luke's shop too? Would he deliberately sabotage his own son's work? But how did he even know about her project? Luke had only found out about it a week ago. Luke. Oh, no. He was involved. He had to be. He was the only one besides her daddy who even knew about her carburetor.

No, no, no. Luke, no.

She thought about what happened to Tom Ogle and a tremor shot through her. She backed away, fled the hospital, and raced home, planning what to do along the way. At home in her bedroom, she threw some things into a bag and started to leave her father a note. No, don't leave any traces. She typed a text instead: I HAVE TO LEAVE FOR A FEW DAYS. I CAN'T TRUST ANYONE AND YOU SHOULDN'T EITHER. TRY NOT TO WORRY ABOUT ME. I'LL CALL WHEN I CAN. I LOVE YOU. She pressed SEND, then searched through her purse and found her external drive. She tucked it back inside, grabbed her laptop, and threw it all into the backseat of the Thunderbolt.

She started the engine, placed her hand on the gearshift, and stopped. Was this the right thing? Maybe she should take her father with her. No, he had crops to plant. This was a busy time of year for him in the fields, and timing was everything when it came to getting the crops in the ground. Exhausted, she closed her eyes. A sleeping bag. She left the engine running while she ran back into the house, grabbed a sleeping bag and pillow, and added them to the pile in the backseat.

Rachel was only a half mile from her house when the headlights of Luke's white Charger came toward her. He hit the brakes, and when she passed him, he spun around in the middle of the dirt road, spewing dust and gravel in his wake. Within seconds he was on her tail.

Now what? She couldn't face him. He couldn't be trusted. Could he? Her phone rang in her purse, but she ignored it. She headed toward the interstate and glanced down at the gas gauge—still almost a full tank. She'd outrun him. He'd follow for a while, but her Thunderbolt could easily outlast his Charger. She had her new carburetor—a hundred and sixty miles to the gallon. As long as he didn't do anything dangerous. He wouldn't risk hurting her, would he?

Luke came up beside her on the interstate several times and tried to get her attention, but she ignored him, shielding her face behind her cupped hand. How did it come to this? She'd trusted him. She'd almost given him everything. Hot tears stung her eyes and she struggled to not let the first one fall. She couldn't think about that now. She'd think about that later. She'd cry for him later.

She turned on the old radio and tried not to look at him in the rearview mirror.

Luke stayed with her. If her carburetor got the mileage he'd seen in her metrics, she'd easily outlast him. His only hope was for her old muscle car to break down. Maybe the radiator would leak and it would overheat, or a belt would break. No. He'd helped her rebuild that engine, practically from the head up, and they'd put all new belts in it. Still, there had to be something, a tie rod, a flat tire even.

So he drove on, his head pounding, while he held on to the hope that she'd either break down or change her mind and stop to talk to him. He wasn't even sure how much she'd overheard, but when she didn't come back, he'd assumed she must have overheard him and his father arguing. *Does she think I'm involved? That I set her up? She must. She's running from me.*

A little over three hours later, as the pale pink glow of dawn began to brighten the eastern sky, he was nearly out of gas, and with a sinking heart he watched her car get smaller and smaller as she disappeared down the highway, and he pulled off at the exit to refuel.

Secrets

L uke screeched to a halt in his parents' circle drive, ready to have it out with his father. He'd had ample time on the long, solitary ride back to think about all that had happened, and he'd concluded that his father had to be involved, at least to some degree. It was late morning and he knew his father would be home. He stormed up the front steps, slammed the front door behind him, and burst through the double doors of his office.

His father was sitting at his desk, talking on the telephone, and held up a finger, signaling he'd be done in a minute. Luke's head was pounding like a woodpecker on maple, and he was close to passing out from the pressure behind his eyes. He went over to the bar and poured himself a whiskey, then remembered the pain meds he wanted to take. He set the glass back on the bar and poured water instead. He reached into his coat pocket and pulled out the bottle of pills, dumped two into his hand, and tossed them back with the water. He took a deep breath, trying to clear his head, and turned around to lean against the bar, folding his arms across his chest and tapping his foot as he glared at his father, his fury growing by the minute.

Luke simmered while his father finished up his call, and when he finally hung up the phone, he turned to Luke with a wary greeting. "What is it, son?"

"You *know* what it is," Luke shouted with barely suppressed rage as he stalked toward the desk. "She's gone. She's running from me. Because of you." He leaned forward to place his hands on his father's desk. "What did you do? Who did you tell? Who knows about my carburetor, and who did you tell about Rachel?"

Aside from the worry that creased his brow, Daniel Brandt appeared unfazed by Luke's outburst. He rubbed his jaw, taking his own sweet time responding. "How's the head?"

"Forget my head." Luke shouted. "Answer the question."

"Son," his father said patiently, easing back in his oversized leather chair, "I didn't tell anyone about your carburetor. I talked to lots of fellas about your great finish at Daytona, though, and your first place finishes at Bristol and Fontana. You know how proud I am of you, and I talk about your racing every chance I get. The guys love to hear about it. But I swear I didn't tell anyone about your carburetor. And I didn't tell anyone about your girlfriend either."

Luke stared across the desk at his father. He wanted to believe him. "Look me in the eye and tell me you had nothing to do with the break-in at my garage or at Rachel's."

Daniel Brandt leaned forward in his chair, and looked him straight in the eye. "I had absolutely *nothing* to do with the break-ins." He walked around the desk to stand in front of Luke. "Come on now. You think I would do that to my own son? My own flesh and blood?"

Luke let out an exasperated sigh. "You know I'm not your flesh and blood."

Daniel Brandt regarded his son carefully, then walked to the doors and closed them both tight before turning back to Luke. "Come sit down."

His father never closed those doors when it was the two of them. Luke's stomach twisted as he anticipated what his father might have to say. He walked over to the sitting area and eased into the chair.

His father sat directly across from him and leaned forward, capturing his attention. "I've thought about this moment for years. Waited for the right time. I pray I haven't waited too long. Luke." He paused. "You *are* my flesh and blood. You *are* ... my son."

Luke stared at him, unblinking for several long moments while thoughts and questions raced through his head. He had a father. All this time he'd felt abandoned, and his own adoptive father was really his birth father? Why would he do that? Keep it a secret? It didn't make sense. He began to shake his head, "No," he whispered.

"Yes." His father placed a hand on Luke's knee. "Listen to me, and I'll tell you everything. Everything I know, anyway. "Your mother was a singer in a little café I used to frequent, but I ..." He paused, lowering his eyes. "I was married to Jilly." Your birth mother and I were together only a couple of times. She never told me about you. She came to me once for help, and I made some calls and got her into a recording studio to create a demo tape, but that was the last time I heard from her. It was only after I read about her death that I found out she'd left behind a young son. I didn't even know if you were mine or not, but I knew I had to find you and discover the truth for myself. It took me two years to find you."

He paused and cleared his throat. "Jilly couldn't have children, so I talked her into adopting. She wanted an infant, but I found you, and ... I knew the first time I saw you—your bright blue eyes and square jaw, your smile." He grinned proudly at his son and Luke's eyes landed on the dimple in his father's cheek. "I convinced your mother it had to be you." He leaned back, giving Luke time to absorb it all.

Luke stood and turned away as he struggled to grasp the fact that the man who'd raised him all these years really *was* his biological father. He spun around and shouted the question gnawing at him. "Why didn't you tell me?" Unshed tears stung his eyes.

Daniel Brandt's eyes went misty. "I couldn't risk losing Jilly. I'd planned to tell you when you were older, but never found the right time. I thought it was enough that I always loved you as if you were my own, I always treated you like you were my own son, and you were such a delightful child, a true blessing. You've made me so proud."

Luke scowled in disbelief, even as a tear escaped to roll down his unshaven cheek. "How could you? You have no idea what it's like to grow up knowing that neither of your parents ..." his voice broke and the last words trailed off to a whisper, "wanted you."

"I did want you. I was driven to find you. And I've done everything I could to make you feel loved, like you belonged. I know your mama must have loved you too. I'm sure she planned to come back for you as soon as she was able."

Luke sank into the chair and put his head in his hands. It felt like it could explode.

His father walked away and a drawer opened and closed. When Luke raised his head, his father was seated back across from him, holding out a cassette tape.

Luke slowly reached out to take it from him. He held it in one hand as the fingertips of the other brushed over the image on the front of it. He'd never even seen a picture of her. He looked up at his father, questioning.

"That's her." After several minutes his father placed his hand on Luke's shoulder. "I'm sorry, son."

Luke stood, and without so much as a backward glance at his father, walked out.

Back at home, Luke threw his keys on the front table, his jacket on the couch, then walked straight to the stereo to put the cassette tape into the player. He sat on the couch and looked at the picture of his mother as he waited for the music to begin. His head jerked up as he heard her voice, sunny and cheerful. "All right now, boys, I'm ready. Let's do this." Then the music started, and her voice joined in and it was soft and sweet, flowing like golden honey in the warm country sunshine.

In the early morning light of a brand new day
On a gentle breeze of a Tennessee spring
With a whisper of God and His love in my heart
You came into my life and changed everything.

A blessing so wonderfully unexpected
A child of my own to love and to name
The son that would light up my darkest days
I knew my life would never be the same.

So many things I had dreamed I would teach you
The love of my life, the light of my days
Things of His world, such as love, faith, goodness, and grace.

A mother loves the child of her heart
The warmth of another who needs her gentle care
There's so much I want to teach you
As I hold you close and keep you near.

If I have only one gift to give you,
The love of my life, the light of my days,
It would be His gift of love, faith, goodness, and grace

The end is near, my time is short,
My heart breaks as I look into your sleeping face.

Don't shed a tear for me when I am gone
My little love, I have to leave this place.

I'll see you again on the other side,
The love of my life, the light of my days,
And you'll bring to me your own tales of love, faith, goodness, and
grace.

Oh, Mama. Did you write that song for me? She knew she was dying and this
had been her final gift to him. But she never even had a chance to teach him. *Oh,*
God, why'd you have to take her so soon? I know nothing of those things: love, faith,
goodness, and grace.

He rewound the tape, falling asleep to the sound of his mother singing to him
and with the comfort of knowing that his father had loved him enough to find
him and raise him as his own.

When he woke several hours later, his first thoughts were of Rachel. Where was
she? Was she all right? He lay there as he tried to fit the events of the past several
weeks into place. If his father didn't tell anyone about his carburetor, then who
would have known about it?

The NASCAR officials knew about it. He'd needed their approval to race
with it. And he'd been running it in his race car since Daytona and the start of
the season. Any one of his sponsors could have easily seen it. But looking at it on
the engine, there was no visible difference between it and a normal double-barrel
model. The Ozonator was inside the unit and couldn't even be seen when the
component was installed.

He called his crew chief. "Good morning, Jimmy Ray."

"Afternoon, Luke," Jimmy Ray said with a slight chuckle.

"Right. I had a little accident last night, and I'm not going be into the shop
today. You guys go ahead and check the car over and work on those chassis repairs,
okay?"

"Sure thing, Luke. Already on it."

"Has anyone asked about the new carburetor we've been running this year?"

"Yeah, now that you mention it. Bobby Carmichael did … at Daytona. He wondered what we'd done to get such good gas mileage."

"What did you tell him?"

"That you'd put a new four-barrel carb on."

Luke thought about that and began to see the pieces starting to fall into place. "Thanks, Jimmy Ray."

"Is everything all right?"

"No, not really. I don't know, man. Rachel's shop was broken into last night and unfortunately she surprised the guy. She's all right, I think. He cracked my head open before she shot him, but he took off. Anyway, she's on the run, thinking I had something to do with it and … I don't know, Jimmy Ray. I'm trying to figure out who would want to break into her shop and why. Mine, sure; but hers? It doesn't make sense." A sudden thought hit him. Unless they think she developed my carburetor.

Jimmy Ray went silent for several moments before he finally spoke. "You know, Luke, when your shop was broken into they took the carb right out of the car, like they knew exactly what they were after. And they trashed the place looking for somethin' … somethin' *else*," he emphasized. "You reckon they were looking for that same somethin' at Rachel's place? Probably wouldn't take too much snooping on the Net to find out she's an engineer. Maybe they figured she's the one who came up with the idea."

"Yeah, Jimmy Ray, that's what I was wondering." He didn't want to tell his friend that Rachel had her own very different version of a superefficient carburetor. "You take care now, Jimmy Ray. And call me if Carmichael comes snooping around, you hear?"

"I will. I'm sorry to hear about Rachel. If there's anything I can do, you let me know."

"I will, Jimmy Ray. Thanks, man."

"Okay. Take care of that head."

"Right." Luke ended the call and stared at the screen as it went dark. Carmichael—Pacific Oil. His father had warned him about his sponsor's interests, and he'd brushed it off. But would they go to those lengths to prevent a fuel-efficient innovation from being tested out? The guy in Rachel's shop had her papers tucked into his jacket at one point. And when he'd surprised him from behind, he was peering into the engine right about where the carb was located. That's what he was after all right. Sure enough.

Luke absently ran his fingers through his hair, wincing at the painful reminder of the staples there. This was all his fault. They were looking for his specs. They probably didn't even know Rachel had her own design. He got her into this, and it was up to him to get her out. But how? Did he dare go to Carmichael and confront him? No, Carmichael was only the front man, a marketing rep for Pacific Oil. There was a surfeit of power and influence behind that front, and he had a feeling they'd only seen a fraction of what that power and influence was capable of.

He showered and dressed and headed back up to the house to talk to his father.

Luke pulled into his parent's drive in his white Charger and waved to a man departing in a black SUV.

Daniel Brandt stood on the front porch, his face a mask of apprehension as Luke took the steps two at a time.

"Was that the mayor?" Luke asked, nodding toward the vehicle disappearing down the lane.

"It was. You feeling any better?"

"I'll be okay. Head's still pounding, but not as bad as it was. Can we go inside? I need to talk to you."

"Of course." His father followed Luke into his office and closed the double doors behind them.

Luke walked over to the bar and helped himself to a cup of coffee. "Want one?"

"No, I'm good, thank you."

When Luke turned back to his father, he was seated on the sofa, eyes closed, bouncing a knee.

"You okay?" His father's eyes flashed open. He looked haunted, older somehow; a mere shadow of the strong and confident man Luke knew and loved.

His father rubbed the back of his neck. "I've been better."

Luke sat across from him. Waited for his father to explain.

"I'm so sorry for keeping things from you. I hope you can forgive me. I can't lose you, son."

"You're not going to lose me." Luke placed a hand on his father's knee, stilling it.

"I figure you have a million questions about my relationship with your birth mother."

Of course he did, but he had more important things that needed tending to. "I do, but right now, Rachel needs my help. Our help. I have a pretty good idea who was behind the break-in at her place last night, and I need your help ensuring it doesn't go any further."

His father leaned back against the couch cushions. "Name it, son. What can I do?"

Luke shared his suspicions with his father, and together they came up with a plan they felt certain would stop Pacific Oil in its tracks.

An hour later Luke pulled into the drive at Rachel's house. When no one answered the door, he walked over to the fields to see if he could find her father there. Not seeing the tractor anywhere, he wondered where the man could be. He walked to the barn next, but again, no one answered his knock, and it was locked up. He walked back to the driveway and stood there looking in all directions, worry starting to set in as he contemplated whether he should sit and wait.

He was walking back to sit on the steps as an old pickup pulled into the drive. It was her father.

"Here, let me help with those," Luke offered as he grabbed a couple of bags of groceries from the back.

Several minutes later, as Luke sat at the kitchen table while her father put away the groceries, Luke asked if he'd heard from Rachel.

"You know, son, you're not exactly her favorite person right now. In fact, I think it's you she's running from," he said, sounding not at all pleased.

"Yeah, I realize that, but she doesn't know everything," Luke explained. "I love her, Mr. Tate, and I want to marry her, with your permission, of course. The last thing in the world I'd ever want to do is to hurt her or make her think she had to run away." He paused. "You know about her carburetor, right?"

"You can call me Will, Luke, and yeah, I know about her carburetor."

"Did she tell you about my design?"

"Nope, she didn't."

"Well, I designed one that uses an Ozonator to induce O3 into the carburetor, so when the air and fuel mix, the flashpoint is a lot lower and it takes less fuel to ignite. Very different approach than Rachel's but, nonetheless, it worked. And it worked pretty well, producing about an eighteen percent increase in fuel efficiency in my test engine. It was enough to capture the interest of Pacific Oil, my primary race sponsor, and I think they're the ones behind the break-ins. Did she tell you that my shop was broken into a few days after Daytona?"

"She mentioned it."

"They took the carburetor out of my car, and totally trashed the place looking for something more. I think they were looking for the specifications, the drawings for it. And I think that's why they were here last night too, looking for something more." Luke paused to let that settle in. "I don't think they even know about her carburetor design. But they know about mine, and by now I'm sure they know Rachel's an engineer. They probably figured she came up with it."

Will nodded.

"Mr. Tate—Will," Luke said, "Did she say where she was going? Did she tell you anything? Have you heard from her since last night?"

Will shook his head. "She sent me a text early this morning to let me know she had to leave for a few days, and that's the last I heard from her. She didn't even tell me why she was leaving."

"Do you think she'd go see Holly in California?"

"I don't know."

"A few days, she said?"

"That's what she said."

Luke gave the older man a look of total desperation. "I want her to come home."

"Me too, son, me too." Will finished with the groceries and took a chair at the table opposite Luke.

"She's not safe out there," Luke said, leaning forward, an intense fear gripping his gut. "I want to protect her."

"I know you do."

Luke looked at him and wondered if he knew where she was headed and not telling him. What else could he say to convince him he wanted to help her? "Can I ask you something?"

"Sure thing."

"Do you believe a man controls his own destiny?" Luke wanted the older man's opinion.

Will thought for a minute before he answered, "I think God helps those who help themselves."

Luke nodded. He liked that answer. "Rachel's my destiny," he said with absolute certainty. "I know my life was meant to have her in it, and I have to do everything I can to get her back, to make sure she knows how much I love her, and that I'd do anything for her."

Will studied him. "I admire your conviction, and I have no doubt your feelings for my daughter are genuine." He took Luke's hand in his own gnarled grasp. "May I pray with you?"

Luke was startled by the request, but gladly acquiesced, bowing his head.

"Oh, mighty Lord," Will began "please bless this good young man, so full of love and energy and confidence. Bless him to discover what true love means. Teach him faith and trust. Help him to believe in something bigger than himself and to trust in your plan for his life. And Lord, please bless my baby girl out there, wherever she is, and bring her safely home real soon. Help her to be brave and smart and please protect her in your loving care. Forever and always, every day. Amen."

"Amen," Luke echoed. "Will you call me if you hear from her?" Luke's pained voice beseeched the older man, "Please?"

Will rubbed his chin. "Tell you what, if she calls I'll pass along what you've told me, and if she's all right with it, I'll let you know. That's the best I can do."

Luke was disappointed, but nodded anyway. "Good enough. Will you at least tell her that I love her? And that I need her? And I'd do anything for her?" He paused then added, "And make sure she knows that I want to protect her, keep her safe. I'm the last person in the world she needs to run from."

"Is that all?" A huge grin lit up Will's face.

Luke chuckled. "Yeah, I think so. That's enough, ain't it?" He stood. "I'm sorry, sir, that I got your little girl involved in this."

"I know you are, Luke. And thank you for caring about her so much." Will stood up to see Luke out.

Luke paused at the door. "Sir, do I have your blessing? To ask her to marry me, I mean?"

Will beamed. "You bet. If she's willing, you two have my heartfelt blessing."

Luke nodded, satisfied. "Thank you, sir." He reached out to shake the older man's hand. Will took his hand in his and pulled him in for a firm hug, patting Luke on the back as he held him close for several minutes.

Will finally let go and stood back. "Take care of that head injury."

"I will, thanks. And you take care now too. They may come back."

"I'll be ready."

Luke slid into his car and a warm feeling came over him. He marveled at the inner peace he felt. Was it the shared prayer? The warm embrace? *So that's where her strong faith comes from. Her father.* He glanced back to the house and gave Will, still standing in the doorway, a quick wave. *That's a mighty fine man, right there.* He wished he had half the faith Will had; wished that he could trust like he did that Rachel was in God's hands and that He'd watch over her and bring her back safely. *Oh, little girl, please come home.*

Questions

L uke was almost home when Detective Landry from the Nashville Police Department called to invite him down to the station to file a statement. When he arrived he was led into a small interrogation room. While he sat across the table from the detective beneath a harsh overhead light, he told him everything he could remember about the previous night's events.

They talked about the break-in at his garage the month before, and the detective asked if he thought the two incidents were related, to which he answered without hesitation, "Yes, definitely." Luke relayed his suspicions about Pacific Oil and his carburetor design. When the detective questioned him about Rachel, including her whereabouts, he held back from telling him about her own carburetor design.

The detective studied Luke carefully. "How many shots were fired?"

"Shots?"

"Your girlfriend shot the guy in the leg. She didn't tell you?"

Luke fell silent, struggling to remember. "I don't remember any shots."

"Where's Ms. Tate now?"

"I don't know," Luke replied, wishing with all his heart that he did.

"Did you get a good look at the intruder?"

"Good enough," Luke said. "You want me to look through your books?"

"Actually, Mr. Brandt," the detective paused and opened a manila folder on the table in front of him. He pulled out three large photographs and spread them out in front of Luke. "Is this the man?"

Luke stared at the pictures placed before him, all of the same man, taken at different angles: a dead man lying on a steel gurney, a white sheet folded back at the shoulders. He swallowed the bile rising in his throat, and his voice was shaky when he finally spoke. "That's him."

"You're sure?"

"Positive." Luke pushed the photos back to Landry.

"We pulled him out of the river this afternoon. There's a shotgun wound in his upper thigh, which is where Ms. Tate thought she hit him ... and another one in the back of the head."

Luke's face went ashen. Rachel wouldn't have shot someone in the back, no way. "Same bullet?"

"No."

Luke's mind raced. Whoever hired the goon to do the job was either mighty displeased he'd failed—displeased enough to kill him for his incompetence—or planned to silence him permanently from the get-go.

"And you don't know where Ms. Tate is?" the detective asked for the third time.

Luke stared at the detective. He was losing his patience, not only with being asked that same question again, but also with the helplessness of his consistent answer. "No," he said through clenched teeth.

"Is it normal for her to disappear like this?"

Luke thought for a minute. *No. I don't know.* "She called in at work. And she sent her father a text telling him she was leaving for a few days."

"A few days?"

"That's what her father told me." *Oh, little girl, where are you?*

"Aren't you worried about her?"

His patience spent, Luke jumped up, his chair tipping over with a loud crash. He leaned forward, hands on the table. "You better believe I'm worried about her. What are you doing to find her? To protect her? Isn't that what you're supposed to be doing?"

Landry leaned back in his chair. "Mr. Brandt, we're doing all we can, but we need your help."

"I already told you who's behind it."

Landry appeared to think about that for several minutes, giving Luke a chance to calm down. "Any idea where she'd go? Family, friends she might turn to?"

Luke turned around and ran his hands through his hair, wincing as his fingertips raked across the staples again. *Ow!* He had to stop doing that. He considered Holly in California. But would Rachel be safer if the police didn't find her? Pacific Oil probably owned cops in every state. No, it would be much better and safer if his father's own private investigator found her first. He turned back to the detective. "No, no one I know of. We've only been dating a couple of months."

The detective stood, reached into his jacket, and handed Luke his card. "If you think of anything more that might help, please call me."

Luke took the card and glanced at it. He carefully considered the question that had been gnawing at him since meeting the detective. "Mr. Landry, how do I know you haven't sold out to them? How do I even know that she'll be safe if the police do find her first?"

Landry met Luke's stare with a sullen resolve. "I'm one of the good guys, Mr. Brandt."

"I surely hope so."

Refuge

It was Friday evening and Rachel was exhausted as she collapsed onto her sleeping bag beneath the willow tree to think about what to do next. She'd been on the run for four days, living in fear of being discovered the whole time, feeling like a pink elephant in her sixty-seven Thunderbolt. It was such a rare vintage car, she felt sure that if someone was looking for her they'd easily find her.

She'd driven at least five to seven hours every day, moving from one small country town to another, working online at coffee shops and sleeping in her car in twenty-four-hour store parking lots. She'd been afraid of using her credit card, so when she ran out of money she drove outside of Nashville to use an ATM machine, emptied her bank account, then drove twelve hours to Texas.

She'd finished the drawings and filed the patent application that morning, then called her daddy from a pay phone in western Mississippi, relieved to discover he was doing fine. His familiar voice almost made her cry.

He told her Luke had stopped by every day wanting to know if he'd heard from her. "Sweet pea, you need to call that boy. He's worried about you something fierce. At least send him a text."

"Daddy, I can't trust him. I think he's behind it. He's one of them. Somehow, whoever broke into our barn found out about my carburetor from him."

"No, darlin'. I think you're wrong about that. When he came by the other day he explained quite a bit. They were looking for specs for *his* carburetor, not yours. No one knows about yours. And he's in love with you like I've never seen before. I don't think it's possible he could have anything to do with that break-in. He wants to protect you, sweet pea ... and I think you should let him."

Rachel contemplated her father's advice as she struggled to decide whether she could trust Luke or not. He seemed to have earned her father's trust. And she sure was tired of running. "You trust him?"

By the length of time it took her father to answer, Rachel knew he was considering it carefully. He wouldn't risk her safety and happiness, and especially not her life. "I do, sweet pea. And I'm worried about you. When you comin' home?"

Oh, she wanted to come home, more than anything but … was it safe? "I don't know. Soon, maybe. Hey, I gotta go. You take care of yourself now, hear?"

"You too, sweet pea. I love you."

"I love you too, Daddy, so much." Her voice broke on the last two words, and when she hung up, her heart ached for him, for home, for the safety and warmth of her own bed, for Luke. She wanted to believe in Luke. More than anything she wanted to trust him, to be able to turn to him to make her feel safe, help her figure out what to do.

Rachel lay on her sleeping bag beneath the giant willow and stared with sleepy eyes at the long branches fluttering gracefully above her in the warm spring breeze. It felt good to be home. She savored the security and protection of her special place.

Was it only yesterday she'd raced across West Texas on I-20, outrunning two men in a black sedan? Her heart pounded thinking about it. Careful not to get below a half tank, she'd stopped to fill up at a Pacific Oil station outside of Fort Worth. When she'd spotted the two men in suits and dark sunglasses pull in behind her, she'd gotten a creepy feeling, certain they were watching her. One man got out to pump while the other one sat there staring straight out the windshield, straight at her. She'd stopped the pump where it was and ran inside to throw a twenty-dollar bill on the counter.

"Sure that's all ya be needin' there, darlin'? That ain't barely enough to git that ol' hog back to the interstate, let alone on down the road," the attendant hollered after her.

"Reckon it's enough to get me where I need to get today," she'd called back as she ran out the door. She hopped into her car and peeked at the rearview to see the man grabbing the nozzle to stop his own fill-up. She didn't panic, but wasted no time getting on the interstate. Then, like a dragster down the straight stretch, she buried the speedometer and never saw them again. After about twenty miles she took an exit and doubled back, keeping to side roads from then on.

Afterward, she'd tried to persuade herself that she'd overreacted, that they were simply two business travelers who had nothing to do with the break-in at her shop, nothing to do with Luke or NASCAR, or fuel-efficient carburetors. But she wasn't convinced; a woman's intuition is a powerful thing, and she'd already learned the hard way it was best to pay attention to it.

She rolled to her side, pushed the incident from her thoughts, and said a nice long prayer, thanking the good Lord for keeping her safe and begging Him to guide her, to help her find refuge, and to keep her father safe. And before she even said amen she was fast asleep.

Luke waited patiently in the faint blush of daybreak as he sat beneath a nearby tree and watched her sleep, ecstatic that he'd finally found her. He wondered if she always slept like that, with her hands palm-to-palm, like an angel in prayer. He'd been there every morning for the past week, waiting, hoping, praying for her to come back.

He'd been a walking heartache for days, unable to sleep or eat, mad at himself for being so angry and untrusting, mad at his race sponsor for the threat they posed, mad at the whole world for taking her away from him. He wanted her back, and he'd been powerless to do anything to help find her.

He thought about what he was going to say when she woke up and saw him. She'd been on the run all week—from him. She'd feel trapped and she'd fight him, sure enough. He'd have to be quick to make her understand how much he loved her. That she could trust him. All he wanted to do was to love and protect her. He had to make her realize that.

She was awakened by bird songs as dawn approached, recognizing the familiar cheerful sounds of home. She nestled in the warmth of the sleeping bag and tried to go back to sleep, but an eerie feeling that she was being watched caused her to bolt upright and look around.

She didn't see him at first, not until he stood from where he'd been sitting against a tree, twenty-some yards away. He began moving toward her.

Before she could get out of her sleeping bag, he must have seen the panic in her eyes that told him she was going to run. He closed the distance in a heartbeat, grabbing her up in his arms. She fought against him in vain for several moments while he held her tight against his chest. "Rachel, stop. I'm not going to hurt you, baby. Please, I love you. Don't you know that by now? Don't fight me. You can trust me. Let me help you."

She finally gave in, her strength exhausted, her courage spent. She let her head collapse against his chest as tears of relief rolled down her cheeks. She'd yearned desperately for the safety of his strong arms the whole time she was running—running from him. And now he'd found her. She held him tight, breathing in the pure male scent of him as she basked in the warmth and security he offered. "How did you find me?"

"I will always find you," he said, brushing the tears from her cheeks.

He held her in his arms for several minutes while the woods awakened around them, and she closed her eyes, relaxing in his embrace. When she opened her eyes, she ran her hand down the arm of his camouflage hunting jacket, coming to rest at the hole in the sleeve. She pulled back and stared at it, recognition cloaking her in a warm comfort. She looked up at him. "This is …"

"Mine." He smiled at her upturned face. "I covered you with it that morning."

She relaxed back against his chest. "Thank you," she whispered and hugged him again.

After several minutes, they sat together on the sleeping bag, and Luke explained his theory about Pacific Oil.

"So, they don't even know about my carburetor design? They think I developed yours? That's what this is all about?"

"Afraid so. I'm sorry I got you involved in this. I'm so sorry, baby."

She tried to take it all in.

Luke stared at her hands in his, and she sensed there was more. "What else, Luke? What aren't you telling me?"

"The man who broke into your shop was found in the river the next day with a bullet in the back of his head. These are bad people. They mean business, and they're not going to stop until they've gotten what they're after. They have virtually unlimited power and influence, and they'll obviously go to great lengths to eliminate any potential threats to their Big Oil money machine."

"But I've already filed my patent. That's it, isn't it? There's nothing they can do now to steal it or destroy it. It's over, right?"

"Baby, these guys are so well connected they could easily ensure your patent application gets conveniently 'lost.' But I have a plan, if you're up for it."

Luke's crew and a four-man security detail—courtesy of his father—met them with his rig and motor home at their next NASCAR venue, Kansas Speedway, where they worked well into the night to fit her carburetor and cooling mechanism into his race car. They knew it wouldn't pass prerace inspections, so they planned to install it at the first pit stop and they practiced swapping out the components over and over, timing the crew each time. They had to be able to do it fast. Any more than a minute and the NASCAR officials would think it was more than a minor adjustment.

"Boiling fuel, huh?" Jimmy Ray moved over beside Luke, leaned back against the wall of the infield garage, and folded his arms across his chest as he watched Rachel and the team work. He leaned into Luke, lowering his tone. "Sounds like a recipe for one mother of an explosion, if you ask me."

Luke glanced at his teammate, his silence offering little reassurance. He simply had none to give.

Jimmy Ray scratched his gray stubbled chin. "How did you say she burned her arm?"

Rachel glared at Jimmy Ray. "That was before—" she stopped herself. "It's not going to explode. I've been running it all week; put over two thousand miles on it. It's fine."

Luke almost choked. So that's how she burned her arm; it did blow up. She lied to him. He could feel Jimmy Ray's stare, and they exchanged worried looks.

Luke rubbed the tightness from the muscles in the back of his neck while Rachel turned her attention back to the engine. The two guys working with her glanced at Luke, and he gave them a reassuring nod.

"We're being timed here," she snapped.

Luke chuckled. That was the feisty little girl he remembered.

"Done," Rachel said seconds later as she straightened.

"Two minutes, fifteen seconds," Cam announced.

"Too long," Rachel said.

"You were distracted," Luke said. "Try it again."

While the others put Luke's old carb back on, Rachel grabbed a shop towel and wiped her hands as she went to stand on the side nearest Luke and Jimmy Ray. Facing them, she leaned back against the car. "So, what if the NASCAR officials discover it?"

Silence. She looked from Luke to Jimmy Ray then back to Luke.

Luke gave Jimmy Ray an almost indiscernible shake of his head. The last thing he needed was for Rachel to get freaked out by what this might end up costing him.

"What? Tell me," she insisted, tossing the rag aside.

Jimmy Ray stared at the floor, then with a passing glance at Luke, looked to Rachel. "We get disqualified. Lose all the points for the race. And more'n likely fined. Maybe even suspended."

"A suspension?"

"Yep."

"One?"

"Maybe. Could be a couple ... could be the rest of the season. Hard tellin'. No one's ever pulled this one before."

"So you could get kicked out of NASCAR for this?" Rachel was glaring at Luke now.

"I'm not going to get kicked out. When we win, I'll make it known. I'll forfeit the win voluntarily."

"Luke, I can't let you—"

He took her hands in his. "Baby, this is the only way. Trust me. I know what I'm doing. It's going to work." He glanced back to Jimmy Ray, and saw the skepticism plain as day on his crew chief's face. "It's going to work," he repeated. It had to work.

As she turned back to the engine for another go at it, he wondered how it would all turn out. Even if they got away with the installation, would it blow up on him? Cause an accident, or worse, kill someone? And what if they didn't win? Would he even have a chance to make her invention public? Stop Pacific Oil from coming after them? He rubbed the weariness from his eyes. There was so much riding on this carburetor of hers.

Finally satisfied they could make the swap quickly and successfully, Luke and Rachel left for the motor home for a few hours' sleep. Luke stretched out on the bed while Rachel took a shower. When she came out minutes later, he was fast asleep. She tucked her Taser beneath a pillow, curled up beside him with her head nestled on his shoulder, and tried to fall asleep.

Sounds in the night made her wonder if they were safe. If these people were so all-fired powerful, they could slip past track security, couldn't they? A stream of scenarios, all of them bad, raced through her mind, and it wasn't long before fear had a firm grip and her heart raced wildly.

She woke Luke with a soft kiss, and when he stirred and began to return her kisses she kissed him with all the passion and desire she'd held in check for so long.

"Make love to me, Luke," she breathed into his ear.

"What are you doing?"

"I don't want to die not knowing what it's like."

"You're not going to die, Rachel. Not while I'm here. There're two guards right up front and another two outside. We're safe, baby, we're safe."

Rachel shook her head. She flat-out didn't believe him.

"Yes, we're going to be fine, Rachel, I've got you, baby, trust me."

"I love you, Luke, and—"

"I love you too, but I want to do this right. Come on." He gently stroked her cheek with the backs of his fingertips. "Here, let me hold you." He pulled her in close in front of him. "Go to sleep, darlin'. Go to sleep."

Luke held her tight and smoothed her hair from her face as he reassured her with words of love, whispered slowly, over and over again, in deep gentle tones until she finally drifted off to sleep. The sound of her soft, even breathing made his heart swell with love. There was something about the way she fit him so perfectly. It felt right, like everything was exactly as it should be. She was beside him, right where she belonged.

As he held her close, her warmth permeated his soul, his heart soared with happiness, and he had a sudden urge to be thankful. He closed his eyes and quietly prayed.

God, I know it's been a long time since I've bent Your ear without needing something, and I'm real sorry about that. But I want to say thank You, from the bottom of my heart, for this beautiful, sweet, and loving woman here beside me. Thank You for keeping her safe, for bringing her back to me, for the precious gift of her love. And God, it's a big day for us tomorrow. Please be with us, keep us both safe as we try to live out Your purpose for our lives, as we try our best to do Your will. And God, most of all, help me to be the kind of man she deserves—a loving, trusting, faithful man. Thank You, God, forever and always, every day. Amen.

Luke kissed her softly on the top of her head and succumbed to sleep, content in the knowledge that God intended them to be together and that his feet were on the right path, walking beside the incredible woman asleep in his arms.

The next morning, almost set to roll the car out onto the track, the race garage was eerily quiet as Luke, Rachel, and the crew finished last-minute preparations under the watchful eyes of the added security guards.

"Aw, man," Jimmy Ray muttered as he stared at his phone.

"What is it, Jimmy Ray?"

"Ain't nothin', Luke," Jimmy Ray said, shaking his head. "Let's roll."

"Don't sound like nothin'. Let me see." Luke reached across and snatched Jimmy Ray's phone from him. It was a news posting. As he read it his heart sank and his stomach twisted violently. Bobby Carmichael, the Pacific Oil rep, their friend, was found dead in his hotel room of a drug overdose. Luke fought anger and pain, and his shock of disbelief.

"He was a good man, Jimmy Ray. A family man—" Luke choked and had to look away. He yanked off his hat and ran his hands through his hair as emotions threatened to overwhelm him. "No way he did that to himself. He never did a drug in his life."

He looked at Rachel, who was donning her new crew suit on the other side of the garage, and when she glanced his way he gave her a reassuring smile, thankful he didn't have to share the news with her; she was freaked out enough. "Jimmy Ray, you gotta do me a favor, man." He couldn't help the note of painful desperation in his voice. "You watch out for her today, you hear?"

Jimmy Ray put his hand on Luke's shoulder. "I gotcha covered, man. She'll be fine. Ain't nothin' gonna happen to her today, not while she's with me. You drive, dude. Bring us home another win today. I wanna see that Winner's Circle one more time before they boot me outta here for good."

"You ain't going nowhere, old man. But I'll do my best, like I always do."

"I know you will." Jimmy Ray gave Luke an affectionate pat on the back. "I know you will."

Luke had been late for qualifications on Saturday, so when the green flag dropped on Sunday afternoon his number eleven Pacific Oil Dodge was starting at the back of the pack. There was a massive crash coming out of the fourth turn after the start of the race that took out several other cars. Luke narrowly escaped it, but when he blew a tire on the debris, it was the perfect opportunity to head to the pits early.

Amid the melee of the damaged cars in the pits, they swapped out the carburetor, and he went on to win the race without incident. Not because Luke turned the fastest laps, but because he'd only had to pit two other times for fresh tires. It was a huge, hands-down win, a good two and a half laps in front of the second-place car.

In Victory Lane afterward, surrounded by sprays of champagne, a throng of press, and the numerous high-ranking politicians Luke's father had personally invited, Luke officially introduced Rachel as his race team's lead engineer, presented her new carburetor design, and described its impact on the race. He then apologized for the necessary deception and gracefully forfeited the trophy.

The excitement was electrifying, the accolades unending. The roar of the fine-tuned race engines had been replaced by a hundred thousand screaming fans cheering wildly, not only for the winner of the race, but for a remarkable innovation that was sure to change the face of modern-day automobiles and the whole oil and gas industry. And with all that publicity there was no way it could get brushed under the rug, no matter how much power and influence those Big Oil cronies tried to exert.

Luke and Rachel posed endlessly for photos, even popping the hood on the number eleven Pacific Oil Dodge to take one with the engine in the background, not realizing at the time that the snapshot would end up on the front page of newspapers across the nation as well as make the cover of *NASCAR Racing* magazine with the tease line "Fueled to Win," and would, years later, earn a spot in the Smithsonian.

Sunrise

The next morning Luke took Rachel to his hunting property, and they hiked out to the sycamore tree to watch the sunrise. He sat down at the base of the tree and guided Rachel to sit with her back to him between his legs. He leaned against the trunk and hugged her close against his chest. They kept each other warm in the predawn quiet as the sun peeked over the horizon, spreading its soft glow across the grassy hills and hollers before them.

"Wow," was all Rachel could say as she looked out at the countryside. A smile as wide as Tennessee spread across Luke's face as he basked in the utter perfection of the moment. His whole life he'd imagined sharing the wonder of a sunrise with someone who would appreciate it as much as he did.

He leaned forward, hugged her close, and whispered in her ear, "I love you, Rachel Tate."

"I love you too, Luke Brandt."

As they sat with only the sound of the birds awakening around them, Luke thought again about the ugly words he'd yelled at her in her shop and all the other times he'd unintentionally pushed her away or hurt her with his anger and mistrust.

He knew she'd forgiven him, but he still felt he needed to set things right. He knew for a fact his life was meant to have her in it, and he didn't want to keep pushing her away. He thought he was starting to understand why he did it, and he hoped that if he shared it with her she could help him learn to get past it. He had prayed she would, and that she'd still love him after he told her his story.

He took a slow breath. "I have something I want to share with you."

"Okay." She snuggled deeper into the warmth of his arms.

"It's a story about a little boy," he began, pausing to swallow back his hesitation, "who for the first few years of his young life grew up with his mama right there beside him. He never knew his daddy, and I don't think he and his mama ever had a real home. They would sleep different places: apartments, shelters, churches, other people's homes. But they were always together. He had his mama and she took care of him, and that was enough. Then one morning when he was about five, he woke up alone. She was gone. And he never saw her again. She didn't say good-bye or leave a note; she was simply gone. He went to live in a children's home for a couple of years with a bunch of other lonely kids."

His throat was suddenly so tight he couldn't swallow as he recalled the cruelty of some of the other boys. That was when he'd first heard the words that had taunted him his whole life: *They didn't want you. No one wants you. No one ever will. Get over it, crybaby.* After that—no matter how much he wanted to—he never again cried himself to sleep.

He let the hot tears that escaped run freely down his cheeks, not wanting to take his arms from around her, not wanting her to turn around and see. Moments passed before he could go on, as he struggled to push away the painful memories. "One day, when he was seven, a real nice couple showed up and introduced themselves, and they told him they wanted to adopt him. They asked if he wanted to come live with them. He said yes, and he went home with Jilly and Daniel Brandt."

He waited, wondering what she thought. Would she pity him for the sad and lonely little boy he'd been? He didn't want that; he wanted her to understand him, to know him, deep down. She snuggled back against him, hugged his arms wrapped around her, and it gave him the reassurance he needed to go on.

"The saddest thing though, my whole life I've felt abandoned. But this week my father told me I'm his biological son. He's my real father." He relaxed, a glimmer of happiness returning as he reveled in the fact that he had a father who loved him, that he belonged, that he was wanted after all. "See, he didn't know about me until after my mama died, and then he searched me out and talked Jilly into adopting me. Jilly doesn't know, but he promised he would tell her."

"All this time, Rachel, I thought I was living with adopted parents, that neither of my real parents wanted me." He hesitated, suddenly unsure. He'd never in his life shared so much with anyone, but he was so in love with her. He needed her to understand.

"I know that doesn't excuse some of the mean things I've said to you or the way I've treated you at times, but I'm pretty sure the reasons behind it are in there somewhere." He swallowed hard, leaned forward, and put his face next to hers and kissed her tenderly on the cheek. "But I don't want to push you away anymore. I want you in my life. I *need* you in my life, Rachel."

She turned to face him, sat up on her knees, and placed her hands on either side of his face. "I love you, Luke Brandt, and I'm not going anywhere. As long as you love me, I will never leave you." She kissed him then and it was soft and sweet and conveyed, without a doubt, everything she'd spoken and more.

He stood and pulled her up with him, holding both her hands in his. "Oh, Rachel, darlin', I am so in love with you. And I know I can be the kind of man you deserve. I want to be. With every breath of life in me I want to love you, Rachel, like God intended a man to love a woman. You're everything I've ever wanted, everything I need. God meant for us to find each other, for us to be together. You said it yourself, right?" He gazed at her expectantly.

She smiled and nodded.

"Rachel, my angel ..." He dropped to a knee in front of her, still holding her hands in his. "I love you more than you could ever know. Will you marry me?" He gazed up at her, their eyes locked in the moment, as he waited anxiously for her answer.

She laughed softly back at him, taken off guard by his impromptu proposal, even as she nodded. "Yes," she whispered, leaning down to kiss him, then throwing herself into his arms. "Oh, yes, Luke. Yes."

His heart soared with unbounded joy as he caught her up and hugged her to him, swinging her around before placing her back on her feet. He reached into his pocket and pulled out a small box and opened it.

She stared at the ring and her mouth fell open. "It's beautiful, Luke." She watched, breathless, as he placed it on her finger.

"I'm gonna live to be the kind of man you deserve," he pledged, holding her hands, his heart overflowing with the love he felt for her.

"You already are."

"Luke Brandt, the race car driver?" Her mama leaned over the white linen tablecloth. "As in Daniel Brandt's son?"

"Yes, Mama." For a heartbeat, Rachel wondered if her mother approved, thankful she'd chosen to share the news on her own, without Luke. "Mama, don't cry."

"Oh, my beautiful girl." Emily Rose Tate stood and pulled Rachel into a loving embrace, then proudly announced the engagement to the rest of the country club lunch crowd. Her mama not only approved, she was thrilled.

When Rachel explained that they wanted to be married as soon as possible, her mother switched into full planning mode, like the green flag on her daughter's happiness had finally dropped.

Rachel could not have imagined a more beautiful wedding or a more perfect day. They were married a short six weeks later in the expansive gardens behind Luke's stately childhood home, a miraculous feat only her mother, with her myriad of event-planning experience and personal contacts, could have pulled off. Only this time it wasn't about the money raised; it was all about what a great time was had by all.

Holly returned from California to be Rachel's maid of honor and help with the last-minute arrangements. Rachel was thrilled when Luke surprised them one evening by showing up to join them for dinner with Dirk Jansen in tow. He and Holly hit it off like country music and cowboy boots, which could not have been more perfect because Dirk was Luke's best man.

Rachel, Holly, and her other bridesmaids, Allie and Becca, got dressed at Luke's house, and a horse-drawn carriage took them to the location for the outdoor wedding. Her attendants went first, all together, then Rachel alone with her father, who helped her out and proudly walked her down the brick pathway to where Luke anxiously waited.

When Luke reached out to shake her father's hand, Rachel was sure her father was going to lose it. His eyes grew misty and he pulled Luke into a loving embrace. The wedding march had long ended by the time they parted. Then, taking Luke's hand and her hand, he put them together and gave Rachel a smile that would stay with her forever. He patted them both on the shoulders before turning to take his seat beside her teary-eyed mother.

The gardens behind the Brandts' home were picture-perfect at the height of their late-springtime flush, with a profusion of daylilies, valerian, and poppies, coneflowers, hollyhocks, and blue flax set on a backdrop of azaleas, rhododendrons, and magnificent white and pale pink magnolia trees. It could not have been lovelier, and the weather was perfect—mild and sunny with a crystal-clear blue sky. Music was provided by Emma Grace, Southern Lights, and a small orchestral ensemble. So there was something for everyone, and the celebration lasted well past midnight.

When Luke and his beautiful bride finally bid their family and friends good night, they climbed back into the horse-drawn carriage and returned to his house. Luke lifted Rachel down and carried her across the threshold, kicking the door closed behind them. He set her down in the middle of the living room and glanced around, satisfied. Everything was as he'd arranged.

"Mrs. Brandt," he bowed low before her, "welcome home."

She laughed at his silly gesture. "Oh, Luke, you get on."

"Some music?"

"Yes, please."

The music began and he walked back to stand before her, thoughts of their long-awaited wedding night crouching like a cornered bobcat between them as they simply stared at one another. "Are you afraid?" He watched her bite her lip. "Don't lie."

She slowly shook her head and flashed a confident smile. "I'm not afraid."

Her calm response was almost enough to reassure him. Almost. "You were terrified before."

"I didn't know you then like I know you now. I wasn't your wife."

"We could wait—"

"Oh, no you don't, Luke Brandt." She pushed hard against his chest with both hands, and he laughed as he stumbled backward. Regaining his balance, he grabbed her wrists and pulled her close against him, capturing her gaze as he'd captured her arms, holding her there while he basked in the overwhelming love he felt for her. She was an amazing woman and she was his wife.

His wife.

He brushed a finger across her cheek. "I don't want to hurt you."

Rachel slowly pushed his jacket off his shoulders, letting it fall to the floor. "You won't." She began to undo his tie.

His hand covered hers, stopping her. "I will."

"I don't care." She pulled the tie free and worked at the buttons of the crisp tux shirt.

Luke admired her courage, her trust in him. He brought his wrists up between them to let her undo his cuff links. When she'd finished and his shirt fell to join his jacket and tie on the floor behind him, he gently cupped her face in his hands. "I have never loved you more, Rachel, than I do right now."

"I love you too, Luke."

When he reached for the champagne that had been left for them, she giggled like a schoolgirl. "I don't need anything more to drink."

"I want to toast my beautiful bride." He poured a little into each glass and handed her one, then stared at her for several moments before he began, "Angel, if you are ever alone or afraid, remember this night, and know how much I love you."

Rachel smiled back at him, her eyes twinkling with mischief. "To my handsome husband, my cowboy hero…" her smile grew wider, "my knight in the white Charger." She touched her glass to his with a ting and they each took a sip.

Luke chuckled. The white Charger—yeah, that was a move he'd never regret. "Baby, I want to be your everything-come-true."

"You already are."

Taking her glass from her, he set it on the side table, then refilled his glass and set it down too.

Rachel watched his every move, the way his muscles flexed in his broad shoulders, the way his strong, bare back narrowed to slim hips. When he turned back to her, her breath caught.

"Can I help you out of that dress?"

Her heart raced as she anticipated his touch, his kiss, his strength. She bit her lower lip to stop it trembling, nodded, and turned her back to him. She held her hair aside as he found the zipper and gently lowered it. Her dress fell to the floor around her feet, and he held her hand as she stepped out of it.

Holding her at arm's length, Luke drank in the sight of her, standing there before him like an angel in her lacy white underthings and heels, all feminine curves and pale softness. She was pure innocence and grace and he felt so crazy blessed to have her in his life, to have her as his wife. This amazing woman whom God had saved only for him.

He swallowed the lump in his throat, and his voice was hoarse with emotion when his words finally found their way out. "You are so incredibly beautiful."

He'd imagined this moment for so many sleepless nights, woke in the mornings with the sweet interrupted dream of her fresh in his memory. Now that the time had come, he wanted to savor every wondrous, fleeting second of it, to commit it to memory—every last taste, scent, touch—to relive for a lifetime. And he wanted to make it perfect for her, a night she, too, would remember forever.

Picking up a glass of champagne, he smiled down at her, dipped his finger into the shimmering liquid and slowly brushed it across her lips before leaning down to kiss it away. His heart soared as he tasted her sweetness, drank in her soft, wet warmth. She melted into him and suddenly all remnants of the fear and hesitation he'd felt earlier vanished as he surrendered his every desire to his beautiful bride.

When she thought her knees would give out, he swept her off her feet and into his arms and started down the hall. Her head rested against his chest, and she heard the wild pounding of his heart in her ears. She nestled against him, safe, secure in his strong arms. At the bedroom, he kicked open the door, and she was wild with excitement. He was her husband now, and this was a new dance she didn't know, the ancient dance of God's design. Like a gust of wind he carried her up, up, and away in arms like clouds. She sighed, content against him, and he stopped to set her gently on the bed. Kneeling beside her, he bent and kissed her with a tenderness and completeness that blew away everything from her mind but the soft ether into which she was floating and his warm, soft breath on her skin.

He trembled, as if driven by a spirit within, and his lips, his fingertips, moved slowly over her. He was whispering things she didn't hear, evoking feelings never felt before. She tried to speak and his lips fell upon her again. She was floating and he was floating and there was nothing else but this moment—only the currents and his body covering hers, yielding to arms that were so strong, lips so soothing, time that passed so slowly.

For the first time in her life she had found someone she could trust completely, someone of this world. Someone she could give everything, who wasn't just taking but giving of himself—giving her everything.

And when she awoke the next morning, he still held her, and if not for his warmth beside her, she would have thought the night before a glorious dream.

Epilogue

L uke rolled over in bed, frowning at the cold emptiness beside him where his beautiful wife should have been. He opened his eyes and ran his hands through his hair as he looked around the close walls of their bedroom in the motor home. He stretched his long frame and relaxed, content, as he listened to the muted voices from beyond the closed door.

"Watch closely and tell me which one has a greater mass," Rachel instructed. "Here, Danny," she said to their five-year-old son. "You hold them, like this, way up high, and let go of them at the same time when I say go. Ready?"

"Yes, Mama."

"Okay, on the count of three. One, two, three, *go,*" Rachel said.

Luke heard a soft thud followed by tiny footsteps scurrying across the room.

"So," Rachel quizzed, "which one has the greater mass?"

"The marble." The answer had come from their three-year-old, Willow.

"The marble," Danny agreed.

"Right. You are both so smart, I can't believe it. Now ... why did you answer the marble?"

"Because it hit the pillow first," Danny answered. "That means it has more mass. The grabity pulled at it harder."

"Gra-*vi*-ty," Willow corrected, enunciating the word to point out his mistake.

Luke's heart smiled. Mornings before a race were absolutely his favorite time of the whole week. This was the time for family—just the four of them—in the small, close quarters of their comfortable motor home, where everything they needed, including each other, stayed within easy reach.

Best of all, there were no demands, nothing left to have to get done. No sponsors to greet, no interviews to do, no last-minute adjustments to make on the car. Most of the time, there wasn't anything left to do until after noon, when they headed over to the track, attended the mandatory prerace meeting, and stood together for the national anthem. Then he'd climb into the car and hit the gas when the green flag dropped.

His stomach growled at the familiar waft of pancakes and sausage coming from the kitchen. Typically he was up before the sun, unable to sleep late at all. The first time he could ever remember sleeping in had been on their honeymoon, after a long night of lovemaking. Tranquility settled over him as he reminisced about their time together in that little cabana on the beach in the Caribbean. Then, he'd felt like the luckiest man alive. Eight years later, that feeling remained.

Luke roused himself out of bed and watched his family from the doorway of the bedroom. The smell of something burning caught his attention, and his gaze flashed to the kitchen and the smoking griddle as the smoke alarm went off. The two little ones covered their ears and screamed as Rachel bolted for the stove.

"I got it, babe," Luke said, turning off the burner. He took the griddle to the door, opened it wide, and set the pan on the ground outside.

When he returned, his children jumped into his arms. "Daddy's up! Daddy's up," they shouted in unison.

"Mama's teaching us God's laws of fisks," Danny announced from his perch on Luke's right arm.

"And making us Mickey Mouse pancakes," Willow chimed in her squeaky-sweet, baby-girl voice.

"Is that right?" Luke grinned at Rachel while she opened windows, then picked up a couch pillow to help direct the smoke out of the room.

She shot him a sheepish grin. "Sorry."

Luke chuckled. "Come here."

"Family hug," the little ones cheered.

Luke bent down to set the children on their feet. "God's laws of 'fisks,' huh?" He looked up at Rachel.

"Physics," she clarified, taking a step back.

"How about I make the pancakes while you show me what you learned," Luke said to their children.

Rachel sat on the floor with her little ones and helped them collect their supplies while Luke retrieved the griddle from outside. He took it back to the kitchen, scraped off the burnt pancakes, and set it on the stove, looking at everything she had going on in the kitchen.

He had to laugh as he took it all in. The sausage was cooked and sitting in the grease, getting cold. The pancake mix was in a large measuring cup that had dripped down onto the counter and halfway down the cabinet door below. She'd washed strawberries, their leaves in a pile in the sink, the berries arranged on plates spread out on the counter. He shook his head and looked to where she sat with the kids on the floor.

One look at her and he knew—she'd been watching him inspect the huge mess she'd made. "You're the best," she said, smiling up at him.

His heart turned to warm wax and melted right there in his chest. He lived for moments like these. He chuckled to himself. There were more important things than having a wife who could cook, but God love her, she tried.

Her patent for the vapor fuel carburetor had not only been unhindered, its approval by the U.S. Patent Office was fast-tracked by several influential politicians, including Tennessee's own, Senator Mitch Davies, and Rachel was able to sell it for millions.

In the eight years they'd been married she'd developed several other ingenious innovations as well, including a new tire compound that extended the life of racing tires. With her as lead engineer on their race team, they continued to qualify for the Chase year after year, even winning the NASCAR Sprint Cup Championship, the pinnacle of American motorsports, three times.

And she'd given him the most incredible blessing of all—his family—their two children. Danny was going to be tall and strong, with Rachel's beautiful green eyes. Willow was small, graceful, and pretty, like her mama, with his own soft-blue eyes. They brought to his life an extreme joy and profound happiness he never could have imagined.

As he watched his wife in her pajamas, sitting cross-legged on the floor with their children around her, he felt an overpowering sense that he had never loved her more than at that moment. She was incredible, the answer to every prayer he hadn't even offered up, the cure for all the pain he didn't even know was ailing him, the hope he didn't even realize was wanting in his sad, lonely life. She'd shown him firsthand what it meant to truly love someone, to have faith in things unseen and unknown. Her patience and perseverance had taught him much about goodness and grace, and forgiveness.

Yeah, his heart smiled again. There were more important things than having a woman who knew her way around a kitchen.

Much, much more important things.

The End